# UNFORGIVEN

## REBECCA SHEA

Tracey,
To my sweet friend... thank you
for your words of encouragement
+ never ending friendship!
            Love you always!
                    Becca ♡

*Unforgiven*
Copyright ©2014 Rebecca Shea, LLC
All rights reserved.

Createspace
ISBN-13: 978-1500359263
ISBN-10: 1500359262

Cover design by: Regina Wamba, Mae I Design
Edited by: Beth Suit, BB Books Editing and Beth Lynne, Hercules Editing
Formatted by: Angela McLaurin at Fictional Formats

# UNFORGIVEN

# DEDICATION

To my readers—for loving this series and always wanting more.
This is for you.

# PROLOGUE

*One year ago*

*Lindsay*

"Whoever thought carrying on a secret affair would be easy was clearly delusional," I mumble against Matt's soft lips. I rest my chin on his firm chest and stretch out on top of his long, muscular body.

"Is that all this is, an affair?"

"You know what I mean." I kiss the sparse stubble along his jawline and press my lips to his neck.

"You'll never be just an *affair* to me, Lindsay." He flips us over on the bed so he's positioned on top of me, his elbows resting on the bed on either side of my head. I run my hands over his defined shoulders and down his biceps.

"Good," I whisper, inhaling sharply when he pulls my earlobe into his mouth. "Why did you fall in love with me?"

"How could I not fall in love with you?"

"Because I'm a neurotic mess."

He laughs quietly. "You're not a neurotic mess. You're driven and independent and strong-willed and beautiful, and somewhere in all of that, I fell in love with you—every part of you."

I wrap my legs around his waist, pulling him closer to me. "Do you know that I'll never forget the first time I ever laid eyes on you?"

"I'd never forget that day either," he breathes against my neck. He always takes his time with me, kissing me, touching me, teasing me until I beg for him to take me.

"Tell me what you remember," I muster in between ragged breaths.

"I remember it was a party at your house."

"Landon's house," I say.

"You share the house with your brother. It's your house too. Stop interrupting me." He pinches my hip gently to scold me. "Anyway, Landon and I had worked together for almost two years and I'd seen pictures of you and had seen you on TV, but anytime I'd been to the house, I'd never met you—I'd never seen you in person. The second I walked through that door that night, you were standing in the middle of the living room and, suddenly, nothing else existed in my world. It was over. I knew I had to have you."

"That's how I felt too." I smile at him.

"Everything about you turned me on. The way you carried yourself, your sense of humor, your excitement about everything we talked about. I don't think I talked to anyone else that night."

"Do you know what I remember? I remember the way you studied me. You saw through the façade – not the TV personality everyone else sees. You saw the *real* me. You looked at me like there was nobody else in the room."

"There wasn't," he whispers.

"I remember how my skin broke out in goose bumps when your hand brushed against me when you reached for a beer. I'd never had that happen before, and I remember how I never wanted that night to end. I didn't want you to leave."

"You do realize there have only been a few nights we've been apart since that night, right?"

"Mmm hmm." I press my lips to his and drink in their softness.

"I'm never letting you go, Lindsay. Before you came along, I was just a thirty-one-year-old cop with no goals or ambitions. Now I have someone I want to live for—live with. I don't ever want to be anywhere unless it's with you."

In this moment, everything in my world is perfect... but as things always go in my life, when everything is perfect, I worry that something will happen to take it all away. I shove those negative feelings aside and fall asleep in the arms of the man I want to spend forever with.

"Good morning, beautiful." Light kisses pepper my face and neck. I grumble and roll closer to Matt, wrapping my arm over his chest, securing myself to him.

"There is only one fault I can find in you," I mumble against his shoulder, my eyes still closed.

"What's that?"

"You're a morning person."

Matt chuckles as he pulls me on top of him and slides his hands down my bare back. I rest my head on his chest while his fingertips trace my spine and I shiver at his gentle touch.

"I like when you wake me up like this and touch me."

"I like waking you up and touching you. I'll never get enough of you, Linds."

I kick the silk sheet off of us and sit up, straddling Matt's hips. I rise and position myself just over the top of him, letting him slide into me.

"Jesus," he hisses and inhales sharply. I use my knees to guide me, rising and falling slowly on top of him, drinking in the feel of him inside me. With my hands pressed to his chest to balance me, I drop my head back and just *feel*. From the day I met Matt, we've had a connection that is indescribable. He understands me and my needs and I the same for him.

"Promise me something," I whisper. "Don't ever leave me." My voice cracks with emotion. His hands grasp my hips, stopping me. I tip my head forward, my eyes finding his.

"Never," he says with conviction. "I will always love and protect you, Lindsay. I promise. Tell me why you're getting emotional?"

"I want us to be like normal couples. I hate being secretive about our relationship and I worry that you're going to get tired of that and leave me. I don't think I could handle life without you."

"Then let's not keep us a secret any longer. Let's talk to Landon and tell him the truth. We love each other and I'm tired of hiding it."

I shake my head. "I'm afraid."

"Of what?"

"That he's going to flip out. I don't want to lose my brother and you can't lose your best friend and partner."

Matt sighs loudly. "Linds, the only thing Landon is going to be upset about is that we've been sneaking around. He loves you and will never disown you. I, on the other hand, may have to deal with something entirely different." He chuckles.

I roll off of Matt and he slides over to me and positions himself on top of me, taking over. "Look at me." His dark brown eyes fix on mine, "I love you," he says, kissing the tip of my nose. I nod and feel the lump in my throat growing larger. "I love you," he says again.

"I love you too."

"Let's not be secretive anymore. I'm ready for everyone to know we're together. I want them to know you're mine and I'm yours."

"Not yet," I whisper and he sighs loudly.

"You're the one calling the shots, Linds."

"Good, then make love to me."

We spend the next hour lying in bed, exploring each other's bodies, minds, and souls. I've never been so intimately connected to another living being and my heart explodes with the feelings of love and contentment I have with Matt. He is my rock when I am unstable, he is my voice of reason when I'm standing on the edge of insanity, and he is the only man I've ever given my heart to.

# Present Day

# CHAPTER 1

## Lindsay

"Mmmm," is about all I manage to get out before Matt slides into me in one heady thrust. I gasp as he gives me a moment to adjust and wake up. "I love that you still wake me up like this," I sputter between breaths. The room is dark except for the sliver of moonlight coming through the skylight.

My arms wrap around his neck and my fingers trail small circles against the back of his neck. His body is damp from a recent shower and he smells like body wash.

"I like when I come home to find you naked in my bed." He presses a kiss to my lips. His thrusts become quicker, needier. "God, you feel so good," he says, biting at my jawline. I lift my hips and match his movements. "You're going to make me come already," he whispers. I wrap my legs around his waist and clench, creating more friction. "Jesus Christ, Lindsay."

"Good; come in me," I groan as I feel my orgasm building. The next few seconds are a flurry of moans, kisses, and perfectly timed releases.

Matt stays inside of me as his erection fades and, for some reason, this is my favorite time… when we're connected as one in the most intimate of ways. It's in these moments, when we connect emotionally, the unspoken words, the intense look in each other's eyes that speak of the love we have without actually speaking a single word.

Matt finally pulls out and rolls off of me and onto his back. He tosses his arms above his head. I roll onto my side, facing him, watching his muscular silhouette in the dark, and listening to his quiet breaths as he falls into a peaceful slumber.

"I love you, Matt," I whisper. Just before his breathing becomes lighter, I barely make out his whispered response.

"I love you too, Linds."

I slap the alarm clock that is blaring on the nightstand next to my head. Matt grumbles and rolls over, and I instantly feel guilty for waking him up. For the last six years, Matt has worked the swing shift for the Wilmington Police Department, patrolling from three in the afternoon to midnight, but doesn't usually get home until almost one in the morning. It's now six and he's had less than five hours of sleep.

Most mornings, he tries to get up with me to see me off to work, which I find sweet, but I feel bad when I know he's tired and needs his rest. We've both been working an insane amount of hours lately and, for the last three weeks, it's those few minutes when he gets home at night, or an hour in the mornings that we see each other.

His tan skin and dark hair stand out against the stark white sheets. I run my fingers down his back, tracing the outline of his muscles all the way down to his perfectly round ass. I press a light kiss to the back of his shoulder as he rolls over, startling me.

"Go get in the shower. I'll meet you there," he says with a groggy voice. He rubs his eyes with his fingers.

"No, go back to sleep, babe. You need your rest. I'll shower, then get ready over at the station." I push myself out of the bed and walk across the wood floors to the master en suite. I close the bathroom door in hopes of minimizing the noise I make so Matt can go back to sleep.

I start the shower and let the water warm up while I brush my teeth. I take note of my curves—this is the healthiest I've been in years. I try to work out on a semi-regular basis, I eat healthy, and my body has finally taken notice.

Stepping into the glass shower, I wash my hair and condition it. I squirt some of my body wash onto a sponge and start washing my body when the shower door opens and Matt steps in. He pulls the sponge from my hands and begins washing me. With one hand, he lifts my long hair and rubs the sponge all over my back before pushing me into the gentle stream of water to rinse me.

He repeats the same process on my chest, breasts, and stomach. He drops the sponge to the tiled shower floor as he presses me up against the wall. His lips find mine, peppering hungry kisses against them. One arm pins me against the wall and another trails down my stomach, parting the soft folds of skin between my legs. He slides one finger inside me, gently gliding it in and out before adding a second finger.

"Need you," he mumbles against my lips, and I reach for his erection. Wrapping my hand around him, I slide it up and down the soft skin as I feel him grow larger the longer I stroke him.

"Turn around," he orders and I press my chest up against the cool shower wall. He places both of his hands on my hips and gently guides himself inside of me from behind.

"Holy shit," I stammer as I try to gain control of my breathing. His thrusts are hard, yet controlled. He kisses the side of my neck as I rest my forehead against the wall. One of his hands moves around the front, paying special attention to the bud of soft skin he knows how to work so well.

With three final thrusts, I feel his release deep within and we stay connected just as we do in bed. As we catch our breaths, Matt withdraws from me and bends down to pick up the sponge. Squirting more body wash onto the sponge, he takes his time cleaning me one last time. I rinse the conditioner from my hair and rinse my body again.

Standing on my tiptoes, I curl my arms around his neck and press a long kiss to his soft lips. "I'll meet you in the kitchen," I tell him as he pulls his body wash off the shelf and washes himself. I wrap myself in a towel and quickly dry off, throwing on a pair of yoga pants and a tank top. I have my dress, shoes, and accessories hanging in the closet, ready to bring to work with me.

I leave my long, wet hair hang loose and let it air dry as I head to the kitchen to make coffee. When I get there, I find that Matt has already made a fresh pot. I smile at how considerate and attentive he is. I fill two mugs of coffee and pour a small amount of creamer in both, stirring them. While I'm scrolling through emails and messages on my phone, Matt joins me in the kitchen.

"Anything exciting?" he asks, pressing a kiss to my cheek before grabbing his mug of coffee and sitting on one of the barstools that sits at his small kitchen island.

"Nothing yet." I smile at him. His eyes have dark circles under them and are bloodshot. "You're exhausted," I tell him.

"I'm fine."

"No, you're not. Go back to bed when I leave. You need your rest."

"You worry too much." He chuckles.

"You work too hard. Stop taking overtime shifts."

"You're telling *me* I work too much? Lindsay, I haven't seen *you* in weeks, which is why I've been working overtime. I'm bored without you here." He raises his eyebrows at me.

"I know. It's just that they're shorthanded and it's a really great opportunity for me to get more airtime. I've been at the anchor desk all week." He sighs in frustration, and I sigh that he doesn't understand how much I love and *need* my career. When my mom left my brother Landon and me, we learned quickly that we had to take care of ourselves. I made it a priority to do well in school and eventually received a full scholarship to college. I majored in broadcast journalism and this career has become an extension of who I am.

"Lindsay, you work for practically nothing. The pay is shit, the hours are long—I feel like they're taking advantage of you."

"You know I love this job, and this is what I've always wanted to do. In a small market news station, you have to put in the hours to get noticed. It's this or relocate somewhere else—it's not for the money, it's about the experience." I raise my mug and take a sip of my hot coffee while he blows on the steam rising from his coffee and watches me with a raised eyebrow.

"So is it always going to be like this? Where do *we* fit into this picture?" he asks, setting his coffee mug down and rubbing his temples. It's a fair question. We essentially work opposite shifts as of late and only spend a few hours together sleeping in the same bed. I don't have an answer for him and that rattles me. We've always been happy, in our individual careers, and as a couple—I hadn't given much thought to the stress that my budding career brings to the relationship.

"We'll figure it out," I say, pouring my coffee into a travel mug. "I have to go or I'm going to be late and I still have to get ready." I stop in front of him and kiss his lips. "I love you, Matt Kennedy, more than anything in the entire world." His dark brown eyes look up at me.

"I love you more than that, Lindsay Christianson. I always will." With one last kiss, I hustle out the door and back to work.

# CHAPTER 2

## Matt

I sit in the large leather chair in the corner of the room and watch Lindsay finish getting ready. She's standing at the bathroom vanity in her black lace bra and panties, rushing to touch up her make-up and hair. The pantsuit she wore to work is in a pile on the bedroom floor and a black dress lies at the foot of our bed with gold jewelry laid out next to it.

"Dammit," she curses as she tosses her curling iron onto the counter.

"Are you okay?"

"Burned myself," she grumbles and sucks on the pad of her thumb.

"Babe, you look amazing. Just get dressed or we're going to be late. You know Reagan is going to flip out if we're late."

"I know, I know." She unplugs the curling iron and washes her hands before shutting off the light. "Maybe we should just stay home." She smiles that devious smile at me. "We haven't had a Friday night all to ourselves in a long time." She walks over to me slowly and I can't help but love the way her body moves when she walks. "Maybe we can just lie down for a little bit." She licks her lips and climbs into my lap, straddling me. She has me pinned, one leg on each side of mine and her chest right in my face. "And, you know, just rest." She winks at me. She places her hands on my chest and slides them up toward the top button on my dress shirt.

"Oh, no. As much as I'd love to have you sprawled on that bed all night, if we miss this party, we won't only be answering to Reagan, but to your brother, and now your mother too. No thanks. Now get your ass in that dress; we have fifteen minutes to be at the restaurant." I lift her off my lap and move carefully, due to the growing erection in my pants. She notices and chews on her bottom lip seductively.

"Are you sure?" She moves quickly and rubs me through my dress pants.

"Dammit, Lindsay. Get dressed." I shake my head at her and try to think about baseball or football; anything to make this erection go away. Lindsay laughs smugly as I adjust myself and she picks up her black dress from the bed. She looks tired and pale with her light skin and blonde hair against the stark black dress. As she steps into tall black heels, I zip up the back of her dress. Wrapping my arms around her from behind, I press her against me. She purrs like a kitten at my touch.

"I love you," she hums and rests her head against my chest.

"I love you too. Now let's go so we can get back here and finish what you started over in that chair."

"I love when you're bossy." She giggles and grabs her jewelry off the bed. "Let's go."

We weave through the linen-clad tables in the small Italian restaurant where Lindsay's brother, Landon, and his fiancé, Reagan, are holding a small dinner party. They have a private room in the back and Reagan stands just inside the open door, waiting presumably for us. Lindsay walks right up to her and gives her a quick kiss on the cheek. "Sorry we're late. Crazy day at the station." Reagan smiles at Lindsay and kisses her back.

"Matt," she says, smiling, "did you two ride together?" It has to be the worst kept secret that Lindsay and I are together. For over a year, everyone has known, but we've just never actually told anyone. We show up to events, dinners, and family functions together. We receive invitations addressed to both of us, but Lindsay has always worried that Landon wouldn't accept me, his best friend and former partner, as her boyfriend. Landon, of all people, would know I would never do anything to hurt Lindsay.

"Yeah, I picked her up on the way over." I wink at Reagan. They love busting my balls over our "secret relationship."

"Matty." Landon shakes my hand and smacks me on the shoulder. "How's it goin'?"

"Good. Hanging in there. How 'bout you?"

"Same here, man. Glad you guys could make it." He chuckles and steps away from me to say hello to Lindsay, who has taken a seat at the long family-style table next to her mom and her stepfather, Louis. Lindsay smiles at her mom and stepfather. I love to see them together making up for lost time.

My heart bursts with pride when I think about how forgiving Lindsay is to her mother for leaving Landon and her at such a

young age with a horribly abusive alcoholic father. The stories
Landon would tell me of the beatings he'd take to protect Lindsay
damn near make me nauseous.

I reflect on my own childhood and how lucky I was to
grow up with two supportive parents who were there for me and
met my every need. My dad coached my little league baseball team
and my mom was the epitome of the perfect housewife. My
brother and I were very blessed. My parents and brother still live
in the area and we're all very close. I can't imagine not being near
them.

A server walks over to me with a tray of filled champagne
glasses and I take two; one for Lindsay and one for myself. I hand
one to Lindsay before leaning over to kiss, Josie, Lindsay's mom,
on the cheek and shake Louis' hand.

"Matt, great to see you," Louis says, squeezing my hand. I
nod and slide into the seat next to Lindsay. Josie is whispering
something in Lindsay's ear and they both laugh. Louis rolls his
eyes and takes a drink of red wine. It's unbelievable how much
Lindsay looks like her mother. Reagan sits down next to me and
Landon sits across the table from her. The rest of the guests find
seats at the end of the long table and the room is suddenly full of
conversation and laughter.

Lindsay slides her hand into mine under the table as Reagan
stands up to greet everyone. "So dinner will be served in just a
minute, but before we eat, I wanted to thank you for coming to
dinner with us. We all get so caught up in our busy lives, careers,
and activities that we sometimes forget to slow down and just
enjoy a few hours with our closest friends and family." She smiles
and looks across the table at Landon. "So dinner will be served
family style. There will be an assortment of pastas, salads, wine,
and champagne." She picks up her wine glass from the table and

raises it in the air. "To amazing friends and family," she toasts before sitting back down.

I squeeze Lindsay's hand, which rests in my lap. "Eat fast so we can go home," she whispers and pinches my thigh.

Reagan leans across me and whispers quietly to Lindsay, "Why don't you use tonight's dinner to make an announcement?" Her eyes shift back and forth from me to Lindsay. I chuckle and sip some more champagne.

Landon pulls some garlic bread from a basket and leans into the middle of the table. "Yeah, Lindsay. Why don't you just tell everyone what we all know already?"

"What does everybody think they know?" Lindsay asks snidely. Narrowing her eyes, she presses her champagne glass to her lips, tips her head back, and finishes the bubbly before smacking her lips.

"Oh, come on, Lindsay. I've probably known before you even knew you were officially a couple. Call it cop's instinct." Landon laughs. Lindsay picks a piece of her dinner roll and chucks it across the table at Landon, who laughs harder as the bread bounces off his chest.

She glances at me and I just shrug. "You're the one calling the shots. Remember, babe?"

"Whatever. Fine. I'll do it." She looks at Reagan, who leans back in her chair smugly and sips on her wine.

"You sure?" I ask Lindsay. I want her to be comfortable in telling everyone and not feel pressured.

"Yeah. I mean, Reagan's right. Everyone's here, so we may just as well get it over with." She smiles and leans in to me, pressing a quick kiss to my lips. Landon chucks a piece of dinner roll back at Lindsay when she kisses me.

"Stop it, you guys," Josie says, picking up the piece of roll from Lindsay's lap. "You'd think you were little kids," she tsks.

"All right, everyone." Lindsay stands up and pushes back her chair slightly. She wobbles a bit on her heels and rests her hand on my shoulder to steady herself. "Apparently, tonight is as good as any night to let you all in on a little secret." She wipes the palms of her hands down the sides of her black dress.

"So, for a little over a year now, Matt and I have been seeing each other." There are a few chuckles, but mostly everyone sits silently listening to Lindsay. "We've kept it quiet for a while simply because it's what worked for us." She shrugs. "It started off casual and just turned into more, and we didn't really make a big deal out of it." She looks down at me and smiles the most beautiful, genuine smile I've ever seen. Her blue eyes sparkle in the lights from the crystal chandelier and her long, blonde hair hangs in waves. She looks almost angelic in the dimly lit room. "So, cat's out of the bag." She laughs and raises her glass. I stand up and raise my glass next to hers. "To Matt and me," she says with a smile on her beautiful face. I lean in and press a long kiss to her lips while everyone hoots and hollers around us.

"I love you, sweet girl," I say between kisses.

Dinner is served shortly after and I look down the long dining table full of family and friends and feel genuine happiness. Most of the people here are those that we've grown the closest to over the last year. Everyone is happy, healthy, and enjoying themselves tonight. Nothing makes me happier than seeing everyone happy.

"We're skipping dessert," Lindsay whispers in my ear.

"You don't have to tell me twice." I press a kiss to her forehead.

"Start saying your goodbyes. We're leaving in five minutes."

"I love when you order me around." I smack her bottom.

I spend the next few minutes chatting with Landon and

Reagan about the building progress on their new house, and chat with Melissa, one of Reagan's medical assistants at the doctor's office she's a partner in. Lindsay sneaks up behind me and slides her hand into mine.

"We're going to take off," I tell the small group. "Reagan, as always, wonderful dinner. Thank you for keeping us all together." I reach over and pull her into a short hug.

"Thanks again," Lindsay says as she all but drags me from the room.

"You in a hurry?" I joke with her as we speed walk through the restaurant.

"I need alone time with you," she smirks.

"We have all night and all day tomorrow."

"It's never enough. I will never have enough of you, Matt."

"Well, then. Let's get my sweet girl home."

# CHAPTER 3

## *Lindsay*

"Well, that went better than I expected." I breathe a sigh of relief as I slide into bed next to Matt.

"Because it's been obvious to everyone around us what's been going on for the last year. We clearly suck at being discreet, Lindsay."

"I'm just glad we don't have to lie anymore."

"We weren't lying; we just weren't being open about our relationship," he says, wrapping his naked, lean, muscular body around me.

"I guess, but it just didn't feel right, keeping us a secret."

"I like when you say *us*." He presses a kiss to my lips, then behind my ear.

"I like it when you do that," I whisper. "And I like it when you…" My work cell phone begins ringing, interrupting us.

"Leave it," Matt growls in my ear.

"I can't." He rolls off of me while I reach onto the nightstand and glance at my agent's name flashing on the screen.

"It's Jack," I mumble as I jump out of bed and pull on a robe.

"Jack," I answer curtly.

"Lindsay, I presume you've gotten my three voicemails, two emails, and endless text messages. Why the hell haven't you returned one of them?"

"We had an important family dinner. I'm sorry." I notice Matt slide out of bed and step into a pair of chambray-colored pajama pants. His tan skin is perfection against the light blue pants. He leaves the room while I talk in a hushed tone with Jack.

"Lindsay, this isn't an opportunity to pass up. This will propel your career and take you places you never envisioned," he says, his voice becoming louder. Jack is my agent and one pushy motherfucker. "People kill to get into a market the size of Phoenix. The money is phenomenal, the exposure…"

"Phoenix," I whisper as I pace the bedroom. "Oh, my god, Jack. I can't believe this." My voice is excited, yet slightly hesitant as I think of Matt and what this will mean to us. "I need a couple of days," I respond, a million thoughts swirling through my head, ranging from excitement to trepidation.

"A couple of days, Lindsay?" Jack repeats me.

"Did I stutter, Jack? I need a couple of days. When we had lunch last week, you mentioned looking for other opportunities, but I didn't realize it would happen so fast and so fucking far away. Do you have any idea where Phoenix is, Jack?"

"It's in Arizona, Lindsay. Listen to me. If you don't take this job, it will be the biggest mistake of your career." His husky voice pulls me from thoughts of everything I'll miss if I leave Wilmington.

"Two days, Jack. I need two days. Give me that. Stall them."

There is a large sigh on the other end of the phone, and what sounds like a hand hitting a table. "You have until noon on Monday."

"Thank you, Jack." He disconnects the phone without saying goodbye. I know he's pissed. I catch a glimpse of Matt leaning against the doorframe of the bedroom. His head has fallen forward and he stares at the ground.

"Talk to me," I say as I walk over and wrap my arms around him.

"What do you want me to say, Lindsay? It sounds like you have a great opportunity—and I'll be damned if I'm going to be the person to hold you back from that." His dark brown eyes meet mine.

"What would you do if you were me?" I ask him.

"That's easy. I'd choose you because I love you and you mean more to me than any job or any opportunity. But Lindsay, I won't stop you from chasing this dream. You'll live with your decision for the rest of your life. I never want to be a decision you regret." He pulls away from me as he turns toward the hallway. "But promise me something, will you?" I nod at him as a lump forms in my throat. "Follow your heart. I know you better than you know yourself and I know how your brain works— listen to your heart." I hear him shuffle down the hall toward the kitchen.

I have no idea how long I've been standing, staring at that damn phone when I pick it up and hit Jack's name on the recent calls screen.

"Lindsay," his deep voice drawls.

"I'll do it." My voice shakes. "I'll take it." My heart sinks and tears fill my eyes.

"Welcome to Phoenix, sweetheart."

My legs are weak and my hands shake as I second-guess my decision to leave, knowing I very well may be making the biggest mistake of my life. My dream of working in a top fifteen market just came true and all I want to do is vomit. Sliding down the wall I've been leaning against for support, I wrap my arms around my knees as I try to calm myself. As I glance back at the open door, I see Matt standing in defeat, broken. His brown eyes are grim and lost, while his face says everything my heart is feeling—shattered.

"Well, that was an easy decision," he snarls at me. He walks across the bedroom and pulls a pair of shorts and a t-shirt from the dresser.

"Matt, listen to me—I have to take this opportunity. It's a year. We can handle a year apart."

"*We*, Lindsay? *We*? I can barely handle one night without you and *you* want *us* to spend a year apart?" His voice is raised and the vein in his neck is throbbing. My heart is racing as I watch his temperament change from hurt to angry. "I can't do long distance, and I know you can't either." I chew on my bottom lip while I search for anything to say to calm him down.

"Then come with me. Matt, you can be a cop anywhere."

"Everything I have, everything I love is here, Lindsay."

He steps into his shorts and pulls the t-shirt over his head. He runs his hands through his mussed up hair and just stares at me. "Who are you? I feel like I don't even know you anymore!" His tone is sharp. "Where is the girl I fell in love with? Remember when you'd sneak over and into my bed every night and share your dreams of what you wanted with *me*? Where'd that girl go? Over the last year, you've become so focused on your career and making it to the next level—and I understand that this is your dream, but it was supposed to include both of us."

My throat has become so dry it's closed up. I'm unable to speak. His dark brown eyes glisten as he looks to me for answers.

"I was fine just being a cop, being your boyfriend, and

supporting your dream—here. All I asked for, all I wanted was for you to love me."

"I do love you, Matt," I barely make out.

He laughs bitterly. "You love me? You love me so much you made what should have been the hardest decision of your life in fifteen seconds."

"I won't go. I'll tell him I made a mistake."

"Don't," he says quietly. "Like I said earlier, I never want to be a decision you regret. I just never thought I'd ever be a decision you could make in a matter of seconds." He walks out of the room and down the hallway.

"Matt, wait." I chase after him.

"Just go." He slides his feet into a pair of tennis shoes and grabs his keys off the table next to the front door. The door slams behind him as he leaves. I had no idea that this would be the last time I saw him before I left for Phoenix.

# CHAPTER 4

## *Lindsay*

Stepping off the airplane, I'm assaulted with hot air—so hot it feels like someone is holding a blow dryer on high heat directly to my face. My cell phone chimes, alerting me to an incoming text message, most likely from Jack. I ignore it as I have with every other text message and phone call that has come in over the last two weeks. I take my time making my way toward the exits that lead to baggage claim, stopping in the nearest restroom to splash some cold water on my face and fix my tousled hair.

The girl looking back at me in the mirror is ashen gray with messy sandy blonde hair and lifeless blue eyes. That's exactly how I feel—lifeless. I pull my stringy hair back into a ponytail and tug at the long, cream tank top I'm wearing over a pair of black leggings. If I had bothered to check the weather, I would have known it was going to be one hundred and fifteen degrees and I would have worn shorts or a dress instead of leggings.

Slinging my oversized handbag onto my shoulder, I take the moving walkway that drops me at the exit where I know Jack will be waiting. I descend on the small groups of people clustered around waiting for loved ones to arrive and locate Jack with his cellphone pressed to his ear, barking orders to his assistant.

"There you are." He pulls me into a side hug before shoving his phone into his pocket. "How was the flight?"

"Long," I grumble as I pull away from him. Jack stands almost a foot taller than me and is built like a linebacker. He's broad shouldered and has a shock of silver hair that stands out against his dark blue eyes that look nearly gray against his backdrop of fair skin. Jack intimidates me. Hell, he intimidates everyone. His voice is deep and demanding and there's no arguing with him. I hired him for this very reason, because he's a pit bull—he doesn't give up and will fight like hell for his clients in this cutthroat industry.

"You look like hell," he observes, taking me in from head to toe.

"Thanks." I offer him a sarcastic smile. "I moved to hell, so I only thought it was fitting to look like my surroundings."

"I didn't force you to take the job, Lindsay…"

"No, but you told me I'd be making a huge mistake if I didn't," I cut him off. He sighs and I notice his jaw muscles flexing as a flush crawls across his face, turning it bright red. He's most likely pondering a brilliant, yet snarky comeback laced with curse words, and it looks like it might damn near kill him. Our foul mouths are so similar one could quite possibly mistake him for my father.

"I'm excited about this opportunity, Jack, but at the same time… I left everything and everyone I've ever known or cared about in North Carolina. I have nothing here but this job." My voice is quiet… tired. I see his face soften slightly when I share my fears.

"It's a one-year contract, Lindsay. That's it. If you hate it, you can move closer to home. I can't guarantee that WXZI will have anything for you, but maybe we can get you to Raleigh or Charlotte." He looks away from me, most likely annoyed at the prospect that I'd take him up on that offer right about now if I could.

"One year," I whisper.

"One year," he repeats and nods his head.

Shoving his hands into his front pockets, he pulls out a key chain that has two keys attached. "Keys to your downtown condo." He drops them into the palm of my hand. "Twenty-second floor, one down from the penthouse level. It has a great view of the Phoenix skyline. You'll love it. It's fully furnished and ready for you."

I nod my head and look at the two keys in my hand before tossing them into my handbag.

"Let's get to baggage claim and get your suitcase. I need to get you to the car dealership so you can get your lease since I'm on an afternoon flight back to Chicago." He begins walking toward the escalators that will take us down to baggage claim before turning back to look at me. Raising his eyebrows, he shakes his head, but keeps walking. "Let's go, Lindsay," he orders me, and I fall into step behind him.

"How do people fucking breathe in this heat?" I complain as the stifling Phoenix heat all but collapses my lungs. Jack lifts my suitcase and sets it into the back of his rented Cadillac Escalade.

"You'll get used to it. It's a dry heat," he smirks at me as he pulls his Ray Bans from the top of his head and pushes them onto his face. "I guess a convertible is out of the question for you?" He chuckles to himself. The trip from the airport to the car dealership takes no more than ten minutes. I study the blue sky that is covered in a light brown layer of smog, but not enough to detract from the beauty of the brown mountains and palm-tree-lined streets. Even though it's August and pushing one hundred and fifteen degrees, people are out and about and not bothered by the extreme heat.

I don't even notice we've arrived at the dealership until Jack cuts the engine and opens his door. I follow him inside and take a seat in the modern lounge. Jack is the master negotiator. He knows what I want and, since it's a lease, it's basically just formalities and paperwork. One hour later, Jack is tossing my suitcase into the back of a silver Lexus IS 350 and sending me on my way to the new downtown condo I'm renting.

"Go get settled. Be positive. You're going to love it here. I promise," he says as he rests both of his hands on my shoulders. "Everything is set up at the condo. All you have to do is get some groceries." He glances at the time on his phone. "I have to get going or I'll miss my flight. Call me if you need anything." I nod and swallow hard. Even though Jack is generally an asshole, he's the only person I have at this moment. He slides into his car and gives me a short wave as he pulls away, leaving me on my own.

I sit in my car for a few moments, letting the last few weeks of my life swirl in my head like a video on replay. To say I left things with Matt on pleasant terms would be incorrect. I crushed him. I broke him into a million pieces and I left him in North Carolina while I chased a dream I wasn't even sure I wanted anymore. His words echo in my head one thousand times a day. "*I'd choose you because I love you and you mean more to me than any job or any opportunity. But, Lindsay, I will not stop you from chasing this dream."*

I sync my phone's Bluetooth to the car and punch in the address of my condo into the navigation system, and then merge my car into traffic. Phoenix is a gorgeous city. In most large cities, the buildings are practically on top of each other. It's not like that here. Every building sits on a perfectly coiffed lot. Cactus and boulders are part of most of the landscapes; so different from everything I'm used to. Driving downtown is easier than I anticipated and I find my condominium easily. Easing my small car into a spot on the street with a parking meter, I put the car in park and take in the downtown skyline.

My condominium must have been a recently converted office building. It takes up a full city block and sits above a bank. Across the street is a gorgeous stone building that is modern, yet not obnoxious, as it blends in well with the other downtown buildings, and a light rail train blows by on the tracks that run down the center of the street. I finally summon the courage to leave the safety of the cool air-conditioned car to check out my new home.

I pull open the large glass doors that lead into a gorgeous modern glass and marble atrium. A concierge desk sits just inside the main entrance and an older man stands behind the desk dressed in a full suit—I feel miserable for him, dressed like that in this heat. I must look lost because he quickly steps out from around the desk and moves toward me with a welcoming smile on his face.

"Good afternoon, miss. How may I be of assistance?" His voice has a heavy Spanish accent and his dark brown eyes dance when he speaks.

"I'm Lindsay Christianson. I'm moving into 2202."

"Oh yes, Ms. Christianson. I've been waiting for you." He holds up his index finger, gesturing for me to wait for him as he quickly walks back to the desk and pulls a large manila envelope from beneath it. "In here is your garage access card. Swipe the card across the pad and the gate will rise. Your spot is clearly marked by your unit number. I've included brochures and pamphlets to all the downtown restaurants, theaters, and the closest shopping areas."

"Thank you," I respond, grateful to have all of this information.

"Any packages that come, I will sign for and hold here at the desk. Mailboxes are over there." He points to a wall that houses an entire section of gold mailboxes just next to the elevators. "Again, yours is marked by your unit number. The key for the mailbox is also in that envelope. Please let me know if there is anything I can do for you, Ms. Christianson." I turn slowly and take in the huge lobby atrium full of large, lush plants and small indoor trees.

"There is something," I say as I turn back toward him. "What's your name?"

"My apologies, Ms. Christianson. Please forgive me. I am Marco."

"Marco, please call me Lindsay."

"Very well. Welcome to your new home." He nods at me and strides back to the tall desk, where he positions himself just as he was when I entered the lobby. I almost snorted when he said the word "home." Phoenix will never be home to me. I make my way to the four sets of elevators that sit across the lobby opposite the mailboxes, making note of where my mailbox is located. I don't have to wait for an elevator, as one is waiting with the doors open. I enter and press the button with the twenty-two on it. The elevator rises quickly and my stomach does a little flip as it quickly halts at the twenty-second floor. The doors open and I step into the hall, which smells of fresh paint. Even the corridors are exquisite, decorated with high-end mirrors and lush plants. I follow the ascending door numbers to the right, which lead me to the end of the hall, a corner unit.

Inserting the key into the lock, I turn the knob and push open the door. My eyes widen as I step into pure luxury. I've never seen a place like this—ever. The floor is covered in real dark wood, laid into a herringbone pattern. The kitchen is huge for a condo, with an oversized kitchen island. Every surface is covered in light-colored granite and every appliance is state of the art stainless steel.

The condo has been fully furnished with top-of-the-line décor and appliances—Jack did this, of course. Cream-colored leather couches and oversized chairs are positioned in the center of the living room. Plush cream throw rugs sit under the furniture, giving the room some warmth. Large throw pillows line the couches and chairs. The entire living area in the condo is floor-to-ceiling windows, with a south-facing view of a gorgeous mountain range. Long, sheer curtains line the walls, breaking up the floor-to-ceiling wall of windows.

Off of the main living area is an open door and, as I approach, I can see it's a bedroom. Inside sits a king size four-poster bed covered in light cream bedding—everything in this condo is cream. Again, there are decorative pillows strewn everywhere in this room; on the bed, covering the chaise lounge that sits in a corner and even on the bench at the end of the bed. I take a seat on the edge of the bed and lie back. With my feet dangling, I take a deep breath and close my tired eyes. While everything here is gorgeous—stunning, to be exact—I'd rather be with Matt in his smaller, cozy house… wrapped in his arms. It's the only place I really feel at home.

# CHAPTER 5
## Matt

Lindsay left for Arizona and I let her go without a fight. I left her standing in my living room weeks ago, crying, and I walked out. I was bitter and hurt and I was a giant prick to her. I didn't say goodbye to her—because I couldn't. It would have destroyed me. A year and a half ago, I almost lost her in a car accident. I almost died that day—thinking of what my life would be like without her. Today, I'm fully aware of what it feels like to be dead—not physically dead, but emotionally. Emotionally, I'm a dead man. She was *everything* to me—everything.

Every time my phone chimes with a text message, or rings—I jump in anticipation that it's her. It never is. Landon and Reagan have been calling and texting non-stop for the last week, but I don't care to talk to them—or anyone, for that matter. I only want to hear Lindsay's voice, see Lindsay's messages on my phone.

I pull the bottle opener from the drawer and pop the cap off another bottle of Dos Equis, tossing the cap and opener onto the kitchen counter. I let the cool, yet sharp liquid slide down my throat as I look around my filthy kitchen. The kitchen island and counters are littered with beer bottles and empty take-out containers. When Lindsay was here, everything in this house was in its place, clean—perfect. Everything was perfect with her. Now my house looks like the bachelor pad of a twenty-two-year-old college senior, not a thirty-two-year-old police officer.

"Matt?" I hear the recognizable voice of Reagan as my front door squeaks open.

"In here," I mumble back, hoping she doesn't hear me and will just go away. No such luck. I hear the front door close and her heels click against the hardwood floor, becoming louder as she nears. She stops and watches me as I toss my head back and take another pull from the bottle of beer in my hand. Her eyebrows raise and her lips curl in disgust. I know I'm a fucking mess, and I can only imagine what I look like.

"It's ten in the morning. How many of those have you had?" She nods toward the beer in my hand.

"A few," I answer her curtly. *A few, or six,* I think to myself, lifting the bottle to my lips and emptying the rest of the cool contents down my throat. I belch loudly and toss the beer bottle into the kitchen sink on top of a stack of dirty dishes.

"Seriously?" she says, scrunching her nose in revulsion as she walks further into the kitchen and sets her purse on the kitchen table.

"What? You live with Landon and that man can burp." I chuckle to myself, realizing how obnoxious I must sound. I reach for the door of the refrigerator and locate another tall green bottle and pull it out.

"Not so fast," Reagan snaps as she snatches the bottle from my hand and pushes the refrigerator door closed abruptly.

"Give it back."

"Not until we talk."

"There's really nothing to talk about." I cross my arms over my bare chest, realizing for the first time since she got here that I'm standing in a pair of jeans that are unbuttoned and nothing else.

"Oh, I wouldn't be so sure about that. There's a lot to talk about—let's start with why you won't return our calls or texts?"

"Because I'm dealing with shit right now and I don't want to talk to anybody." She leans back against the fridge door and juggles the cold bottle of beer back and forth between her hands.

"So drinking your life away and living in squalor is how you're going to handle this?" Her eyes move from the stack of dirty dishes to the kitchen island full of empty bottles and take-out containers.

"For right now, yes."

"Matt," she whispers. "Let us help you."

"Help me what, Reagan? I'm fucking lost. I can't think, I can't sleep." I turn my head to look out the kitchen window as my voice trails off. "I fucking miss her."

"I know you do," she whispers as she sets the beer bottle on the counter and pulls me into a hug. "We all miss her. But, Matt, we miss you too. You shut us out." She pulls away, but rests her hands on my biceps. Reagan's mannerisms, even the simplest of touches, remind me of Lindsay. Her soft eyes and caring nature remind me of everything I'm missing—everything I no longer have.

"Let me help you get this house in order. It looks like a fucking frat house." She shakes her head as she lowers her hands and begins pulling empty beer bottles out of the sink. I take the beer bottle from the counter and stuff it back into the fridge.

"You don't have to do that, you know," I say as I watch her pull the recycle bucket out of the kitchen pantry and start stuffing it with the empty bottles.

"I know." She smiles softly. "I want to. Why don't you go shower? It looks like you could use one."

"Is that your way of telling me I look like shit?" I jokingly ask her.

"Yes. And you smell like it too," she smirks.

Standing under the scalding water, I inhale sharply as the water bites at my skin. The pain feels good. It momentarily pulls me away from the pain that is tearing through my heart. I reach for the shampoo from the corner shelf and am instantly reminded of Lindsay when I see a bottle that she left behind. I pull it from the shelf and open the lid, bringing it to my nose. I inhale the sweet floral scent and am flooded with memories of my nose pressed to her head. Opening the shower door, I toss the bottle across the bathroom until it lands on the floor next to the trash can. I scrub my tired body and pray I can scrub away the hurt at the same time.

The house smells of cleaning solution and looks like it did weeks ago before Lindsay left me. Reagan is loading the dishwasher and I walk in to find a sparkling clean kitchen. Everything is neat and tidy and in its place, a far cry from how it was when she got here.

"Almost done." She smiles.

"You didn't have to do this. I would have gotten around to it eventually."

"Pfft," she snorts. "After the mold started taking over? I'm glad to help. But in return, you're going to do something for me." She wipes her hands on a kitchen towel and cocks her head to the side just a little bit. She's demanding, and gorgeous. I can understand why Landon is hopelessly in love with her.

"Oh, I am, huh?"

"Yeah, you are. You're coming over for dinner tonight. I know you're off work for the weekend—and we decided this morning to have a little impromptu dinner party. So your house is clean—sleep off the beer you've been drinking like it's what's keeping you alive…"

"It *is* what's been keeping me alive," I mumble.

"Matt, what I'm trying to say is, this sucks. I know it does. Trust me. But you need to start moving on. You're a gorgeous and fun guy…"

"Does your fiancé know you just called me gorgeous?" I joke with her. She rolls her eyes at me and sighs.

"Please?" she asks.

"Okay, I'll be there. What time and what do you want me to bring?"

"Be there at six and you don't need to bring anything. Just shave that fuzz off your face," she teases me about my lame attempt at growing facial hair as an act of rebellion against Lindsay leaving. "And, Matt…" She pulls her purse off the kitchen table and takes out her car keys. "You better show up."

"I'll be there. I promise."

"Sober."

"Yes, ma'am." I wink at her.

"See you in a few hours."

"Thanks again, Reagan. I mean it."

"Anytime." She smiles at me and gives me a little wave as she leaves me standing in my kitchen. Looking around, I see that Reagan has put her own little touches in my kitchen. A towel hanging from the handle on the oven door, a scented candle that has never been lit is now making my kitchen smell like sugar cookies, and a post-it note on my refrigerator reads *"Look Forward With Hope"* with a little smiley face underneath it. For the first time in weeks, I feel a smile tug at my lips.

I drive up the long, newly paved driveway at Landon and Reagan's new house and am in complete awe of the gorgeous home. Enormous isn't sufficient enough a word for this custom house. I park my Tahoe and take notice of the spectacular multi-colored pavers that circle a large fountain in their driveway. *They have a fountain in the middle of their driveway.* I chuckle to myself. I grab the bouquet of flowers I stopped and picked up for Reagan as I step out of my car and take in the enormity of this house. *Over the top.* I wouldn't expect anything less from my best friend. The oversized glass and wrought-iron front doors swing open and Reagan bounds down the stone stairs.

"You're here!" She pulls me into a tight hug.

"What can I say? I'm a man of my word," I mumble and squeeze her back.

"I'm glad you're here. Tonight is going to be fun." She pulls away and gives me a good looking over. "You clean up nicely too." She laughs.

"These are for you." I hand her the large bouquet.

"And you're amazingly sweet too. Thank you," she says as she loops her arm through mine. "Let's go inside. Landon is showing everyone around."

"Who else is here?" I'm suddenly curious because I didn't notice the other cars that were parked off to the side of the garage until she said there were other people here.

"Oh, Melissa and Ashley from my work, and Detective Weston and his wife; you know him from the police station, right? It's just a small group," she reassures me.

Stepping into the foyer, I'm instantly in awe of how open and inviting the house is. For a home this large, I expected it to be cold and stark, but Reagan has outdone herself with making it feel warm, comfortable, and cozy; nothing like the modern feel of Landon's old house. The walls are painted in rich, deep colors, and oversized mirrors, paintings, and pictures cover most of the walls surfaces.

I follow Reagan down the travertine-tiled floor to the massive kitchen. The kitchen island is covered with platters of antipasti, cheese boards, fruit, and crudité. "How many people did you say were here?" I ask Reagan, who has positioned herself next to the stove as she sips from her glass of white wine. "There's enough food here to feed an army," I remark.

"Just wait," she says, setting her glass of wine on the marbled granite counter. "I have lasagna in the oven and a huge tray of homemade meatballs covered in marinara." She opens one of the doors to the double oven and peeks inside.

"You two never do anything small, do you?" I ask, pulling a bottle of beer from the metal bucket that sits full of ice and a variety of beverages.

"I don't think 'small' is in our vocabulary." She winks at me.

"The house is gorgeous, Reagan. Seriously, I'm almost overwhelmed."

"Is it too much?" she asks, the smile dropping from her face. "You know I don't like extravagant…"

"No," I cut her off. "I didn't mean it like that. It's just gorgeous and huge… but it's homey. I like that it feels lived in— comfortable." The smile creeps back across her face.

"Are you flirting with my woman?" I feel his hand smack my back before I see him. The rest of the guests follow him inside from the glass doors that slide open to the back patio. I hadn't even realized that the wall of windows opened like that.

"Better look out; I'm a free man now." I realize how insensitive that sounds the second it rolls off my tongue. Missing Lindsay and acting like an asshole aren't allowed here tonight. Reagan grabs the flowers I brought her and starts unwrapping them and places them in a crystal vase. Everyone else stands around, awkwardly sipping on their drinks. "Sorry," I mumble. Landon takes a deep breath and gives my shoulder a squeeze.

"Everyone, please help yourself to some appetizers," he says as he steps around me and grabs an olive off the antipasti tray. Everyone gathers around the large island and helps themselves to appetizers while I slip out the door they just came from to the back patio. Patio isn't quite how I'd describe this either—it's more of an outdoor living area. It's huge and decorated with outdoor furniture that looks like it should be inside a house. There is even a flat-screen TV mounted up in the corner. Soft music is being piped from the speakers that are built into the ceiling. Along the edges of the stained concrete, lush potted plants sit encasing the patio.

I walk to the open edge of the patio where it's no longer covered and is truly outside. The backyard is fenced and enormous. It has to sit on over an acre. Green grass is growing and you can barely make out the outlines from the rows of sod that were most likely laid not more than a week or two ago. The backyard is illuminated with large lights from each of the back corners of the house, along with landscape lighting around the yard.

"Hey," Landon says as he approaches me from behind. "Glad you could make it, buddy."

"Thanks for the invite." I stand with my arms crossed over my chest and just look out into the yard. I don't know how this is supposed to go. My best friend's sister just broke up with me to take a job across the country and I'm fucking angry—actually, no; I'm hurt.

"How are you doing?" he asks. Nothing like cutting straight to the chase, not that I'd expect anything different from him.

"Been better," I admit.

"Have you heard from her?"

I let out a small groan before answering. "Nope. Last time I heard from her was two weeks ago when she came to get her stuff from my house." He looks at me and nods his head once.

"Have you?" I ask, curiosity getting the better of me.

"Yeah, when she first got there she called but it was really brief. We haven't heard from her since."

"Sounds like her." I let out a little laugh.

"For what it's worth, I was really happy to hear about you two. There is no one else in this world that I would trust my sister with other than you."

I swallow hard at his admission. "Kind of a moot point now, huh?"

"Never say never," he says quietly. "Let's go inside. There is something I want to show you after dinner." His face lights up with a huge smile.

"This place is insane," I comment. "I had no idea how big it was going to be."

"Reagan wanted a place with lots of room for visitors and... kids."

"Kids? Is Reagan ready? Hell, are you ready for kids?"

"I don't know." He shrugs. "You know I'll give her anything she wants."

"Yeah, but is that what *you* want?" I ask.

"It is, when the time is right," he answers firmly. "But right now, we're just focused on the wedding and we like to practice making kids," he smirks.

"Good plan." I laugh.

Dinner was amazing. I wouldn't expect anything less from Reagan. Even the company was nice. It was nice to be out of the confines of my stuffy house and in the real world, having normal conversations with adults instead of sulking in my pitiful misery at home. I even made plans with Melissa, Reagan's medical assistant and mutual friend, to go hiking tomorrow. I felt guilty accepting her invitation, like it was something I shouldn't be doing, but she's a friend, that's it, and it will be nice to start doing normal things again.

As we gather around the outside fireplace with our after-dinner drinks, the girls naturally circle around each other and giggle about the latest celebrity gossip while we guys gravitate toward the fire and talk sports.

"Oh, hey, I wanted to show you guys the game room," Landon says, stepping back into the house.

"Game room?" Weston questions.

"Yeah, it's the only room Reagan let me have complete say in." He laughs.

"One room?" I can't help but laugh at how much Landon has changed since his single days. "Does she carry your balls around in her purse?"

"Fuck off," he barks at me. But we all laugh. When Landon opens the oversized interior double doors, we walk into a massive room that holds a pool table in the center of the room.

"Holy shit, man," I say, admiring the room. It's decorated in a sports theme with framed football jerseys and autographed pictures. There is a small wet bar in the far corner, and tall barstools that line one wall.

"Want to play?"

"Yeah!" Weston and I say in unison. I set my drink on one of the tall pub tables and pull a pool stick from the stand on the wall and rack the balls. My phone vibrates in my pocket and I scramble to pull it out in hopes that it's Lindsay. My heart stops when I glance at the screen and her picture stares back at me. The one I took of her on the beach only a few short weeks ago. Her blonde hair curls around tan shoulders and her sunglasses are propped on top of her head. Her bright blue eyes glisten against the backdrop of the Atlantic Ocean. I slide my finger over the screen to accept the call and walk out of the game room and into the hallway.

"Linds?" I answer the phone. She doesn't respond. "Hello?" Still no answer. "Lindsay, is everything okay?" The phone clicks and she hangs up. Pulling the phone away from my ear, I stare at the screen, whispering a silent prayer that she calls back. She never does. I lean against the wall, a million thoughts swirling through my head. Is she okay? Why did she call? What is she doing? Where does she live? Is she alone? Does she miss me as much as I miss her?

"Everything okay?" Landon asks as he walks toward me.

"I don't know." I shrug. "She hung up. I'm really worried about her," I admit. Landon runs his hand across his chin, but doesn't say anything else. "I think I'm going to call it a night. I'm going to go say goodbye to Reagan and the girls."

He nods his head. "Thanks for coming by, and if I hear anything from Lindsay…"

"Yeah. Please let me know."

# CHAPTER 6

## *Lindsay*

I hung up. I miss him. I needed to hear his voice, but hearing his voice about killed me. I lie in this oversized bed, crying into a pillow and wanting him—needing him. I left the sheer curtains open, in hopes that I wouldn't feel so alone, yet all I feel is emptiness and isolation. I toss and turn for hours, my eyes never closing as I watch the minutes on the digital alarm clock tick by in slow motion.

Just as my eyes begin to feel heavy, I can hear the deep bass line penetrating through my bedroom wall. The large mirror that hangs above my headboard rattles with each thump. "You have got to be fucking kidding me," I grumble. I ball my hand into a fist and bang on the wall a few times in a heed of warning.

The music continues for another thirty minutes before I finally break down. In between bouts of laughter and tears, I come unglued. I throw shoes at the wall, throw pillows, and kick the wall so hard I damn near leave a hole. I'm so angry, lost, and sorry. Pulling myself together, I stand up and brush the tears from my face. I realize that I look like a wreck and I don't care. I need to sleep before I lose my mind.

I walk through the living room, dodging end tables, and into the kitchen, where I flip on the light over the kitchen island. I twist the deadbolt lock and step into the carpeted hallway. The music is noticeably louder out here, and only gets louder as I approach the door marked 2200. I knock, tentatively at first, and wait. When no one answers, I smack the door hard with my open hand and wait again. This time, the door flies open and the obnoxious club music fills the hallway along with sounds of laughter from the party.

"Can I help you?" the obviously drunk man says as he steadies himself with the open door.

"Yeah. I'm Lindsay, your next-door neighbor who is trying to sleep. Think you can turn down that atrocious music and ask your friends to keep it down? I mean it's *only* three twenty in the morning. I hope that's not too much to ask." My voice is loud and laced with anger and sarcasm.

"I'm Jonah, and three o'clock is usually when we just get started. Want to join us?" His eyes trail slowly down my barely clothed body and he smirks. I look into the condo and see a couple snorting something off the granite countertop and an island full of liquor.

"Just fucking keep it down," I hiss at him and begin walking back to my condo. "And quit acting like a twelve-year-old boy with a boner, who has never seen a girl in a pair of shorts and tank top."

"Those are fucking underwear, not shorts." He laughs and slams his door shut before I get the chance to slam mine first.

"Prick," I mutter to myself and lean against my door. My hand is trembling and I'm not sure if it's out of anger or exhaustion, but I know I need to take a pill and relax. I spot my purse on the couch and quickly make my way to it. Reaching inside, I pull out the brown pill bottle and pop open the top. I dump two little white pills into my hand and toss the bottle on the couch as I scramble back to the kitchen for a glass of water.

Pressing the glass to my lips, I let the water carry those two little pills that will bring me relief down my throat. I'd been doing great at not using these pills until three weeks ago—until I made the decision to take this job and move here. I clench my right hand in hopes that the trembling ceases. The thumping music is less noticeable here in the living room than it is in the bedroom, so I lie down on the cool leather couch and release a deep breath. Knocking the small bottle of pills onto the floor, I hold a large throw pillow against my chest and close my eyes. My heart beats wildly while I wait for the little pills to dissolve and bring me relief—relief from the anger and self-hatred I feel—but mostly relief from the pain in my heart.

I find myself stuck somewhere between deep sleep and semi-consciousness when I hear the loud knocking that doesn't let up. "What?" I mumble incoherently. I finally open my eyes, only to be assaulted by sun streaming in from the wall of floor-to-ceiling windows in my living room and another round of loud knocking on the door. "Hold on," I holler as I push myself off the couch and get my bearings.

I stumble to the door just as the knocking continues. "Jesus Christ! I said 'hold on,'" I bark as I fling the door open.

"Well, well, well. Look who's finally awake," Jonah, my obnoxious next-door neighbor says as he stands holding a cardboard tray with two coffees and a small, white paper bag.

"What do you want?" I glare at him.

"Peace offering," he says as he raises the bag and tray and a wide smile stretches across his face. "Are you going to be neighborly and invite me in, or do I have to take this back to my place and share with the girl who's passed out on my couch?"

"Classy, aren't you, Jonah?" I say, opening the door wider and motioning him in. He walks to the center island and sets down the bag and tray of coffees. I shut the door and stand with my arms crossed over my chest and wonder why in the world I just let this asshole into my condo. But the smell of the coffee reminds me why: I have a headache the size of the Grand Canyon and coffee is what I need. Jonah pulls out one of the tall chairs and waits for me to take a seat.

"I might not be the classiest guy around, but I'm not a complete asshole either," he breathes into my hair when he bends down to push in my chair. I inhale sharply when his warm breath meets my ear and goose bumps crawl across my arms. He notices my reaction and smiles again smugly. "So, Lindsay, let's start over, on the right foot this time." He takes a cup of coffee out of the cardboard carrier and hands it to me. "I'm Jonah Murphy, your awesome and handsome next-door neighbor." I can't help but smile at him.

Jonah is cute in a frat boy kind of way. He's tall and has sandy blond hair and dark brown eyes with just a sprinkling of dark facial hair along the jawline. He wears khakis and a polo t-shirt, his appearance telling me he's stuck somewhere between party animal and prep student.

"How old are you?" I ask.

"Twenty-four," he says with a small chuckle. "You?"

"Twenty-five, almost twenty-six."

"See, we can be friends." He smiles and takes a sip of his coffee. I roll my eyes.

"Let's not put the cart before the horse, shall we?" I say

sarcastically. "I saw the company you keep last night, and that's not really *my* crowd." I realize I sound really bitchy, but snorting what I assume was cocaine off a kitchen counter isn't my thing.

"Yeah, about that… that's not really *my* thing either, but it's my friends' thing… so I deal with it." He pauses. "Where are you from? I heard a little southern in that snippy tone of yours last night." I like his wittiness and can't help but smile at his remark.

"North Carolina. I moved here yesterday."

"Ah, that makes sense. I've been the lone occupant on the twenty-second floor for almost a year now. So to say I was surprised about having a new next-door neighbor would be an understatement."

"Sorry to disappoint you," I mumble and take a sip of coffee.

"I'm hardly disappointed," he says, raising an eyebrow. "And I'm sorry about the music last night. Now that I know I have a neighbor, I'll be more respectful."

"Well, I appreciate that. And thank you for the coffee."

"Oh, there are muffins too." He reaches across me and grabs the paper bag.

"Thanks, but I'm not feeling all that great." I place my hand on my stomach.

"Why is your hand shaking like that?" Jonah questions me.

"I'm just tired and not feeling well. It's been a long couple of days," I say as I scan the living room, looking for the pill bottle that I kicked off the couch last night. I spot it peeking out from underneath the coffee table. Sliding off the tall chair, I walk over to the table and pick up the pill bottle. I open it and pop two pills and toss the bottle onto the couch. Jonah watches me intently, taking in every move I make. His eyes follow me back to the island, where I wash down the pills with a swallow of coffee.

"That going to make you feel better?" he asks suspiciously.

"Yes. But that's really none of your business, is it?" I reply sharply and his eyes widen in surprise.

"Well, on that note, neighbor... I'll be leaving." He pushes his chair away from the island and stands up. "It was nice to formally meet you." He smiles. "And I promise to be a better neighbor." He walks to the door and opens it. "If you need anything—sugar, eggs, a friend—I'm just next door." He glances back to me before he steps through the threshold and disappears with the click of the door behind him.

Cinching the belt around my waist, I stand back and study myself in the mirror. I'm exhausted, but I look good. First impressions are everything in this business and I plan to rock my first day at work. This red silk sheath dress with three-quarter sleeves and nude heels screams power. I've curled my long, blonde hair so that it hangs in loose tendrils and my make-up is perfect—smoky eye shadow makes my light blue eyes pop. Gold accessories complete the outfit and I'm ready to go.

I swap out my oversized handbag for a more chic clutch and grab my car keys and cell phone. "Let's do this," I mumble to myself in the mirror.

The elevator is waiting for me as I approach. Just as I step in, I hear Jonah's voice. "Hold the elevator." I close my eyes and take a deep breath.

"Well, well, well... look at you," he says with a whistle. "Aren't we stunning this morning? Where are you off to, looking like that?"

"First day at the new job," I grumble as I glance at him out of the corner of my eye. He looks like he's fourteen as he's dressed in a pair of athletic shorts and t-shirt, and his blond hair is tucked under a baseball cap turned backwards. "Why are you wearing a backpack?" I inquire as he presses the L on the elevator keypad to bring us to the lobby.

"I'm going to class," he smirks.

"Class?"

"Yeah. I'm a fifth-year senior." He laughs.

"A fifth-year senior?" I repeat.

"Yeah. It's still to be determined if I'll be making it to sixth-year senior."

"Unbelievable," I say under my breath. "So how is it that a college student can afford to live in a condo like that?"

"Ah, it's my dad's place. It's nothing but a tax write-off for him and a party palace for me. I mean, former party palace, now that I have a next-door neighbor." He winks at me. The elevator slows to a stop and the doors open. "After you." He holds the door and smiles at me.

"Thanks. Have a good day at *class*," I say, my tone snarky as I step out of the elevator and cut across the lobby.

"Have a good day at work," he offers back and jogs away in the opposite direction.

The bustling newsroom and the number of people buzzing around seemingly oblivious to my presence immediately intimidates me. I've been here all of three minutes and have already received two dirty looks and an eye roll. "Good times," I whisper to myself as I toss my purse on my desk and sit down in the ergonomic chair. My cell phone buzzes inside my purse and I pull it out to see who's calling. Reagan. I hit ignore and set it on my desk.

"You must be the infamous Lindsay Christianson. I'm Michael Wilson. You can call me Mike; it just sounds more manly." I look up to find "Mike" standing inside the entrance of my small cubicle, his arms resting on each side of the short walls, making the space feel even smaller than it really is.

"Infamous? No. Lindsay Christianson? Yes." I smile at him and offer him my hand to shake. "Nice to meet you."

"Likewise," he says, reaching out to take my hand in his. His handshake is weak, but his smile is contagious, welcoming. I feel an instant connection to Mike and am happy he's so friendly. "Well, you've been quite the talk around here for the last week." His eyes dart around the newsroom as he lowers his voice.

"Why?" I ask, confused.

"You really have to ask that?" He chuckles and tosses his head back dramatically. "Are you all settled?" he asks as he changes the subject quickly. I make a mental note to follow up with him on that declaration later.

"As much as I will be for today." I exhale loudly and look around the newsroom. People are moving around quickly as the morning news broadcast is coming to a close in a few minutes. Leaning in to me, Mike lowers his voice again and raises his eyebrows.

"I'll help you navigate your first few days. The rumor mill is rampant already, so get your thick skin on and prepare yourself," he says.

"I've been here for five minutes," I say quietly, although I'm honestly not surprised. This industry is full of arrogant, self-absorbed, claw-your-way-to-the-top-and-take-out-anyone-in-your way assholes—I've heard the stories.

"Started last week. What can I say? You've ruffled feathers and made waves even before your first day."

"Awesome." I shake my head.

"Just giving you fair warning. Come on; we have our morning production meeting and Rob will introduce you to everyone."

Rob is the news director and my new boss. I tuck my phone into my clutch and shove it into one of the empty desk drawers. Grabbing a notebook and pen, I follow Mike through the newsroom to a large conference room where people have already taken seats and are chatting casually over cups of coffee and bottles of water.

"Good morning, everyone." Rob's voice is boisterous for this early in the morning. His smile is forced, but he commands attention. The room quiets quickly and everyone finds a seat either around the conference room table or along the wall, which is lined with chairs. Mike and I stand awkwardly just inside the conference room, all eyes on us. "This is Lindsay Christianson," he announces to little fanfare. I get a few nods and tight smiles, but it's as cold as a North Dakota winter in this conference room.

"Over here," Mike mumbles, walking toward two open chairs that sit along a wall behind the conference table. I spend the meeting taking notes and observing everyone in this room. I can tell without even talking to most of them if I'll like them or not. I judge people based upon their fake smiles, their uppity attitudes, and all around basic lack of kindness. I guarantee that Mike will be my only friend at work. Rob wraps up the morning meeting and everyone hustles to start on their assignments. I close my notebook and take a deep breath.

"Ready?" Mike says as he stands and waits for me. I was lost in thought, recalling everything we went over in the meeting.

"Ready," I repeat after him.

"So, tomorrow, you'll get your first assignment. Rob is going to make it rough on you the first few weeks. He likes to see what his reporters have. How they handle the pressure. He's going to throw stories at you, offer you a photographer, then pull that photographer out from under your feet to see how you react." As we walk back to our desks, Mike preps me on what to expect and my stomach clenches at the thought of shooting my own stories. Even in Wilmington, I had a photographer with me at all times. "Don't panic. You're going to do fine." He smiles at me. "And I'm taking you to lunch today, so be ready around eleven-thirty."

"Eleven-thirty," I mumble as I fire up my computer and review all the notes I'd taken in the meeting. I can hear my phone buzzing from my desk drawer, but I ignore it—again. I spend the next few hours jotting notes and making a list of questions to ask Mike. There is a flurry of activity in the newsroom right now— this is the part of the job I love. The fast pace, the stories—the multitasking and working to put together a great newscast just seconds before it goes live.

I notice the time is almost 11:30 and I take a minute to powder my face and freshen my lipstick before I go looking for Mike. With one last brush over my cheeks, I shove the compact and lip-gloss back into my clutch.

"No matter how much of that you put on, it's not going to help you," the high-pitched voice comes from behind me.

"Excuse me?" I spin my chair around to find a leggy brunette standing in the entrance to my cubicle. One of her hands is resting on her hip, her eyes are narrowed, and her lips pursed. If I remember correctly, Rob called her Amanda in the production meeting earlier.

"Make-up isn't going to help you," she says a little louder as she takes a step forward into my small office space. Her tall stature should intimidate me, but it doesn't. "You're not pretty enough to ever make anchor. Rob will keep you around for a little while because of your *wholesome* appearance—it's what he does. It's good for ratings. But that baby fat you're carrying around isn't going to help you and your face…" She taps her finger to her chin. "It's just that you're not *pretty* enough to ever sit at that desk." She nods her head to the large anchor desk that sits surrounded by glass walls in the studio. "But depending on how good you suck dick, he might keep you around longer than he usually keeps them." She winks at me with a smirk on her face.

I stand up and take a step closer into her space. I want her to know that she doesn't intimidate me. I've heard the stories about the catty behavior in newsrooms across the country, and I knew I'd get some backlash in regards to this job. I'm young. This is a top twelve market and I came from a much smaller market in Wilmington. I am an unknown in this business and I get that the perception of how or why I got this job is probably because I got on my knees and sucked some dick, when in reality, I worked my ass off to get this job. I work hard and I earned this job.

"Well, the skank look isn't working for you, sweetheart. So tuck those tits back into that blouse and lay off the black eye liner. There is a difference between smoky eye and Goth. We want to *attract* viewers, not fucking scare them," I say, nudging her shoulder with mine as I push past her. I find Mike standing just outside my cube, stalled in his tracks, his eyes wide.

"Did I just hear you call her a skank? Because if you did. I might kiss you." He flashes a huge cheesy grin at me. "Except I'm gay, so that might be weird for both of us." I can't help but laugh at him.

"I might be from the South, and I really am a nice person, but when bitches come at me, I won't back down."

"Good, because that bitch is out for blood. Watch out for her, Lindsay."

"Noted," I say as I follow him out the doors.

A rush of cool air greets me as I push through the glass doors and into the lobby of my building. Juggling a large paper bag with three bottles of wine for dinner, I head for the elevators in a hurry. "Ms. Christianson, I have a delivery for you," I hear Marco say as I almost make it to the elevator. He's hot on my heels. "Let me help you," he says as he strolls over, carrying a large vase of roses.

"Hi, Marco." I can hear the strain in my voice, a sign of the utter exhaustion I'm feeling.

"These just arrived for you." He shifts the vase of roses into one arm and reaches for my bag of wine. The bottles clink together as he shifts the bag in his arm. He gives me a suspecting look, and I can't help but smile.

"It was a rough first day," I joke. "However, I don't plan to drink all three bottles tonight."

"They won't always be bad, Ms. Christianson," Marco says politely, then nods. I hope he's right. My upset stomach is a constant reminder that I may have made the biggest mistake of my life thinking I could make it in a market this size. I'm a little fish in a big pond here. I feel defeated and I've been in Phoenix for less than a week.

Marco is a complete gentleman as we ride up the elevator

together and he holds everything while I scramble to find my keys and open the condo door. He sets everything on my kitchen island while I search my clutch for some cash to tip him.

"Thank you for your help, Marco." I pull five dollars from my clutch to tip him and he immediately pushes the money back at me.

"No tips, Ms. Christianson. It was my pleasure."

"Lindsay," I correct him.

"Glad to help you, Lindsay."

"He might not take tips, but I will!" Jonah says from the open doorway.

"Mr. Murphy. Nice to see you," Marco acknowledges and nods at him as he leaves.

"I'm not really in the mood for company tonight, Jonah," I say, pulling a bottle of wine from the grocery bag and setting it on the granite counter. I shuffle through drawer after drawer, looking for a wine opener. I didn't think to pick one up at the store. After coming up empty, I feel tears sting at the back of my eyes. Resting both of my hands on the kitchen counter, I drop my head forward and I breathe. Taking deep breaths in and out, I try to calm the nerves I feel bringing me toward a breakdown.

"Hey, what's wrong?" Jonah's voice is quiet, but full of concern. A lump begins forming in the back of my throat, not allowing me to answer, so I shake my head back and forth, a silent answer. "Don't get upset over a wine opener. If you need a wine opener, I have one I can bring over." He lets out a small laugh, his voice calming. I know he's trying to cheer me up, but that's when the tears spill from my eyes. I swat at the traitorous tears that roll down my cheeks, angry that I let myself get emotional.

"I'll be right back. I'm going to go get a wine opener from next door." Jonah hurries to the door, giving me some privacy. I kick off my pumps and my aching feet begin to relax against the cool, wooden floor. Traipsing across the living room, I begin unbuckling my belt as I make my way to the bedroom. With each piece of clothing and accessory I remove, a bitter reminder of my day is torn from my body.

I stand in nothing but red lace panties and a bra and stare at myself in the full-length mirror. My long, blonde hair falls down past my shoulders in loose curls. My long arms have lost much of their definition and are starting to look thin—lanky. The red lace waistband of my panties sits below jutting hipbones. I haven't seen my hipbones in a couple of years. *Hello, old friends. Nice to see you again.* Raising my arms above my head, I turn to the side and am still able to see some of my curves, although most of them are noticeably gone. *Baby fat*, I hear Amanda's squeaky voice in my head, as I run my hands over my ribs and down to my stomach.

"Got the… wine… opener…" Jonah's voice breaks when he finds me standing in my bedroom in next to nothing. "Sorry, the door was open, so I figured …" He pauses. "I'll just be in the kitchen." He turns away quickly, closing the bedroom door behind him as he leaves. I stop my fervent body inspection and pull on a pair of yoga pants and a tank top. I give myself a quick inspection in the mirror and head to the kitchen.

I find Jonah standing at the kitchen island, pouring a single glass of Riesling. His eyes are downcast, watching the wine slowly fill the glass. "Thanks for the wine opener," I say, startling him. Wine spills from the bottle and splashes against the stone countertop.

"You're welcome," he says as he sets the bottle down and reaches for a small hand towel to wipe up the spill.

"Don't worry about that. I'll clean it up." I move toward him and tug at the hand towel he's just picked up.

"I got it, Lindsay. Sit down and enjoy your wine." His voice sounds as tired as I feel.

"Will you join me? I have more than enough wine and, clearly, I'm not planning to toss back three bottles of wine by myself tonight."

"Thought you said you weren't in the mood for company?" He smirks and pulls another wine glass down from the cabinet.

"I'm not, but..." I pause, looking away and out the long windows. The sun is just beginning to set and the sky is a beautiful combination of pink and orange. "I'm lonely."

"I'll stay for just a few minutes." Pulling up a stool, he sits next to me at the island while I swirl the white wine around in my wine glass.

"Jonah, why are you so nice to me? I have been a complete bitch to you ever since we met."

He nods his head in agreement while he squeezes his chin. His eyes focus, deep in thought. "Because behind that bitchy façade you have going on, it looks like you need a friend."

Once again, I'm reminded of how truly alone I really am. "I do need a friend. Thank you," I choke out.

# CHAPTER 7
## Matt

The doorbell ringing pulls me from my thoughts. "Coming," I holler. Pushing myself up from the couch, I turn the deadbolt and pull the door open.

"Hi!" Melissa's voice is perky. Her long, red hair is pulled up into a messy pile on top of her head, and she's dressed for hiking.

"Hey, come in. Let me just grab a bottle of water and I'll be ready to go." For the past two weekends, I've hiked with Melissa on Saturday mornings and enjoyed myself. I've always loved the outdoors and hiking was something Lindsay and I never did. Lindsay was never the outdoorsy type. This is one activity I can do without becoming overly sensitive about missing Lindsay, since I have no familiar memories of us doing anything like this.

I grab a bottle of water from the refrigerator and pull my keys off the hook in the kitchen. "Ready?" I ask as I step into the living room. Melissa quickly sets a picture of Lindsay and me from last Christmas back on the mantle. That picture has been my lifeline to Lindsay since she left. Her head is tilted back and she's laughing. Her smile is large and infectious. My arm is wrapped around her, pulling her into me, and my lips are pressed to her forehead. Reagan snapped this candid picture of us on Christmas Eve last year and, the second I saw it, I knew I wanted it framed. It summed *us* up perfectly—comfortable and content.

"Sorry. I didn't mean to snoop," she whispers.

"Don't be," I reassure her.

"You look so happy."

"I was." I swallow tightly. "You ready?"

She nods her head. "I mapped out a new trail for us," I say as I open the door and wait for her to step outside in front of me. I glance back to the eight or so picture frames, all in varying sizes, staggered across the mantle. Each frame holds a picture of Lindsay or Lindsay and me together. My chest tightens when I see those piercing blue eyes, as if they're watching me. I miss her eyes, her lips, the smell of her hair on my pillow, and her soft skin pressed against mine. My stomach turns as I tear my eyes away from those pictures and close the door behind me.

"How far in do you think we've hiked?" Melissa asks as she props her hands on her knees and bends down to catch her breath. We've kept a steady pace at a pretty good incline and I know I've probably pushed her farther than she was ready for. We've barely said two words to each other since we left the trailhead—a good sign that I was probably moving too fast—but I'm not really in the mood for conversation today anyway.

"I'm not sure. Maybe three miles or so."

She stands up and reaches her hands above her head to stretch.

"Are you okay?" I ask, finally feeling guilty.

"I'm great." She smiles at me. She twists the cap on her bottle of water and presses it to her lips. Her lips are light pink and full. In the sun, I notice the light freckles sprinkled across her nose. She looks younger than I expect her to be.

"What are you looking at?" she smirks and takes another drink of water.

"I just noticed you have freckles." I'm embarrassed that she caught me looking at her.

"They're usually covered up under make-up, but they're light... so most people never see them." She presses the plastic bottle to her lips again and, this time, I look away. The trail is lined with large trees with full green leaves and the late summer air is moist and fragrant. For a brief moment, I feel at peace.

"Matt." Her voice tears me away from my thoughts. "It'll get easier. I know right now, it doesn't seem like it, but I promise you it will. Every day will get easier and the memories won't hurt nearly as bad, and then one day, you'll finally be able to breathe again without feeling like you're going to be sick." She speaks as if she knows this from experience. I turn to look at her and find her green eyes are fixated on a large cloud in the sky. Her voice is quiet, yet knowing. "You'll learn to live without her, Matt."

"What if I don't want to?"

"What if you don't have a choice?"

I close the front door and press my forehead against the

doorframe. I still expect to walk through the front door to find Lindsay spread out on the couch with her magazines and a diet Coke. That giant smile she'd give me every time I walked in the door made my day, no matter how bad the day had been. I still hear her voice say, "Hey, babe." She always called me babe. No other woman will ever be able to call me that... that is Lindsay's name for me.

My cell phone chimes in my pocket, but I ignore it, as usual. The clock on the wall tells me that the Braves game is about to start. Nothing sounds better at this moment than losing myself in a game of baseball and a few beers. Walking toward the kitchen, I kick off my tennis shoes along the way and toss my phone onto the couch as it chimes again.

Opening the fridge, I find a foil-covered glass dish with a sticky note on it. *"Lasagna. Eat. Call us. Reagan."* I smile at the note and pull the dish out of the fridge and set it on top of the stove. Reagan continues to take it upon herself to treat me like an orphaned child. As much as I find it annoying at times, I also don't know what I'd do without her. Reaching back into the fridge, I pull out a bottle of beer and pop off the top, tossing the cap into the kitchen sink. Pre-heating the oven, I place the dish inside, setting the timer for forty-five minutes. I can't remember the last time I cooked for myself. Lindsay did all the cooking; even when she would work evenings, she'd have a huge meal waiting for me when I got home. I always felt guilty and offered to help her, but she insisted on cooking and I didn't argue with her over it.

Throwing myself down onto the couch, I position a throw pillow under my arm and push the power button on the remote control. Changing the channels, I find the baseball game and prop my feet on the coffee table. Some semblance of normalcy creeps over me for the first time in weeks, except I realize this is my new normal—alone.

The screen on my phone lights up, pulling my attention away from the game. The screen flashes the two text messages I've missed, but it's the background screen I fixate on, a picture of Lindsay sitting on my lap at Landon and Reagan's engagement party. Her blue eyes shine against the royal blue dress she's wearing, her long, blonde hair falling in waves over her bare shoulders. She's petite, small in my lap. My long arms wrap around her waist, holding her close to me—an embrace that says I'd never let her go.

I swipe my finger over the screen lock, opening my phone. I tap the contacts icon and slide my finger over Lindsay's name. A small photo of her blowing a kiss to me pops up on the screen and a smile tugs at my lips. I pause, looking at the screen, at her face, at her name staring at me and, without a second thought, I tap the phone number and wait—and wait—and wait. By the fourth ring, I know she's not going to answer. Just as I pull the phone away from my ear, I hear her faint voice. "Matt?"

"Linds?" I ask, unsure if I'm imagining this.

"Hi," she says quietly.

"Hi," I say back, my heart beating rapidly as I scramble to sit up. "I didn't expect you to answer," I admit. She exhales loudly and pauses before she answers.

"I'm glad you called. I miss you." And those three little words break me. *I miss you.*

"I miss you too." It's a silent plea, my final resolve breaking.

We sit in silence, letting the weight of those words sink in. Weeks of silence, stubbornness, and anger lifted by the admission of those three words I needed to hear so badly. There are so many questions I have for her. How is she doing? Does she like

Arizona? So much I want to know—but I'll take sitting in silence on the phone with her, listening to nothing else but her faint breath if that's all she can offer me.

"Matt?"

"Hi. I'm here."

"Talk to me. Tell me a something funny. Tell me anything." The pitch in her voice rises before it breaks. She's crying. I can hear her sniffles and envision her chin quivering. My girl is alone, across the country, and hurting. I search for anything to tell her. There is so much I want to say, but now is not the time.

"I don't have anything funny to share," I muster, clearing my throat and trying to contain my own emotions. "I saw your brother and Reagan. Their house is insane, Linds." I pause, waiting for her to respond, but she doesn't. "You should call them. They miss you and want to hear how you're doing."

"They have enough going on with their new house and planning their wedding." She pauses for a moment. "I'll call Landon this week. Just let him know I'm okay, will you?"

"Yeah, of course." A now awkward silence settles between us.

"I should probably go now." *No. Don't hang up. I need you, Lindsay. I need your smile, your laughter—I need you.* "Thanks for calling." Her voice is short and the line goes dead.

Numbly, I sit on the couch, the Braves game on mute playing in the background. My bottle of beer has warmed and I push it to the center of the coffee table. I sit for god only knows how long, trying to feel anything other than absolute devastation.

# CHAPTER 8

## *Lindsay*

"How do you feel about Starbucks?" Mike asks as he leans into my cube with a grin on his face. His tan face looks tired, but in this business, you learn to "fake it till you make it."

"I feel like that's the best thing I've heard all morning." I reach for my clutch and slide out of my office chair. "My treat," I say, wiggling the clutch in front of him as I step out of my cubicle.

"Even better," he smirks. We walk side by side down the long aisle lined with cubes that lead out to the front lobby. Mike holds the large glass door open as we step out into the sweltering Phoenix heat.

"It's only nine in the morning. When does this heat end?" I complain and fan my face with my hand.

Mike chuckles and shakes his head, "Late November—so toughen up, buttercup. We have at least three more months of this."

"I feel like this is the gateway to hell."

"So dramatic, tsk tsk," he scolds me with a laugh.

We walk quickly down the sidewalk, cutting through one of the downtown office buildings for a reprieve from the unbearable heat. My heels click along the travertine floors as we slow our pace, drinking in the cool air until we find the line for Starbucks that wraps around the outside of the store. Apparently, 112 degrees does not deter Phoenicians from drinking coffee.

"So your first week is almost done. How are you feeling?" Mike asks as we wait in line.

"Like I made the biggest mistake of my life," I admit quietly.

"That bad, huh?"

"You could say that."

"Has Amanda backed off yet? She usually has her claws out for a couple of days, but then backs down fairly quick."

"Eh, I don't give a shit about Amanda. I just feel like maybe I bit off more than I can chew by coming to Arizona."

"Can I make an observation without you getting upset?" Mike asks.

"Of course."

"If there was anyone who has ever come from a small market and jumped right in and owned this job, it's you. In the first week, you've impressed the hell out of everyone. Why do you think Amanda hasn't backed down? She's threatened. You are the real deal, the total package."

"You're adorable when you're blowing smoke up my ass. You know that, right?" I laugh at him. However, his words are comforting. I've second-guessed every decision I've made in the last month—and honestly have been waiting to fail, my excuse to go running home with my tail between my legs.

"It's the truth, Lindsay. The camera loves you, the viewers love you, and Rob loves you." He wags his eyebrows and I can't contain the eye roll that just happens so naturally.

"What's his deal anyway?" I ask, referring to Rob's overly friendly personality. He is always floating around the newsroom, popping into say hello, or wanting to chat it up.

"He likes blondes."

"Shut up." I smack him on the shoulder.

"No, he really does. You're young… presumably single?" He backs away, posing it as a question.

I nod my head. "Yeah, recently single. Not looking; especially not looking at my boss." I shake my head.

"Well, in my expert opinion, he's looking at you. So just keep it professional, would be my advice." I like Mike. I like that he's looking out for me and concerned with appearances. "So, your recent break-up; tell me about it."

I swallow tightly against my dry throat, thinking of Matt. I loved nothing more than seeing him off to work in the mornings. He'd wake up early and make coffee, then join me back in bed while it was brewing. I loved when he'd wrap himself around me, his warm skin pressed against mine. Mornings were *our* time together. With my crazy schedule, evenings were difficult to plan around. Matt made sure every morning that I was thoroughly *taken care of* in every possible way. A smile tugs at the corners of my mouth when I think of our morning routine.

I glance at the time on my phone and assume he's at work. It's noon in Wilmington and, if I was home, I might be meeting him for lunch right now. My stomach turns as I wonder who he meets for lunch now.

"Hello?" Mike says, snapping his fingers in front of my face to get my attention. "Are you okay?"

"Yeah, sorry… just got lost in my thoughts for a moment."

"I could see that. I didn't mean to bring up any bad

memories," he says as we scoot forward in the seemingly never-ending line for Starbucks.

"No. No bad memories. Just remembering…" I trail off.

"Want to talk about it? I'm a great listener."

"I left him to take this job," I say quietly, trying to keep my emotions at bay. "I love him more than anything in the world, but I left him very selfishly to take this job."

"Why do you say 'selfishly'? Don't you deserve to be happy, even if that comes in the form of a job opportunity across the country?" Mike questions me.

"I suppose, but I think I might have been happier if I had stayed in Wilmington, at the station there, *and* had Matt."

"So then why'd you leave?"

I contemplate his question. It's a question I have asked myself over and over—nonstop since I left, and I cannot find the answer. I'm not sure I have an answer. I shrug.

"I don't know, Mike. I honestly don't know."

"You know, Lindsay, I've known you for all of what… five days now, but there is one thing I know about you. You have a great head on your shoulders. You're smart. You're driven. You may not have the answer today, but you'll understand someday why you left and took this job. It might not be the answer you like, but you'll figure it out." He smiles at me as we approach the counter to place our order.

We wait at the end of the counter for our coffee in silence, as I get lost in memories again. Matt dragging me from our bed after our morning marathon lovemaking session and pulling me into a hot shower. He loved to take his time washing my body, then promptly pressing me against the shower wall for another quick round of lovemaking—it was his *thing* to do in the shower. God I miss him.

"Skinny vanilla latte?" the voice asks from behind the counter as I reach for the piping hot cup of coffee.

"Thanks."

"You look sad," Mike says as he casually wraps his arm around my shoulders, nudging me forward.

"I'll be okay. It's just really hard right now."

"Every day will get easier."

"You say this like you know this."

"Sweetheart, who hasn't had a broken heart before? Just stay positive. Oh, and don't make plans for tonight. You're coming out with me."

"Out?"

"Me and a couple of friends are going to hit the town. You should come along. I promise we're a good time," he smirks.

"I don't know."

"Come on. I guarantee you every drag queen in Phoenix is going to want a piece of you."

I can't help but laugh.

"Maybe for just a little bit."

"You're not going to sit in that high-rise condo all alone, play Peter Gabriel songs, and mope." He gives my shoulder a little squeeze. "And I've now declared it my job to make sure you love Phoenix."

"I hate Peter Gabriel, so you don't have to worry about that, but loving Phoenix... that's not going to happen either," I say bluntly.

"Well, I'm going to do my best to try," he says.

Our walk back to the office is quiet, weighted by my somber mood.

With one swipe of bright red lipstick, I step away from the bathroom vanity and give myself a once over in the mirror. Black skinny leather pants and a silver sequined tank top with black patent-leather stilettos to complete the outfit. My long hair hangs in loose waves and my blue eyes pop with the extra dark eye shadow. My stomach flutters a little in anticipation of going out and meeting Mike and his friends.

I grab my small, black clutch and head for the front door. As I weave through the living room, I can't help but notice how cold and lonely this condo feels, even though it has million-dollar views and would be the envy of most people my age. I miss my home. I miss my home with Matt.

Pressing the elevator button, I wait patiently and pick at my fingernail. A shrill whistle sounds behind me along with the sound of a shutting door.

"Well, well, well… where are you headed?" Jonah sidles up next to me. I haven't seen him since Monday night when we had wine.

"Out," I answer him curtly. There is something about him, an innocence that I'm drawn to, but something inside me tells me I need to keep my distance.

"Out, huh? On a date?"

"Not that it's any of your business, but no. It's not a date. Speaking of, where are you headed dressed like that?" It's the first time I've seen him in anything other than gym shorts or preppy schoolboy clothes. He actually looks nice in a white dress shirt with his sleeves rolled up and a pair of dark jeans. His face is freshly shaven and his hair is styled.

"Same as you. Out."

I don't inquire further, or care to carry on meaningless conversation, so we wait together quietly. The elevator arrives and we ride down in silence; neither of us have much to say, apparently. I press my body into the back corner while he stands up front near the doors. We arrive and the doors open. Always the gentleman, he stands back and holds the doors open while I exit first.

"Thank you," I mumble as I step into the cool lobby.

"Do you have your phone?" he asks me as I begin walking away, catching me off guard.

"Yes."

"Let me see it."

"Why?"

"Just let me see it, Lindsay."

I reach into my clutch, pull out the slim iPhone, and hand it to him. He swipes his finger, opening the screen, and begins tapping.

"First of all, put a passcode on this. Second, my number is in there. Call me if you need anything and be safe." He hands me the phone and saunters away.

"I should be telling *you* to be safe," I mutter.

He waves me off without ever turning back to look at me. That man is ballsy.

⌒

Pulling up to the nondescript building, I check the navigation system to be sure it has taken me to the right place. The parking lot is full and I can hear music, so this must be it. I check my lipstick and hair in the visor mirror one last time before stepping out into the torrid air. My leather pants are stuck to my legs and a light sheen of sweat instantly forms across my forehead and upper lip. I move quickly toward the large, wooden door, which has a flashing neon light hanging over it, screaming that the bar is open.

I pull open the heavy door and am greeted by a blast of cold air and the sounds of Justin Timberlake singing through the speakers. The bar is dimly lit and packed with bodies. Flashing lights from the dance floor make it hard to focus on finding anyone. I try to look for Mike over the sea of people and I squeeze in between sweaty bodies that are swaying to the music, excusing myself every few feet. I finally see Mike standing at a tall pub table that is surrounded by two other men.

"Lindsay!" Mike shouts as I approach. He leans in and presses a wet kiss to my cheek. "Look at you, gorgeous!" He lifts my hand above my head and twirls me around to look at me. "You look amazing in those pants." I laugh at his fashion observation.

"Thanks, and look at you!" I raise my eyebrows at him. He's wearing a skin-tight tank top and faded jeans. His arms are firm and muscular, but lean. He looks so different from how he dresses at the office in a shirt and tie. I notice a tattoo on his shoulder and make a mental note to ask him the meaning behind it.

"Nick, Javier, this is Lindsay. Lindsay, this is Nick and Javier." Both men reach out to shake my hand. Nick is tall and slender with dark hair and trendy dark-rimmed glasses. His hair is styled back away from his face. His smile is slightly crooked, but he's a good-looking man. Mike and Javier dance around the small table when the music changes and Lady Gaga starts piping through the speakers, leaving me with Nick.

"Don't believe anything he tells you about me," Nick says with a laugh as he leans in closer to me. "Only half of the stories are true." The music is loud and it's hard to hear in the bar. "Javier and Michael are adorable, aren't they?" He changes the subject.

"I didn't realize they were a couple, and did you just call him 'Michael'?"

"He only goes by Mike at work. It's more 'masculine.'" He makes air quotes with his fingers and rolls his eyes. "And yes, they've been together about a year. Michael is lucky; just look at Javi." Nick smacks his lips. Nick tosses back the remainder of his drink and slams the glass down on the table. "I'm going to go get another one. Can I get you anything while I'm there?"

"I'd love a vodka cranberry, please." I reach into my clutch to pull out some cash.

"I've got this." He waves off the cash that I try handing to him. I slide onto one of the tall stools that surround the pub table and laugh at Mike and Javier dancing and acting goofy. Lady Gaga's crooning comes to an end and both men saunter over to the table, sweaty and laughing. Javi excuses himself and leaves Mike with me.

"Soooo... Michael." I say his full name, eliciting an eye roll. "How long have you been with Javier?"

"A little over a year, but we've been friends for over five years."

"He's adorable."

"I know." He winks at me.

"One vodka cranberry for you and one appletini for me," Nick announces as he sets down the drinks on the table. "A toast to new friends." Nick raises his glass. I grab my drink and meet the rim of my glass with Nick's and Mike's, and we all toast.

"To new friends," I say, letting the vodka slide down my throat. Something about the slow burn makes me feel better.

"Let's dance!" Mike says, pulling me off my stool, and I don't argue. I need to let loose and have fun.

Four hours, six vodka cranberries, and endless minutes on the dance floor later, I'm done. I'm ready to go home.

"I need to call a cab," I announce, reaching for my cell phone, which has been tucked away nicely in my clutch all night.

"We will give you a ride. Javier doesn't drink, so he always gets to drive. Just call me tomorrow and I'll come pick you up so we can get your car."

"I don't want to inconvenience you. It was nice enough of you to invite me to come out with you tonight."

"No trouble at all," Javi says as he holds out his arm for me. I'm unsteady in these heels and tipsy after my over indulgence of vodka cranberries this evening. We weave through the still standing-room-only crowd and find the front door. Javi pulls me out into the warm air, guiding me toward his car. For being in the middle of a major metropolitan area, you can still see the bright stars against the crystal clear night sky. Javier opens the front door and I slide into the front seat. Mike sits in the back like a gentleman.

"Where to?" Javi asks as he puts the car in reverse.

"Central and Washington, the condos on the corner."

He whistles. "Someone's living the good life." He glances in the rearview mirror to Mike.

"Hardly," I mumble. "It's just temporary anyway."

"Why temporary? Not staying long?"

"Not planning to," I admit honestly. "My agent thought it would be a good career move…"

"It is," Mike pipes in from the back seat.

"But I gave up a lot to take this job."

"Sweetheart, if you're miserable, no job will ever make this move worth it." Javier's voice is sympathetic.

I nod my head, knowing that he's right. "I know," I whisper.

Javier pulls up to the curb outside my building and parks. He meets me at my door as I'm getting out. "Thanks again for driving me home."

"Call Michael in the morning. We'll pick you up and take you to your car." He walks with me toward my building.

"You don't have to walk me to the door." I nudge him with my shoulder.

"Well, I'm not dumping you on a street corner in downtown Phoenix and driving off." He laughs. I reach out to give him a hug.

"Goodnight, Javi."

"Night, Lindsay. It was really nice to finally meet you. Mike talks a lot about you." He gives me a hug in return and a small wave as he jogs back to his car. Crossing the lobby, I wait for the elevator when I hear a commotion in the lobby. In walks Jonah with a group of people. Loud, billowing laughter fills the open atrium and I press the up button for the elevator again, hoping to catch a ride before the group gets near. The elevator chimes its arrival and I quickly step inside, when I hear Jonah's deep voice.

"Hold the door, beautiful."

*Shit.*

# CHAPTER 9

## *Lindsay*

My feet move quickly, carrying me forward into the solitude of the elevator. I push the door close button quickly, but a large hand reaches in and holds the doors open. A small, defeated sigh escapes me.

"Perfect timing," Jonah says as his group of friends filter into the elevator.

"Yeah, perfect," I mumble under my breath. My fingers fidget with the small clutch in my hand. With the elevator full, Jonah nudges himself in behind me. I can feel his warm breath on the back of my neck, telling me he's closer than he should be. I try to focus on remaining steady in these heels.

Jonah's friends are discussing the evening's events and laughing as the elevator glides upward. One of them carries a case of beer, another holds a paper bag with what appears to be a bottle of alcohol. As the elevator slows to a stop, I stumble, and a firm set of hands grabs my hips, steadying me. His chest presses against my back and I shiver again when I feel his warm breath on my ear. "Easy there." His voice is raspy.

"Thanks," I say quietly. The doors open and everyone begins to exit. I stay firmly rooted in the corner, letting everyone off first. Jonah stays put behind me the entire time, his hands still holding me firmly on the hips.

"After you," he says, nudging me toward the open elevator doors. He releases my hips, but grabs my hand and pulls me gently out of the elevator and down the hallway.

"I'm fine, Jonah. I've got this."

"You're not fine. You're drunk and were swaying all over that elevator."

"I said I'm fine." I pull my hand from his and fumble with my clutch to get my key out. Jonah pulls his keys from his front pocket and tosses them at one of the guys standing outside his door.

"Let yourselves in," he says as he pulls the clutch from my hand and unzips it.

"Jonah!"

"Lindsay, quit acting childish and let me help you." He opens the clutch and pulls out the key, tossing the black leather clutch back to me. I of course miss catching it, and it falls to the ground, spilling my license, credit cards, cash, and those little white pills that have become my best friend everywhere. He pauses as he looks at everything spilled on the ground, then bends down to pick up the scattered contents. I scramble to my knees to grab the pills, but he's too quick for me.

"What are these?" he questions me, reaching out and picking up a couple of the white pills. He studies them, then closes his long fingers around the pills. I stay silent, reaching for the cash and my license that are still lying on the ground. "Tell me you aren't mixing pills with alcohol, Lindsay." I remain silent as I stuff the cash and license back into my clutch. His large hand wraps around my wrist and squeezes me tightly, causing me to gasp.

"Answer me," he bites out. "I know what those are. Tell me you aren't taking those with alcohol."

"Why do you care?" I whisper.

"Because that's what those assholes do." He nods his head toward the door of his condominium. "And they're fucking stupid," he says, releasing my wrist and running both of his hands through his hair.

We sit for a moment in silence, looking at each other, both contemplating what to say, what to do next. In one quick movement, he stands up and holds out his hands for me take. I reach out and let him pull me to my feet. He wraps an arm around my waist, pulling me toward him and into a hug—and I let him hug me and hold me while I fall apart in his arms.

I cry because I'm sad and embarrassed, but mostly because I'm angry at myself for using pills to hide everything I'm feeling. Jonah holds me while I cry, his grasp firm and tight. He's silent, but sometimes no words are needed, just the presence of a friend when you're coming unglued and a firm hug are all you need.

"Come on; let's get you inside," he whispers against the top of my head. I nod and sniffle while I swat at tears that continue to fall from my eyes. He keeps me close as he unlocks the door to my condo and reaches in to flip on a light. A single hanging light flickers to life above the kitchen island, and I kick off my heels just inside the door. Jonah stands and watches me for a moment before closing the door and turning the deadbolt.

"Go. You have people at your place waiting on you." I begin pulling off my earrings, bracelets, and necklace, piling them up on top of each other on the granite island.

"I'd rather be here—with you," he says quietly.

"I'm just going to shower and go to bed."

"No. Talk to me," he says as he crosses the kitchen and takes a seat on the oversized sofa.

"Jonah, I'm tired… and I've had a lot to drink." I hiccup as if on cue. He smirks at me, then pats the cushion next to him.

"Sit."

My bare feet pad against the wood floor and I throw myself down on the couch dramatically. "What do you want to talk about?"

"You." His voice is direct, firm. His dark brown eyes drink me in. He watches my every move.

"I'm very boring, I promise."

"Why the pills, Lindsay?" Whoa; he just jumps right in there, doesn't he?

"Jonah, look…"

"I'm worried about you, Lindsay. You're all over the place—happy, sad, and angry. One minute I'm the only friend you have and the next, you act like you can't stand me. You won't make eye contact with me and you act like a bitch. What's going on?"

I contemplate how much I should tell him—how much I want to tell him. I find myself chewing on my bottom lip, my tongue running over a small piece of dry skin, while his dark brown eyes watch me intently.

"I take the pills for pain caused by a car accident I was in about a year and a half ago," I finally admit. My heart begins beating a little faster as I remember the accident.

"And you still take them?" His brows furrow and he looks at me skeptically.

"No. Well, I didn't. I just started again." I look away from him and fix my eyes on a large floor vase full of long, bare branches. I'm ashamed to admit I use pills to deal with the mental pain I'm in, no longer the physical pain from the accident.

"How serious was the accident?" He shifts, causing his body to move a little closer into me.

"It was bad. I broke my leg, my future sister-in-law broke her pelvis, and she ended up losing a pregnancy because of the accident," I tell him quietly. "I was driving; it was my fault."

"Accidents happen all the time, Lindsay. It was an accident. You can't blame yourself."

"But I do. I shouldn't have been driving in that storm. I should have turned around, but I was trying to get Reagan to the airport. It just came up on us so quickly and I swerved to avoid a tree in the road and over corrected. I'm not even sure how many times the car rolled; they think three or four. I'll never forget hearing Reagan's sobs and thinking she might not survive," I choke out. A chill runs through me when I think about that afternoon.

"Reagan is your future sister-in-law?"

I nod my head. The lump that has formed in my throat won't allow me to speak.

"Come here." He leans back into the arm of the couch and turns toward me with open arms—an invitation that I'm hesitant of. "It's just a hug, Lindsay." His small, concerned smile tells me he's being genuine and, without a second thought, I crawl into his arms and settle in. While his unfamiliar arms wrap around me, I finally let go of all the anger, the sadness, the confusion, and the heartache I've been holding onto.

I wake up with a kink in my neck and warm arms wrapped around me. I fell asleep in the arms of another man. Innocent, but feeling guilty, I unwrap myself from his body and push myself off the couch, stumbling across the living room and into my bedroom.

I peel off the leather pants that are stuck to my legs and pull my tank top over my head, tossing both of them into a pile on the floor. I kick them aside as I saunter into the bathroom and turn on the shower—even though the water is on cold, it's scalding hot, a side effect of the scorching Phoenix temperatures I've quickly learned.

The hot water pricks at my skin and my tense muscles finally begin to relax. Steam billows from the shower and fills the air—a light cloud enveloping me. I scrub my body, hoping the water will wash away the ache inside of me. My head pounds from the drinks and crying myself to sleep last night, but nothing hurts as much as my heart.

Slipping into a pair of cotton lounge pants and a loose t-shirt, I run a comb through my tangled mess of blonde hair. My blue eyes are lacking spark; they're lifeless, just how I feel. I make a mental note of how I look and plan to make a greater effort to take care of myself—on the outside. A knock on my door pulls me away from my self-loathing.

"Come in," I murmur. The door swings open and Jonah peeks in. A smile spreads across his face. His smile is infectious and his brown eyes bright. His morning hair is a tousled mess, but it fits his personality.

"I made coffee," he stammers.

"Exactly what I need. I'll be right out." He shuts the door and I pick up the pile of clothes I left lying in the center of the floor. I catch a glimpse of a pill bottle on my nightstand and quickly move to hide the bottle in the drawer, but before I do, I toss two in my mouth. I've become an expert at swallowing pills with a dry mouth. I hear Jonah rustling around out in the kitchen, so I tuck the bottle of pills away under a sleep mask and decide to face Jonah for coffee.

I find Jonah standing at my kitchen island, all Adonis-like. His tan skin glows against his dirty blond hair and brown eyes. This is the first time I've noticed him in a way other than my pesky college student neighbor. He looks older than twenty-four and his looks are out of place in Phoenix. He definitely belongs on a beach with a surfboard. He smiles when he catches me watching him, and I'm slightly embarrassed he caught me. I blush and head for the island, where a cup of coffee waits for me.

"Hmmm…" I growl when the black liquid hits my tongue. There is nothing like the feeling of hot coffee sliding down your throat, when you can feel it travel from your throat to your belly, finally settling into your veins, where it delivers that first kick of caffeine your body craves. It's intense… and I love the first sip of coffee every morning.

"I like that sound you make when you drink coffee," he smirks. I shake my head and smile at him. "You did it last week when I brought coffee and muffins."

"I don't even think that I realize I do it."

"Do it again."

"I can't force it. It just happens." I laugh at him.

"I like when you laugh, Lindsay." His voice becomes more serious.

"I do too." I press the large mug to my lips again, hoping to avoid a repeat of last night's conversation.

"So," Jonah sets his mug down and sits on one of the stools at the island. "Tell me something about yourself. Something I don't know about you."

"What is this, like twenty questions or something?"

"Something like that." He steeples his long fingers together and places them under his chin while he waits for me to answer.

"Hmm... let me think." I tap my finger to my chin and scrunch my face as if I'm thinking really hard about how to answer.

"I'm really funny and sarcastic," I say with a smile.

"See! That's something I didn't know about you. I haven't seen that side of you." My mood sobers a bit as I think about what he's just said. An awkward silence settles around us when I don't say anything in return. He pushes himself up from the stool and walks toward me, placing himself directly in front of me. It's a bold move, but I don't back away from him. In my bare feet, he towers over me, and I realize how small I am in comparison to him.

"I want to see the funny Lindsay," he says quietly, brushing a piece of wet hair away from my face. I swallow hard, at a loss for words. "Have dinner with me tonight. Let me get to know you." His fingers play with a strand of my hair; he rubs it back and forth between his thumb and forefinger.

"Okay."

"Okay?" he says with a giant sigh of relief and a smile stretches across his golden face.

"Yes, okay," I repeat with a smile this time.

# CHAPTER 10
## Matt

There's a knock at my door and I know it's Landon and Reagan. "Doors open!" I holler from the kitchen. I'm stocking the fridge with beers and opening bags of chips. When I invited Landon over to watch the pre-season football game, I didn't realize it was going to turn into a party. But where Landon goes, Reagan goes. Where Reagan goes, it's a party.

"Hey, Matty," Reagan says, leaning in and planting a quick kiss to my cheek. She's juggling a large crockpot in her hands while a shopping bag dangles from her arm.

"Hey, Reag. Let me help you." I pull the crockpot from her hands and plug it into the outlet on my kitchen island. I see her do a once over on the kitchen and a small smile tugs at the corner of her lips when she realizes I haven't reverted back to my ways of caveman living since she helped me clean up the place a few weeks ago.

"Smells good. What's in there?"

"Buffalo chicken dip. It's amazing and for you guys, since I'm on a diet." She pats her stomach. "Watching my weight for the wedding."

"You're not getting married for months. I think you'll be fine if you have some chips and dip, Reagan." What is it with these women and obsessing about their weight?

"You try to squeeze into that fitted wedding gown and tell me if you'd put a crockpot of melted cheese in your mouth," she jokes with me, then starts pulling jars and packages from her shopping bag.

"Do you have a platter?" she asks as she starts flinging open cupboard doors and searching for one.

"In the cabinet above the fridge." I reach above and pull down the large, wooden platter.

"Perfect!" She claps her hands together. "I'm putting together an amazing antipasti tray."

"Dudes don't eat antipasti when they watch football!" Landon bellows as he comes around the corner.

"*These* dudes are eating antipasti," I say with a laugh when I see the look of death Reagan just gave him. I open a bottle of beer and take a long pull.

"Maybe some of the other guys will eat antipasti—and appreciate it," Reagan says, glaring at Landon as she arranges cuts of meat, cheese, olives, and peppers on the tray. Landon and I both start laughing. She stands back from the tray she was just arranging and places both hands on her hips and shakes her head in disgust at us.

"This is a party! You need more than ruffle chips and onion dip."

"Babe, we're just giving you a hard time. We'll eat your antipasti," Landon says, pressing a kiss to her temple, a sign of peace. He nods his head toward the living room, and we leave

Reagan in the kitchen to do what she does best when we get together—make food and force us to eat it.

Landon and I take our usual seats on the leather couch and I turn on the surround sound. The pre-game show roars to life on the TV; the Panthers are playing the Steelers and, as usual, this should be a good game.

"Did you want to get tickets for a home game again this season?" Landon asks. It's been our "guys' weekend" every year for the last five years. We spend the weekend in Charlotte and catch a Panthers' home game and visit some of the guys we used to work with that now live there.

"Hell yeah. Wouldn't miss it." The sound of my cell phone ringing interrupts our planning.

"Need to get that?" he asks, eyeing the ringing phone on the coffee table.

"Nah, just going to let it go to voicemail." He looks at me skeptically.

"It's not Lindsay; she has a different ringtone." He nods his head and takes a long pull on his beer. "I did talk to her last week, though. She told me to let you know she's sorry she hasn't called. She's been busy."

"Busy?" he scoffs. "I haven't heard from her since she called right after she arrived. I've left her voice messages and text messages and, quite frankly, I'm pissed off," he snaps at me.

"She's adjusting," I remind him. I can't believe I'm actually making excuses for her. "She didn't sound good, honestly. She sounded tired and emotional."

"Emotional? That's not like her," Reagan interrupts as she comes into the living room from the kitchen, carrying a bowl of Doritos.

"I know. We only talked for about a minute before she cut

me off." I feel guilty for not having told Landon and Reagan about our conversation earlier.

"So you called her?" Reagan asks as she arranges the magazines on the coffee table into a neat pile as she moves our beers to the center of the table.

"I did," I admit humbly. "I had to," I whisper.

"What time is it there?" Landon asks, reaching for his phone. You can hear the agitation in his voice.

"Three hours behind us, babe," Reagan reminds him. "But you're not calling her right now, so put the phone away. You're angry and if she's having a hard time, you being upset with her isn't going to help. Let's watch the game, relax, and maybe we'll all call her later. Put her on speakerphone. We'll make it a light-hearted call, tell her we all miss her, and to call us when she has time. You know, keep it short and sweet, and *pleasant.*" She raises her eyebrows at Landon and plasters a stiff smile on her face. Landon and I both nod before turning back to the football game on the TV.

Other friends from the police department have stopped by to catch the game and even my brother dropped by for a short bit. I will admit the company was nice and reminded me of old times, having everyone over. Reagan is in the kitchen, cleaning up, and Landon and I catch the game highlights on ESPN.

"What's this?" Landon grabs a magazine off my coffee table.

"Travel magazine."

"Are you taking a trip?"

"Nah. I had ordered it before Lindsay left. I had thought

about seeing if she wanted to take a short European vacation this fall."

"She would have loved that. She always talked about going to Europe. You know she's never left the country, right?"

"I know—something about flying over water." I laugh.

"Speaking of Lindsay now that things have calmed down, should we call her?" Reagan asks as she sneaks back in the room and pulls her phone from her back pocket. She clicks the speakerphone function and grabs the remote from the coffee table, muting the TV. The phone rings three times, then a fourth before it finally clicks and we all hear the muffled sounds of Lindsay and another man. Reagan shoves the phone back in her pocket and offers me a sympathetic look before excusing herself to the kitchen.

"Matt?" I can hear Landon trying to get my attention, but I can't focus on anything right now. Landon and I sit in silence as every thought imaginable runs through my head.

I'm not sure how long I sat lost in visions of another man with Lindsay. My ears fill to the sound of blood rushing to my head. I remember very little, other than Landon pulling me off the wall I was punching holes into. Everything happened in a blur. Reagan is holding ice on my hand. Time ceased to exist for a matter of moments, or maybe hours. I now know that I believe in nothing I thought I believed in when it came to Lindsay and me. Is this what hatred feels like? I feel nothing but anger and rage, and I want nothing more than to kill the male voice on the end of that phone line.

# CHAPTER 11

## *Lindsay*

There's a knock at the door, but before I make it over to open it, it flies open, and Jonah lets himself in. Carrying a square, pink box, he sets it on the kitchen island and gives me a little whistle.

"You look stunning, Lindsay," he remarks as my cheeks redden. I threw on a dark gray silk tank dress and paired it with large, yellow jewelry. It's different, but fun for summer. I paired it with a pair of open-toe, tall-wedged shoes.

"Thanks. You clean up pretty well yourself." I laugh. Again, I notice Jonah looks older than twenty-four, although his hair is still wild, but he's styled it and he's wearing a pair of tan dress pants and white pressed dress shirt, the sleeves rolled neatly.

"What's in the box?" I ask, trying to steer the conversation away from how I look. I spent an hour on my make-up, trying to bury the dark circles beneath my eyes under a layer of concealer. My hair is becoming dry and lifeless, so I spent another twenty minutes trying to blow it out so that it had some body. Arizona is sucking the life out of every part of me.

"Cupcakes." He smiles.

"Cupcakes?"

"Yeah. There is this bakery that makes the most amazing cupcakes. I thought maybe, after dinner, we could come back here and have cupcakes."

"Pretty bold of you, Mr. Murphy." He blushes, rocking back on the heels of his feet; a sign of nervousness. I can't help but laugh a little. He's cute in a boyish way, and handsome in a grown-up way. He's stuck somewhere in the middle.

"Ready?" he asks as I reach for my purse.

"Yep, let me just go grab my phone," I say, remembering I left it charging on my nightstand in the bedroom. I turn on a lamp that sits on one of the end tables as I make my way to the bedroom to get my phone, shutting off other overhead lights as I go.

I unplug my phone and toss the charger into my nightstand, noticing the pill bottle I stashed away earlier. *Just one*, the devil that sits on my shoulder taunts me. *It'll help with your nerves.* So, for good measure, I take two. I take one last look at myself in the full-length mirror and take a deep breath. "Let's do this," I whisper to myself.

"So, where are we going?" I ask as I find Jonah waiting by the front door.

"I made reservations at a new restaurant a few miles away. I've never been there, but I've heard great things." He offers his arm for me to hold on to, and I accept it.

The conversation is light and carefree as we drive the few miles to the restaurant. Jonah taps the leather-encased steering wheel of his Audi A8 as Dave Matthews sings through the speakers. I settle into the rich leather seats and watch Jonah navigate with ease the busy downtown Phoenix streets.

The restaurant is quiet and dim and we're at a small table that sits along floor-to-ceiling windows and overlooks a small outdoor patio seating area. It's too hot, so no one is seated outside, even though misters blow cool water throughout the patio area. There are only a few other people in the restaurant, so we're seated in a back corner away from others.

"Wine?" Jonah asks as he scans the wine list.

"Sure. White okay with you?"

"Pinot Grigio?"

"Perfect," I tell him as I go back to scanning the menu. I don't have much of an appetite and the pills I took before I left are kicking in. I'm finally starting to feel really good, less anxious. The waiter arrives, setting down a basket of breads and two glasses of ice water. While Jonah orders our wine, I sip from the glass of ice water that was just delivered in hopes of quelling my dry mouth.

"Have you decided on dinner?" the waiter asks and Jonah looks at me. I nod and order first.

"I'll take the wedge salad please," I tell the waiter and close the menu. Jonah shoots me a strange look and shakes his head, but doesn't say anything before ordering himself the filet mignon. He flashes a genuine smile as the waiter leaves us alone. There is a moment of silence while Jonah just looks at me—studies me, as I study him in return. His eyes are telling; there is something he wants to say, but he's not going to.

"What?" I finally ask him.

"Nothing. I just like looking at you." He pulls a dinner roll from the breadbasket and sets it on the small plate in front of him.

"There's not much to look at," I mumble under my breath and take a sip of my water.

"Why so much self-hatred?" he asks as he pulls apart the bread. "I mean, from the moment I met you, Lindsay, you're just so…" He pauses as he chooses the right word. "You're so angry," he says quietly. "From the outside, you have it all. You're stunning. You have a new job, a kick-ass condo—"

"Excuse me." I choke on the water. "You really don't know anything about me."

"Exactly. I want to, though, Lindsay. I want you to tell me why you're so angry, and I want to see the funny Lindsay we talked about this morning." I roll my eyes, more so out of habit, but also because I don't want to share the ugly parts of me.

"What do you want to know?" I ask, my voice flat.

"What's your favorite movie?"

"*Pitch Perfect.*"

He laughs.

"What's so funny?" I ask him.

"Nothing. That's a good answer," he says and continues to chuckle.

"What else?" I ask him, prompting him to move on.

"What's your favorite color?"

"Gray." His forehead scrunches together, seemingly not buying my answer.

"What's your favorite animal?"

"I don't have one. I've never had a pet."

"You've never had a pet?" I shake my head. I'm not about to get into my fucked up childhood with Jonah. I can barely take care of myself, let alone an animal.

"Tell me about your dreams." He twirls his empty wine glass while paying close attention to me.

"My dreams?" I question him. "I don't dream. I'm usually too tired."

"Not those dreams, Lindsay. The dreams you think about when you're alone. When you catch yourself daydreaming. What do you want to do before you die? Those dreams."

Our waiter returns with the bottle of wine just in time. He uncorks the bottle and swishes a small amount in a glass for Jonah to taste. Jonah approves and the waiter fills our glasses and disappears just as quickly as he arrived.

"So where were we?" he asks as he sips his wine. "Dreams." He smiles across the table at me.

"Dreams," I repeat quietly. "I don't know that I have any," I tell him.

"Oh, come on. Everyone has a dream, Lindsay."

"Well, then. Tell me one of yours?" I turn the tables on him. If I can keep him talking, I can avoid talking about me.

"I want to be a charitable entrepreneur, but I don't want to work in a stuffy little office. I want to travel to third-world countries and help those who don't have medical care, or basic human needs—all while getting to see the world at the same time."

"That's an amazing dream," I admit. Here I thought he was just a little rich kid who liked to get high on Daddy's money. He sips some more wine, and I play with the stem of my wine glass.

"So what's your dream, Lindsay?"

I pick up the wine glass and press it to my lips, letting the cool white wine slide down my throat. It pools in my belly, spreading a warmth that starts in my abdomen and quickly spreads to my legs and arms.

"It might sound funny, but I've always wanted a real family." I toss back the rest of my glass of wine as his brown eyes pierce mine. He's quiet as he watches me, and I shift in my seat nervously.

"Then a real family is what you'll have—if you want it badly enough."

The rest of dinner is less stressful. Our serious conversation turned into light-hearted discussions of local news and the insane political environment in the state of Arizona.

"This state is a fucking madhouse," I say, telling him about my interview this last week with the craziest politician I've ever encountered. "Who elects these people? I just don't get it."

"There's nothing to get, Lindsay. Politics is the evil of the world, run by money and idiocracy."

"No shit," I admit. We then toast to the idiots that run the state of Arizona and our hopes for better elections in November. We laugh and enjoy dinner and each other's company, even taking a selfie together with our glasses of wine. I feel good—happy, even if it's medicated and temporary.

"Let's go have dessert." Jonah stuffs a wad of cash in the black folio on the table and rises, helping me out of my chair.

The ride home is quiet, but I catch Jonah watching me out of the corner of his eye. We pull into the parking garage and he hurries around the car to open the door for me. He reaches for my hand, and I let him hold it, leaning into him just a bit to steady myself. Mixing the pills with the wine was probably not a great idea and I'm really starting to feel the effects of it. My feet feel heavy and I can tell I'm leaning into him as we walk down the hallway to my condo.

Jonah opens the door and turns on the kitchen lights as I kick off my heels and pull a bottle of water from the fridge.

"Want one?" I ask as I twist off the cap and drink.

"No thanks," he says as he opens the pink box of cupcakes. I walk over to the island and peek inside the box. Each of them is decorated differently.

"What kind are they?" I ask as my mouth starts watering. *A second on the lips, forever on the hips,* I hear that bitch at my work saying. "They look amazing, but I think I'm going to pass."

"You can't pass on dessert, Lindsay. It's a rule."

"A rule, is it?" I laugh.

Jonah snakes his arm around my waist, pulling me up against him. His arm tightens around me, steadying me against him. I inhale the expensive cologne that lightly floats from his skin. "Pick a cupcake," he whispers into my ear. His warm breath causes me to shiver. His fingers lightly brush against the bare skin of my waistline where my shirt has snaked up.

"The pink one," I stutter.

"Good choice. Strawberry. I love strawberries," he says, pulling the pink cupcake from the box. He sets it on the island, moving me in front of him, pinning me between the kitchen island and himself. His hips press against me, holding me in place while his deft fingers move quickly to remove the wrapper from around the base of the cupcake. He tosses the wrapper back into the box.

"Turn around," he whispers, and I do. He takes his index finger and scoops some of the fluffy pink buttercream frosting onto it, bringing it to my lips. My lips part and his eyes darken as he watches me take his finger into my mouth and lick the frosting from his finger. He removes his finger and scoops some more frosting, this time rubbing some on my bottom lip before sliding his finger back into my mouth.

"Taste good?"

"Mmm hmm," I muster against his finger, sucking it clean.

"I think I need to try some," he says, removing his finger from my mouth. His eyes are intense and focused on my lips. I can feel the sticky frosting he rubbed on my bottom lip and instinctively my tongue goes in search of it. "No. That's mine," he says just before his tongue finds my lip and lightly licks at the frosting he smeared on my lips moments ago. "I fucking love strawberries," he says, pressing his lips against mine in a deep kiss.

There are no fireworks, no immediate impressions of love… but I *like* the feel of his lips on mine. I like being held in his strong arms. I like feeling wanted—and I *need* to be touched. His large hands hold my head firmly as his tongue explores my mouth. His lips are soft but greedy. He knows what he wants and he's taking it.

"Jonah," I breathe against his lips, a plea for him to stop… or maybe a plea for him to continue. I put my hands on his chest to put some distance between us and break our kiss. He pulls back just enough to look at me, his hands resting on the space between my shoulders and my neck, his thumbs rubbing against my jawline.

"Don't fight this, Lindsay."

My body is a traitor as my breaths come quick and shallow. My heart pounds frantically against my ribs as his dark eyes search mine for permission to continue. His grip on my neck tightens as my cell phone begins ringing in my purse.

"Leave it. Focus on *this.*" He presses his lips to mine again as my phone continues to ring. I can feel him reach behind me and search for the phone to silence it, all the while his lips continue their exploration. With a thump, I hear my phone land on the granite counter, no longer ringing.

"Kiss me," I mutter against his lips, begging for more… and he does.

# CHAPTER 12

## *Lindsay*

Another Monday, another assignment. My life is seemingly routine, aside from the fact that I'm falling apart on the inside. On the outside, it appears I've got this handled—cool and confident. The pills help me cope with the mental pain I carry around, and not eating or eating very little provides me something I can control. I'm losing weight and feel I look good—better. I'm proving to Amanda that I've got and will do what it takes to make it.

Mike lets out a little whistle as he watches the complete story we just finished editing. He loves to help me, and I'm so thankful for his guidance. He has an eye for storytelling and a knack for making the imperfect look perfect.

"Amazing, Linds—that's how you tell a story."

"Thank you for always helping me. I honestly don't know what I'd do without you," I admit as we sit and play back the story one last time just to make sure it's perfect before I submit it.

"You ready to anchor this weekend?"

"What?"

"Brian and Kim are on vacation this weekend. Did you forget it's a holiday? It's you and me at the anchor desk Saturday morning!"

"Us? Together?" I can't stop smiling. I knew it was a long shot coming into this market that I'd get to sit at the desk, but it's something I've always dreamed of doing, and for it to happen this soon is truly remarkable.

"Amanda is fucking pissed," he says under his breath. "She's been vying for a seat at that desk for almost a year, but look at her." He taps and rolls his fingers on the desk. "She's just not cut out for the desk, Lindsay. She meddles, her work is subpar, and she's a complete bitch to everyone. You came in here, kept your nose down, produced some amazing stories, and killed it with your live report the other night. Rob has taken notice; hell, viewers have taken notice. Have you seen the social media feed on the station's home page? Hashtag Lindsay Christianson is hot." Mike's smile is big, genuine, infectious.

"Yeah, that hashtag is from a subset of two seemingly lonely male viewers." I roll my eyes and laugh.

"Lonely or not, Amanda doesn't have a fucking hashtag and it's eating her alive," he smirks. "Submit the story, Lindsay. We're going to lunch to celebrate." Mike stands up and waits for me just outside of my cubicle.

"I'll meet you in the lobby in five minutes. I need to use the ladies' room and return an email."

I pull my purse from my desk drawer, walking out of my way to use the restroom as I always do—just to avoid the devil in the flesh, Amanda. I push open the bathroom door and am greeted by bright lights and mirrors everywhere. Full-length mirrors line every wall, and aside from the bathrooms in the back, there are four seating areas where we can sit to do hair and make-up before going on air. Even in a market the size of Phoenix, we don't have the luxury of hair and make-up professionals. It's "do it yourself" around here.

I pause, finding myself scrutinizing every inch of my body. From hair, to face, to chest, to hips, all the way down to my calves. My taupe pencil skirt hangs loose around the waist and makes me feel sloppy. My long curls hang, dry and heavy, and my once crisply pressed white blouse is wrinkled. "Get it together, Christianson," I mumble to myself. A trip to the mall is in order to get some smaller clothes that fit.

I unzip my tan purse and pull out a pill, tossing it into my mouth. I watch the muscles flex in my throat as I swallow, and while it will take nearly a half hour for the effects of my magic pill to begin working, I immediately feel better, more confident—yet inside, I continue to feel the shame of using drugs to numb what I'm really feeling.

I turn to the wall lined with sinks and turn on the water. I wet my fingers and begin fixing my hair, twisting the ends in hopes that my damp fingers will help bring some life back to the dry curls. I pull my lip gloss from my purse and dab some on my lips, noting that the nude color I chose works well with this outfit.

A toilet flushes and a bathroom stall opens as I'm finishing up and washing my hands. "Well, well, well, if it isn't Little Miss Sunshine." Amanda's voice seeps out agitation. I don't respond. I continue lathering the soap and rinsing as quickly as I can. Running my hand in front of the paper towel dispenser to trigger an automatic towel, I wait anxiously. Nothing happens.

"Shit," I mutter to myself. Instead of walking past Amanda to the other dispenser, I opt to wipe my wet hands on my skirt.

"Classy," she drawls with a little snark in her tone.

"Fuck off, Amanda." I pull my purse from the counter and quickly open the door that leads to my escape. I can hear her laughing in the bathroom as the door shuts behind me. *Why do I let her get to me? I never let people like this get under my skin.* For good measure, I open my purse and dig out another pill. I can tell one just isn't going to cut it today. I take a deep breath and leave quickly to meet Mike in the lobby.

I settle into a little two-person table tucked away in the corner of the sandwich shop while Mike purchases our lunches. I take these few minutes to check messages and emails on my phone and am surprised to have a voice message from my friend Jessica. Jessica and I interned at WXZI in Wilmington almost two summers ago. She's one of the few friends that I have that I know I'll always keep in touch with. I hit play on the voice message and press the phone to my ear.

*"Linds!"* Her voice is shrill—excited. *"I'm coming to Phoenix this weekend. Please tell me you'll be there and I can stay with you? Gabe is meeting some buddies from U of A and I don't want to be holed up at a resort all weekend by myself while he's playing golf and reliving the glory of his football days. Call me, please. I miss you."*

A smile creeps across my face. God, I miss her too. I haven't seen her in person since she moved back to California, but we keep in touch via text, email, and Facetime. I don't have time to call her back right now, but I pound out a quick text message to her.

*I'll be here. Stay with me. I love you and can't wait to see you. Text me the details. Xoxo*

Mike sets a lunch tray on the table with two salads and two bottles of water. "Greek for you, chicken salad for me," he says, pulling his plate off the tray. Our lunch conversation is comfortable and I manage to choke down a few bites of salad, mostly artichoke hearts, but it's something.

"Eat, Lindsay," Mike instructs as he devours his salad and breadstick in record time.

"I'm not really hungry."

"You never are. You can't live on coffee." He raises his eyebrows at me and purses his lips.

"I love coffee."

"We all do, but, girl, you need some calories. You're getting too skinny."

"You can never be too skinny," I mumble under my breath.

Mike drops his fork and glares at me. "What the hell is this all about, Christianson?"

"I love it when you get all *gay-mad* at me and call me Christianson." I smile at him.

"I'm serious. Is this about Amanda? She tells everyone they're fat. It's her 'go-to' method of watching new girls self-destruct… and, Lindsay, you're self-destructing. Your clothes hang on you. Your cheekbones are starting to stick out, and you look fucking exhausted all the time. Eat."

"I'm fine, and nothing Amanda says will get me to self-destruct, so stop worrying."

"You're my friend, Lindsay. I will worry."

"Thank you for being my friend." I appreciate Mike's concern and love that he considers me a friend. I need a friend. Mike's phone rings and, with an eye roll and a grumble, he answers it just as my phone starts ringing. My news director's name, Rob, flashes across the screen.

"Hi, Rob," I answer with a tone of confusion, as he never calls me.

"Lindsay, I stopped by your desk, but you weren't there. When can I expect your story? You said it'd be done by noon."

"I uploaded it to the server before I left for lunch."

"Lindsay, it's not there."

"Shit. I'm on my way back now." I jump up and grab my purse, not waiting for Mike. I'm only a couple of blocks away, but I'm in almost a full sprint, even in my heels. I keep replaying the minutes before we left for lunch. Mike is hot on my heels as he yells for me to slow down.

"What's wrong?" he asks as he finally catches up to me.

"Rob called. The story didn't upload to the server."

"Don't panic. It's on your computer. Just hit upload when we get back. It was a mistake."

"I don't have room for mistakes, Mike. Everyone is watching me."

"I know, Lindsay."

He jogs in front of me and holds open the glass door as I run through the main lobby toward the hall that leads down to the newsroom and offices. Amanda stands just outside her cubicle with her arms crossed across her chest, a chest she paid for, no doubt, and a smirk on her face. She's talking to another reporter and says something inaudible as I pass her before she breaks into a fit of laughter.

I toss my purse onto my desk and throw myself into my chair. I struggle to catch my breath as I punch in the password to my computer and my screen opens up. The software that I use to edit has been closed out. I don't remember closing the application after I submitted the story. Mike stands in the open doorway of my cubicle, hovering over me. The application opens and there is nothing there. I stare at a blank screen. The story is gone. The original raw footage is gone. Everything is gone.

"It's gone."

"What do you mean 'it's gone,'" Mike says, pushing his way next to me. "Move over." I roll my chair away as Mike clicks away on the keyboard.

"Did you lock your screen when you got up to leave?" Mike looks back over his shoulder at me.

"I think so. I mean, I don't know for sure. Mike, this is bad. The story is gone."

"Lindsay, go talk to Rob. I have someone else I have to talk to." His eyes narrow and his tan face turns bright red.

"Shit. Shit. Shit. Shit," I curse at myself, rubbing my temples, trying to remember everything I did before we left for lunch. I don't remember hitting submit and sending the story to Rob, but I know I saved the story in the application. It was there. I am confident it was there—in fact, I *know* it was there.

I grab my purse off my desk and shove it into my desk drawer aggressively, slamming it shut. Anger fuels my bad attitude as I storm down the hall and past Mike, who is dragging Amanda into a conference room. I hesitate before knocking on Rob's office door, my heart racing in anticipation of his verbal lashing. I knock twice.

"Come in." My hand shakes as I twist the doorknob and push open the large office door. "Lindsay." He looks at me, perplexed. "I still don't have your story."

"I know. It's gone."

His brows furrow as he spins back and forth in his high-back office chair. "What do you mean 'it's gone'?"

"I finished the package and saved it. I thought I had uploaded it to the server, but I was distracted and left for lunch. I'm almost positive I didn't lock my computer when I left and now it's gone."

"So what are you saying?"

"I'm saying it was there when I left for lunch. Now it's not."

"So you're saying you think someone deleted it?"

I pause for a moment and clear my throat. "I believe someone did delete it, along with all the raw footage—the SIM card is also missing."

He sighs loudly. "Why would anybody do that, Lindsay?"

"I'm honestly not sure why. I just know that I put together an amazing package. It was on my computer, the SIM card was there, I went to lunch, and now it's gone—all of it is gone and the SIM card is missing." My palms are sweating and I can feel my cheeks flush. "Rob, I swear the package was done and I know this sounds like it's just a bunch of bullshit excuses, but you can ask Mike. He sat there and watched it with me. He said it was some of my best work yet."

A sarcastic laugh escapes Rob's lips and his hands are steepled in front of him—watching me intently, pondering his next move.

"So we don't have your story for the five o'clock. What do you suggest we do to make up for that?" His tone is flat, annoyed.

"I'll work with…" I look away from him, trying to remember the assignment manager's name.

"Jan?" he says sharply.

"She's the assignment manager, right?" He nods his head quickly. "I'll work with Jan to find a relevant wire story." I stand quietly, waiting for confirmation that this is what I should do.

"Lindsay, this isn't Wilmington anymore. This is the big leagues. If you can't handle the pressure, I need to know now rather than later."

"I'm fine. I've got this," I say quietly, leaving his office.

"Prove it, Lindsay," he barks as I shut his office door behind me. I walk quickly back to my cube, not wanting to talk to or see anyone. I settle into my chair and bury my face in my hands. My entire body shakes with anger as I feel tears stinging at the backs of my eyes.

"Lindsay, it's been handled." Mike's voice is calm, comforting.

"Not now," I snap at him and jump up from my chair. "I have to find Jan." I push past him, but not before he catches my arm, abruptly stopping me.

"It's going to be fine. Take a deep breath, get it together, and find Jan." I sigh and reach out to hug him.

"Thanks, Mike."

"Anytime, sweetheart. Now go. Go find Jan."

# CHAPTER 13

## Matt

Since Landon took a detective position last year, I've patrolled alone. At times, I've missed the partnership of having someone ride patrol with me, but no one could replace Landon. I've trained a few of the new recruits, but when the department asked if I wanted another partner, I declined. My beat is usually pretty quiet and, thus, here I am—alone. In so many ways that single word, *alone*, defines everything about me right now.

The days both at work and home have been long and slow, but I actually find solace in work. It's a pleasant distraction—an escape. I've picked up some off-duty work as well as some additional shifts to help cover vacations. Today, I'm working the day shift, from seven in the morning to three thirty in the afternoon, which is a change for me. The day shifts are usually slower, less going on. I pull into the small strip mall that houses one of the best sandwich shops in Wilmington and take myself out of duty. Landon pulls into the spot next to me at the same time and nods in acknowledgement.

"What's up, buddy?" he asks as we greet each other with a fist bump. "Glad you could join me for lunch. It's been a while."

"Thanks for asking. Just been trying to stay out of trouble," I joke.

We step into the air-conditioned sandwich shop and take a seat in one of the booths tucked away in the far corner. Being cops, both of us have a sense of paranoia about sitting in front of glass windows—call it a quirk of ours, but we both understand each other. In a glass window, you're an open target for anyone that has a beef with the police.

Our regular server, Margie, greets us with two glasses of water and doesn't even bother to bring us menus. "My boys!" she bellows. "It's been too long."

"Hi, Margie," I greet her with a smile. Margie has served Landon and me lunch or dinner for years. We'd usually come in at least twice a week when we patrolled together. I come less often now that I patrol alone and Landon probably even less, now that he's a detective.

"The usual, boys?"

"The usual, Margie." I smile at the aging older woman. She has worked here for as long as I've been coming and that's been well over fifteen years. My dad used to bring my brother and me here after our baseball games.

"So what have you been up to?" Landon asks, sipping his iced tea.

"Honestly, not much of anything. Work, mostly. Picked up a few overtime shifts, hitting the gym—that's about it. What about you? How's Reagan?" I don't bother to tell him I spend a good portion of each night looking into possible transfers to Phoenix or its surrounding suburbs. I haven't made any calls or any decisions, but I've started looking into opportunities.

"Reagan's great. We honestly haven't seen each other much lately. She was on call last weekend and spent most of her time at the hospital, and I've been working with the feds on that drug bust we had last weekend. Hey, thanks for the tip on that house."

"I've been watching that house for a while. We arrested a guy a couple of weeks ago and I just had a bad feeling about what was going on there."

"You've always had good instincts. You should consider applying for detective. We've got a guy leaving narcs; we could use a guy like you," Landon tries to convince me.

I shake my head. "I like patrol. Always have. I don't see myself anywhere but here."

"That's what I thought too, but I love it."

"If I didn't know you better, I'd assume you're working your way up the ranks, detective."

"Nah. This is it. I love narcs too. We're working a case over at the high school right now—it's crazy the drugs running through that school."

"Too many rich kids playing with nose candy on Mom and Dad's money, huh?" I laugh.

"Nope. Smack. Pure… black tar. We just need to figure out where it's coming in from. We know our local distributor; we just can't narrow down where he's getting it from."

Margie strolls over with our sandwiches and a pitcher of iced tea to top off our drinks.

"If I hear anything, I'll let you know. Most of the guys I pick up aren't selling; just possession."

Landon nods his head. "Thanks, man."

We eat and observe the people coming and going from the sandwich shop. It's part of the job; we're always watching everything—observing people and their behaviors. Landon turns sideways in the booth, as he doesn't like not being able to see what's going on behind him. He used to do this when we rode patrol together as well.

"So I was thinking," he says, pausing to take a drink of tea. "We need to start doing poker nights again."

"Yeah, we kind of let life get in the way of that," I admit.

"We did. But let's do it. How about Thursday night, my house? I'll let Reagan know that a few of you are coming over."

"Will she care?"

"Nah. She doesn't mind. Plus she loves to cook for all of us."

"Think you can tell her no antipasti tray?" We both laugh.

"It'll be pizza and wings. Trust me."

"I'm in."

When I finish my sandwich, I toss a twenty-dollar bill on the table to cover our lunches. We take turns buying lunch and, if memory serves me right, today was my turn.

"Thanks for lunch." Landon wipes his mouth with a napkin before tossing it onto his empty plate. "Let's plan for seven o'clock on Thursday. Does that work?"

"What can I bring other than some beer?"

"Nothing, unless Reagan insists on salami and artichoke hearts." He rolls his eyes. "Then I'll have you bring the man-food."

I laugh. "Deal." Landon's cellphone rings and he gestures that he needs to take the call.

"See ya Thursday."

As we exit the café, I notice Melissa, wearing her work scrubs, walking toward me—a smile on her face.

"Hey," she says as she approaches with a to-go bag in her hand. She stands a little closer than she normally does, and I take a step backwards. I catch Landon watching us out of the corner of my eye. He stands next to his unmarked police car, taking his call.

"Hey," I respond and take another step back, putting even more distance between us.

"Did you get my voice message the other night?"

"I did. Sorry I haven't responded—just been busy." *That's a lie.* I have more time than I've ever had. I just spend it thinking of Lindsay.

"Did you want to hike this weekend? Maybe on Saturday? I haven't been out in a couple of weeks, and the weather is supposed to be great."

"Um, yeah, sure."

She looks at me hesitantly, as if she wants to say something. "Okay. Well, I have to get this lunch back to the office." She lifts up the plastic bag in which she is carrying several to-go boxes. "So, I guess I'll see you Saturday." She raises her hand in a small wave. Landon stands leaning against his car, pretending not to pay attention to me, but I know he was watching me talk to Melissa. He waits until I get into my squad car and put myself back on duty before leaving. Today, I'm thankful to work some overtime and use this time to focus on something other than Lindsay or Melissa.

# CHAPTER 14

## *Lindsay*

I glance at the screen on my phone when it pings, alerting me to a new text message. Jess. I swipe my finger across the screen and smile when I see her message.

*Tomorrow. Tomorrow. Tomorrow. I can't wait to see you.*

I tap out a quick response.

*Me too. I'm anchoring this weekend. Found out Monday. You're coming to work with me Saturday morning.*

She immediately responds.

*Perfect. So proud of you, Lindsay.*

Something in those words makes my heart smile. I feel like I've let everyone down, so it's nice to hear someone say they're proud of me. I pull my thoughts away from Jess and her visit to focus on the list of story ideas I plan to submit at our morning production meeting.

"Venti skinny vanilla latte, madam," Mike says as he sets the paper cup on my desk in front of me.

"You're a life saver."

"You've been antisocial since Monday, sweetheart."

"I'm on Rob's shit list. I need to keep my nose buried in work."

"Lindsay, you're entitled to a break every now and then. So tell me, what did he say anyway?"

I sigh, remembering the conversation I had with Rob two days ago over my deleted story. "He just couldn't understand how my story was deleted from my computer and the raw footage from the SIM card."

"Did you tell him you thought that dirty whore Amanda did it?" He chuckles.

"No."

"No? Why the hell not?"

"Because it's just not worth it. I'm not going to snitch her out. I'm going to work my ass off and prove that I'm better than her."

"There's nothing to prove. You're a better reporter, a better person…"

"Well, I want everyone else to see that."

I lift the cup of coffee to my lips and Mike leans back against my desk. "Look at me," he says. I lift my chin and look at him as I swallow the coffee he brought me.

"Lindsay, I get what you're doing. You're young and you're motivated—and you don't want to start shit with Amanda. But you're worth it. Your career is worth it—do not let her destroy you."

We sit and sip our coffee while I let the weight of those words sink in. "Come on; let's go." I smile at him as I grab my notebook and pen. We walk side by side and I bump shoulders with him as we walk down the hall to our morning production meeting. We normally sit along the back wall, away from the conference table, but today we grab chairs around the table and settle in. Amanda sits directly across from me, turned slightly, her chest extended forward, her attention focused solely on Rob. I don't miss her sarcastic eyes and her long sighs, as if she's bored when I speak.

Out of the corner of my eye, I catch the dirty look Mike flashes at Amanda and can't help but smile. I'm so thankful for Mike, my little pit bull of a friend, for looking out for me. I present all of my story ideas during the meeting—damn good story ideas. Jan, the assignment manager, smiles and nods her head, frantically taking notes, but Rob quickly kills all of my story ideas. I'm being punished for my slip-up on Monday. I bite my tongue, smile gracefully, and take diligent notes, trying not to let being snubbed bother me—at least not here in the meeting. *Keep it together, Christianson*, I repeat over and over in my head.

My hands begin to betray me and start shaking as I write notes. I feel little beads of sweat form across my upper lip and forehead and I discreetly try to wipe them away with my shaking hand. I fold my hands into my lap in hopes that the shaking isn't noticeable to anyone other than me, but Mike reaches out and places his hand on top of mine under the table to stop the noticeable shaking. A wave of nausea overcomes me and I jump up from the conference room table.

"Excuse me; I'm not feeling well." I take off for the bathroom, hoping that I make it in time. Pushing the door open so hard that it slams against the wall behind it, I stumble into a stall and heave the little bit of coffee in my system. Another wave of nausea hits and I heave again—this time just bile. There's a knock on the bathroom door, which I choose to ignore.

"Linds," Mike's voice echoes through the tile bathroom. "You okay?"

"Can you grab my purse from my desk drawer? And my cosmetic bag too?"

"Sure thing, sweetheart."

One more bout of dry heaves and my stomach aches—the muscles burning from clenching over and over. I hear the bathroom door open again. "Are you going to be okay?" he asks. "Coffee just didn't settle well with me, I guess."

"I'm just going to set everything on the counter and go back to the meeting, unless you need me here."

"No, go. I'll be back as soon as I clean myself up."

I hear the door close and I pull myself up from the cool tile floor. I straighten my coral shift dress and blow my nose with some toilet paper, tossing it into the toilet as I flush it one last time. My legs are wobbly as I walk to the sink and wash my hands and use some paper towel to wipe the tears that have leaked from my eyes.

I pull my toothbrush and toothpaste from my cosmetic bag and brush my teeth and tongue. I splash some cool water on my face to ease the red splotches before reapplying my make-up. Thankfully, I pulled my hair up into a twist and that came out unscathed. Inside my purse, I reach for my little pill container and shake two of the OxyContin pills into my hand. I toss them into my mouth and use my hand to scoop some water from the faucet into my mouth to help them go down.

Gathering my belongings, I head back to my desk, dropping my purse and cosmetic bag into my drawer. The newsroom begins bustling with activity and I glance at the clock, noting that the morning production meeting must have just ended. I rest my elbows on my desk and drop my head into my hands for a moment, willing the pills to start working. I close my eyes, rub my temples, and breathe deeply, knowing that relief is minutes away.

"Found this. Heard you lost one." Amanda's voice is cynical. I open my eyes just as a SIM card lands on my desk directly in front of me.

"I didn't lose it." I try to contain my voice as I spin my desk chair around to look at her. She's standing in the open entry of my cubicle. Her hands are on her hips and her mouth is twisted into a devious smile. She leans forward just a bit and whispers, "Better keep track of your stuff. If this becomes a habit, there won't be any room left for you here."

And that's all it takes for me to snap. I lunge from my chair and push her backward. She stumbles on her heels, out into the hall. "Don't fuck with me, Amanda. I'm the wrong person. I will take you down with me," I scream in her face. I have her backed against the wall, holding her by the shoulders. She has a look of shock on her face.

"You're fucking crazy," she seethes.

"Keep this shit up and you're about to find out how fucking crazy I am," I spit out.

"Lindsay." Rob's voice is strong, angry. "In my office. Now!" I look down the hallway where he stands with Mike and a few of the other daytime reporters.

"This isn't done," I mutter through gritted teeth before I back away from Amanda and walk down the hall to Rob's office. He's waiting for me and shuts the door with a loud bang as I step through the entrance.

"Take a seat," he barks.

"I'd rather stand." I remember reading that if someone is standing, so should you. It keeps the playing field even. Plus, I'm fucking angry and I'm tired of Rob treating me like I'm the one who did something wrong.

"Sit down," he demands and gestures toward the chair that

sits in front of his large, mahogany desk. I cave, sitting down and quickly crossing my legs. Taking deep breaths, I hope it helps calm me down as my pulse races. "What was that out there?"

I choose my words carefully. "Amanda mysteriously *found* my SIM card that went missing."

"What's going on with you and Amanda?" he asks as he circles behind his desk and places both of his hands on the back of his high-back leather desk chair.

"She's been at me since the day I started. I'm not pretty enough, I'm too fat, I'm too young—accusing me of doing lewd things to get this job." My voice trails off as my throat tightens and my words become weak. I clear my throat and choke back my emotions. "I know it was her that stole the SIM card from my computer."

"How do you know that?"

"Because who else would do that, Rob? She's mad because you gave me the desk this weekend with Mike. She's jealous because viewers are responding to my stories. She's just a vile person," I say angrily. He stands still, watching me. I can almost see the wheels in his brain turning. He watches me closely as I fold my hands together in my lap and breathe loudly.

"There won't be a desk this weekend, Lindsay."

"What?" I interrupt him. "But I earned it."

"And you lost it," he quips.

I snap my mouth shut. I can feel myself on the verge of losing control. My hands ball into tight fists and I look away from him.

"Lindsay, you're done for the week. I'm placing you on leave until Monday. You physically placed your hands on Amanda, and you verbally threatened her. If she really wanted to, she could come after you for assault. At the very minimum, I cannot have that happening in this building on my watch. You're off until

Monday. Take this time to think about what's important to you; this charade with Amanda or your career."

He walks out from around his desk and opens his office door. I remain seated, trying to gather my thoughts before I push myself up from the chair I'm seated in.

"Guess I'll see you Monday," I say with an attitude as I walk past him to my cube to get my purse and shut down my computer.

"Linds," Mike says as he catches up to me in the hall. "What happened?"

"Not now, Mike. I'll call you later."

"Where are you going?"

"To my condo."

"Shit," he mumbles as he stops following me.

I kick the solid, wooden door closed behind me and juggle the large grocery bags over to the kitchen island. Setting them down, I rub my arm, which has gone numb from carrying all of the heavy bags at once instead of making more than one trip back to the car. I stopped by one of the local specialty grocery stores to pick up some food to make while Jess is here, but as I unpack, I realize there is less food and more wine. *Typical.*

I open the drawer of the island, pulling out the wine opener, and twist the metal corkscrew into the cork on a bottle of Pinot Grigio. I twist and twist, then try to pull it out, and nothing. My hands are shaking again and I fish out the small container in my clutch with my pills, along with my cell phone. As I toss a pill to the back of my throat, I text Jonah to see if he can help me.

While I wait to hear back from him, I stuff cheese and meats into the fridge and wash fruit. The door swings open and Jonah steps in.

"Do you ever knock?"

"What's wrong? Your text sounded urgent."

My head falls back as I laugh. "I said I needed your help. That's not urgent."

Jonah eyes the bottle of wine with the corkscrew stuck in the top. He points at the bottle. "Is this what you needed help with?" His eyebrows lift and he shakes his head in disbelief. Reaching for the bottle, he gives it a pull. In one swift tug, the cork frees itself and Jonah gets a smug smile on his face. He pours me a glass and sets the bottle on the island.

"Want to stay for a glass?"

"Yeah, but I need to run next door for a few minutes. I have to finish something."

"I'll be here. Not going anywhere until Monday," I say sarcastically, raising my glass of Pinot in the air.

He looks at me suspiciously. "Sounds like there's a story there. I'll be back in just a few minutes." The door shuts quietly behind him and I pull my phone and the little container of pills from my purse. I rattle the bottle, noticing that it's almost empty. I put the remaining grocery items away and sigh to myself when I realize how I'm going to have to get more pills.

Checking my phone, I realize I have no missed calls, no voice messages, no text messages, and no emails from anyone I love. I've pushed them all so far away that I fear they've given up on me—rightfully so, I think. I've all but given up on myself. I pour another glass of wine and lean against the kitchen island, waiting for Jonah to return. Needing more than one pill and wine, I toss my phone aside and open the small pill bottle, pouring another single pill into the palm of my hand. I place the pill on my tongue and roll it around my mouth before washing it down with two swallows of wine… the burn in my throat from the wine is both soothing and painful all at the same time. The warmth settles in my belly and I wait for the relief the pill will offer—an escape from feeling anything—physically or emotionally.

I close my eyes and let my head fall back slowly as I wait for numbness to take over me. Focusing on my breathing, I inhale and exhale slowly three times, allowing the deep, cleansing breaths to calm me. My cellphone rings, but I ignore it as I feel myself slipping into a place I've become so familiar with lately—oblivion. My cellphone rings again and again. I ignore the calls until it begins ringing a fourth time. I snatch the phone from the counter to see Jack's name glaring brightly at me.

"Jack," I answer it coldly. I know Rob must have called him. I haven't heard from Jack since he boarded his plane back to Chicago.

"Lindsay, goddammit! Robert called me; what the hell happened today?" I hear the door click shut and I glance up to see Jonah watching me. He keeps his distance as I talk to Jack.

I chuckle. "No 'nice to hear your voice'? No 'how are things going'? Just, 'Robert called me; what the hell happened today'?"

"Lindsay…" His tone is argumentative and I can tell he is pissed.

"I pushed Amanda Stephens. She's been fucking with me since the first day and I lost it today. I pushed her up against a wall and told her to quit fucking with me. Got a problem with that?"

I hear him sigh loudly. "Lindsay, you cannot lose control. You have to prove yourself to Robert. This dream of yours is hanging by a thread."

"I don't want this dream, Jack. I thought I did. I thought I wanted all of this, but if this is how it is, I don't want this," I scream through the phone at him, my voice full of emotion. "I don't want this." My voice breaks.

"Lindsay, you're in a one-year contract. That is unheard of in this business. Give it a year. Focus and give it one-hundred percent and don't let bullshit like Amanda Stephens get in the way of your career."

"Jack, I'm losing control. Everything is slipping through my fingers."

"No, it's not, Lindsay. Pull yourself together." With those words *pull yourself together*, there is an abrupt click and the phone call ends. I set the phone on the counter and feel my shoulders begin shaking at the same time an arm wraps around my waist from behind, giving me support.

"Come here." Jonah's long arms spin me around and he pulls me into his chest.

"Jonah, now's not a good time. I need to be alone."

"You need me," he says firmly. "The last thing you need is to be alone." His embrace is comforting yet foreign as I stand in his arms and let him hold me.

"Look at me, Lindsay," he finally says as his arms release me. "You are stronger than you think you are, but you need to believe it."

"I don't believe in anything right now," I confide in him. Jonah rests his hands on my shoulders and tips my head back so that I'm looking at him.

"You're beautiful, and strong, and..." His voice trails off. His hands move from my shoulders to my neck and he rubs his thumb gently across my bottom lip. "... and beautiful." His eyes search mine, looking for resistance or an invitation, but I am numb. Without waiting any longer, he leans in, pressing his lips to mine. His lips are warm and soft and everything I don't want right now, yet I can't say no—I am weak, and he has the upper hand. Closing my eyes, I welcome his kiss, needy and hungry.

My hands rest low on his sides, my fingers brushing the warm skin just under the hem of his shirt.

"Lindsay," he mumbles between desperate kisses, but I ignore his warning. My hands move under his shirt, finding the rigid muscles of his stomach. My hands explore his solid stomach, brushing against a light sprinkling of hair as they find their way up to his chest. He breaks our kiss and pulls away from me slightly before pulling his polo shirt over his head and tossing it onto the kitchen floor.

His skin is a perfect golden color, and a slight tan line peeks out just above the waistband of his shorts. I reach out, pulling him closer to me, pressing my lips to the center of his chest. His skin is soft and warm and he smells like body wash. He wraps his arms around me again and holds me tightly. He gasps quietly as I fumble with the button on his khaki shorts and, in one swift motion, I pull down his shorts and boxer briefs at the same time. I follow their descent to the floor and kneel before him.

"Lindsay." He reaches for my arm, pulling me back to my feet. "Not here." I nod and he laces his hand through mine as he steps out of his shorts and leads me toward the bedroom.

A flood of emotions and thoughts cross my mind as we walk quietly, hand in hand. It's late afternoon, so the bedroom is light. Jonah pulls the long, sheer curtains as I step out my heels and unzip my dress.

"Let me," he says quietly as he approaches from behind me and finishes unzipping me. The dress falls to the floor and pools around my feet. His finger trails down the curve of my spine, tracing it from neck to bottom, slow and soft before he lifts my silk slip over my head. He sweeps my long, blonde hair over my left shoulder and I feel the press of his lips against the back of my neck. His erection pushes against my backside and my body falls back into his.

His fingers unclasp my bra and he pushes it forward down my arms. "Turn around," he says as he guides me by the shoulders. My arms instinctively wrap around my waist, hiding the sagging skin and my small breasts.

"Don't do that," he instructs as he pulls my hands down so they rest at my sides. "You're beautiful—all of you," he says, his eyes inspecting me from head to foot. "Lie down." I step backwards slowly until the backs of my legs hit the soft down comforter of my bed. I hesitate momentarily before sitting down on the edge of the bed and sliding myself to the center. The bed sinks as Jonah lies down next to me. There is a moment where I have a fleeting thought of stopping this, telling him to leave, but I don't—I welcome his touch, even though I hate myself for wanting it.

"Touch me," I whisper and close my eyes. He accepts my invitation and presses himself up against me. He runs his hand from my stomach up to my breasts, squeezing each one gently. He's slow and methodical in his exploration. He traces my collarbone, which sends a shiver down my spine, and lightly traces small circles down my belly to the top of my panties, the only thing I'm left wearing.

"I love the way you look in red lace," he whispers against my stomach as he runs his tongue across my skin, kissing my bellybutton.

His fingers hook the top of the panties and I raise my hips as he tugs them down my legs, throwing them on the floor behind him. He rubs each of my legs starting at my ankle working his way up. My body trembles at his touch, a combination of fear and shame.

"Relax," he says, pressing his mouth against my inner thigh and kissing it delicately. He holds me firmly in place. The wetness from his tongue mixed with the cool air spreads goose bumps across my skin. His mouth moves higher from my thigh upwards. I gasp when I feel his warm body hovering over me... my body aching with need, with want... with guilt.

His firm hands press my thighs apart and hold me captive as I hold my breath waiting—wanting. "Jesus, you're beautiful, Lindsay," he says just before his tongue slides into me. I gasp at the sudden, yet welcome intrusion. My body deceives me when it reacts to Jonah's touch, flooding me with warmth. I lie open, vulnerable—aching—and Jonah is fulfilling a need I only want Matt to fulfill. I close my eyes and swallow back the disgust I have for myself.

"Lindsay," I hear him say my name as I breathe deeply, the effects of the Oxy finally taking hold. Jonah kisses his way up my body from my stomach to my neck. His breathing is ragged—heavy. "Condom," he mumbles as he presses kisses to my neck and jawline. I lie numbly as my body tumbles over the edge—an adulteration of pleasure and anguish swirled with anticipation. *I'm truly fucked up*, I think to myself.

"Lindsay," he says again, pressing more kisses to my neck. "We don't have..."

"Drawer," I respond. Jonah leans across me and slides the bedside drawer open, pulling out a condom. I hear the tear of the wrapper and feel the bed move as he prepares himself. I lie motionless, one arm pressed against my side, the other raised above my head. Jonah settles between my legs and holds my face in his hands.

"Look at me, Lindsay," I hear his voice as I fall further away with the help of the pills. I find his beautiful brown eyes just as he slides into me with one gentle push. "Lindsay," he says as he laces his hand in mine above my head and steadies himself with his other. His movements are slow, caring, and gentle and I hate myself for the conflicted feelings I have. My eyes fill with tears as I look away from him, my head falling to the side as I fade away and feel nothing at all.

I awake to the moon peeking through the sheer curtains of my room and the sound of the television on in the living room. My body is sore and my head is pounding—the repercussions of combining alcohol, Oxy, and another man's touch—I hate myself.

I crawl out of bed and into the bathroom, where I hover over the toilet and dry heave. My stomach muscles cramp as I heave over and over and yet my body expels nothing. I should be used to this by now, but my body still insists on punishing me. Resting my head on the toilet seat, I breathe deeply as my stomach begins to calm. With just enough strength, I push myself up to a standing position and walk to the sink. The reflection in the mirror disgusts me as I wipe my nose with a tissue and toss it onto the bathroom counter.

I brush my teeth and run a comb through my long, stringy hair. Twisting it up into a makeshift bun, I secure a hair tie around it and turn on the shower. While the water warms, I find some aspirin and take four in hopes it will ease the pounding in my head and the ache that has settled throughout my body.

Stepping into the hot water, I inhale sharply as it pricks my skin. I rest my forehead against the ice-cold tile and close my eyes. My body shifts from side to side ever so slightly as I'm overcome with a dizzy spell. I place my hands on the wall to steady myself as the water washes away my sins.

I finish my shower and throw on a pair of pajama pants and a tank top. I pull the hair tie from my hair, leaving it long and loose. When I open my bedroom door, I find Jonah lying on the couch, watching a baseball game on the TV.

"Hey, sleepyhead," he says, pushing himself up to a sitting position. I lean against the doorjamb and watch him as he turns the volume down on the TV. He's put his shorts back on, but his chest remains bare. He runs a hand through his messy hair and smiles at me. "Come here." He pats the space on the couch next to him. I walk toward him hesitantly, my palms sweating. As I squat to sit down, Jonah pulls me into his lap and I'm too weak to resist. He holds me as one would hold a small child in their lap.

He presses a kiss to my temple, then wraps his arms around me before he rests his chin on my shoulder. "I ordered pizza about fifteen minutes ago. You're going to eat," he says quietly.

"Okay," I say, my voice as shaky as my body.

"You're trembling," he says and runs his hands up and down my arms. "What's wrong?"

"Nothing." I lie, turning my head away from him in an attempt to locate my purse.

"Lindsay, talk to me."

"There's nothing wrong, I promise," I say, turning back to him and offering him a fake smile. Just then, the doorbell rings and Jonah kisses my forehead as he lifts me off his lap and sets me on the couch.

"Pizza's here." He jumps up and pulls his wallet from his back pocket. While he gets cash and pays for the pizza, I jump from the couch and head toward the kitchen island, where my purse sits. Reaching inside, I push and twist the white cap off the pill bottle and shake two pills into the palm of my hand. Jonah is closing the door as I toss them in my mouth and swallow hard.

"Wine?" I ask as he sets the large, cardboard pizza box on the counter.

"Sit down. I'll get it." He pushes me toward the tall barstools that sit at the kitchen island. "So I was thinking." He smiles as he pulls plates down from the cupboard. "Maybe this weekend, we could go out again, maybe get some Mexican food and a movie?"

I watch him as he carefully pulls the slices of pizza from the box and sets a piece on a plate for me.

"I can't this weekend. My friend Jess is coming into town with her fiancé, Gabe. She's staying with me while he reconnects with some of his friends." Jonah shoves the plate with pizza in front of me.

"So what are you guys going to do?" He takes a bite of pizza and waits for me to answer.

"Not sure. She was supposed to come with me to work on Saturday. I was given the morning anchor desk on Saturday before everything happened." I pause. "Anyway, she was supposed to come with me. We met while interning together at a TV station back home in Wilmington." I pick at the crust of the pizza and put a small piece in my mouth.

"So now you're just going to hang out?"

I shrug. "Something like that. We'll find something to do. Besides, it might just be nice to sit back and catch up."

"Well, I'm sure the guys will be over tomorrow night if you guys want to stop by."

I shake my head rapidly. "No, she's not like that."

"Like what, Lindsay?"

"Into the drugs..."

"Neither am I. I don't do that. What Dominic does is Dominic's business, not mine."

"I watched him snort something off your kitchen counter the first time I met you. I think that qualifies as your business," I say angrily.

"Well, isn't that the pot calling the kettle black."

"What the hell is that supposed to mean?" I sit up tall and toss my shoulders back.

"The pills, Lindsay. I know you're using. I can see it in your eyes. I can tell when you take them and all of the sudden you relax, you stop shaking, you calm down—and you laugh. It's the only time I see you smile," he says with an edge of irritation.

I swallow hard against my dry throat and plan a snarky come back, but he cuts in before I have a chance.

"It worries me, Lindsay."

"Don't worry about me." I drop my eyes to the wine glass that sits in front of me. I can't look at him as he confesses his concern, knowing I just swallowed two more pills.

"I will worry. I care about you."

I snort as I pull the wine glass to my lips and swallow the cool Pinot Grigio. "What?" he asks, glaring at me.

"So if you know I'm using, why did you fuck me while I was high?" In a flash of anger, he moves around the kitchen island and pulls me from the chair I'm sitting on. It's sudden and quick and it scares me. My heart beats wildly as he grips my arms—hard.

"What the hell did you just say? Are you accusing me of something?"

"No, no accusations. I'm just curious; if you're so concerned about me, why did you fuck me while I was high?" I raise my chin in a show of defiance.

He just stares at me and shakes his head in disgust. *Good. Hate me. Everyone else does.* He lets go of me and grabs his wallet off the kitchen counter and stuffs it into his back pocket. He pulls his shirt off the floor and puts it on.

"Get this through your head, Lindsay. I *never* fucked you. Never. It was more than just a fuck to me. Second, I didn't know you were high until you started crying, slurring your words, and called me 'Matt.'" In four brisk steps, he walks out my door and slams it behind him, startling me. I bury my head in my hands and wonder what else I can fuck up.

# CHAPTER 15

*Lindsay*

My phone vibrates on the nightstand, pulling me out of a hazy slumber. The sun is shining brightly through the sheer curtains and my head swirls in dizziness. "Shit," I mumble as I roll onto my stomach and reach for the buzzing phone. With one eye open, I see Jess' name flashing on the home screen and I swipe the answer icon.

"Hello," I say, my voice hoarse.

"Linds, we're almost there!" Jess squeals into the phone. "You're probably still at work, so I'll just have Gabe drop me off tonight." Glancing at the alarm clock, I see that it's almost two o'clock in the afternoon. I exhale loudly and roll onto my back.

"No, change of plans. I'm home this weekend. I'm not working. You can have Gabe drop you off as soon as you get into town."

"Even better. I'll be there in about thirty minutes."

"Sounds good." I tell her before I drop my cell phone onto the floor and stare at the ceiling above me, watching it spin in slow circles. I close my eyes and breathe deeply as I run through the mini-checklist of things I need to do in the next thirty minutes before Jess arrives. Forcing myself out of bed, I stumble into the bathroom. Turning on the shower, I twist my hair into a messy bun and brush last night's two bottles of wine from my teeth and tongue, gagging as I do it.

I stick my head under the water faucet and lap at some of the cool water, swishing it around my mouth before swallowing. I still feel parched as I step into the warm shower and quickly wash my body and face. Drying myself quickly, I pull on a short silk robe and strip the sheets from my bed, stuffing them into the washing machine and turning it on.

My room is a complete disaster with piles of clothes, accessories, and shoes strewn everywhere. I haven't cleaned this place since I moved in. While a mess like this would have sent the old Lindsay into a fit of OCD-induced rage, I just step over the piles of clothes and look forward to losing myself in the numbness that only the Oxy can provide. I sit on the edge of the bed and bury my head in my hands, rubbing my temples gently, urging the pounding headache to go away. My stomach turns and nausea overcomes me again. I've come to realize how much I appreciate the comfort of the OxyContin pills. They kill the nausea, the shakes, the trembling, and the headaches—I've become dependent on these stupid pills simply to function.

I punch the mattress and flex my shaking hand at the thought of needing the pills, no longer just wanting them to keep my emotions at bay. Yanking open the nightstand, I pull out the bottle of pills and take two. I'm down to my last four. *Shit.* On wobbly legs, I walk back to the bathroom and turn on the water. Popping the pills into my mouth, I fill my hands with water and drink from them.

Standing up, I use a hand towel to wipe the newly formed sheen of sweat from my forehead and cheeks. I close my eyes and will the pills to start working before Jess arrives. Just then, the doorbell rings and I whisper a silent prayer to whoever it is that's answering them today, take a deep breath, and push myself away from the bathroom vanity and toward the front door.

I take note of the condition of my living room and kitchen as I dodge throw pillows and empty wine bottles. "Coming," I holler as the doorbell rings again. I pull the door open and Jess launches herself into my arms. I can't help but laugh at her. She's taller than me, so my chin rests on her shoulder and I get a mouthful of her long, wavy hair.

"Linds," she whispers and squeezes me tighter. My throat tightens and tears sting the back of my eyes. "I missed you so much."

"I missed you too," I admit. And I have. Jess was my only girlfriend in Wilmington. My friends from high school moved away for college and never came back. When I returned after graduating, I dove head first into my internship at WXZI and it was me and Jess. I hear a man clear his throat and Jess pulls out of our embrace.

"Oh my gosh. Lindsay, this is Gabe. Gabe, Lindsay." He sets down the two bags he's carrying and reaches out his tan hand to shake mine. Gabe is tall and gorgeous with dark brown hair and almost golden eyes that stand out against his tan skin and dark lashes. He's striking—and muscular. I notice his arms flex as he shakes my hand. I realize I'm standing in a silk bathrobe and I make sure I'm covered and tighten the belt on the robe. I catch Jess looking around the messy condo and she looks back tentatively to Gabe.

"Sorry for the mess. I've been so busy at the station this week that I just haven't cleaned up."

"Don't worry about it." Jess smiles. "I'll help you." She sinks into Gabe's arms and gives him a quick hug and kiss and all but shoves him out the door. I smile as I watch her assure him she'll be fine and will call him later.

"I can't believe it's been almost two years since we've seen each other," Jess says as she kicks off her shoes and sits down on the couch. She pulls a throw pillow into her lap and tucks her feet underneath her. She's exactly as I remember her; casual and stunning. Then, when I sit opposite of her, I take in how much she's changed since the last time I've seen her. She looks older, but better. She's gained a little weight, but in a healthy way.

"So talk to me; what are you doing these days?" I ask, curious to catch up with my old friend.

"A little of this, a little of that. I've been teaching some online classes. English," she says, "And also taking some classes in social work."

"Social work?" I question. "That's a far cry from broadcast communications." She nods her head and twists her fingers around each other.

"I don't know if Landon ever told you…"

"He never told me anything about you two," I interrupt her. She looks away from me, her attention focused on the mantle that hangs above the gas fireplace. "I'm not sure exactly what went down with the two of you, but Jess, he loved you and respected you. He never discussed what happened."

"Nothing happened," she sighs, "except he helped me find myself again when I was lost," she says quietly. "I was in a pretty dark place, and I'll never be able to repay him—for loving me the way he did." Her voice cracks.

"What happened, Jess?" I shift on the couch and pull a pillow into my lap.

"So much." Her voice trails off. The smile on her face slowly fades. "We'll talk—before I leave, but not right now. I just got here and I want to see this amazing condo and hear about *you*." She clears her throat and swallows down her emotions. "I mean, look at this place, Lindsay. Holy shit," she says, trying to sound excited.

I can't help but smile. "I know. I'm so embarrassed by the mess, though," I stand up and begin picking up all the throw pillows that are all over the floor. I arrange them neatly on the couches and the oversized chair.

"I don't care about the mess. Tell me about you. How's Matt?" And there it is. A knife directly to the heart.

"Ah, we're not together anymore." I stand up straight and turn around.

"What?"

"Yeah, we decided long distance wasn't our thing."

"Christ, Lindsay." She places her hand on her heart and her face twists into a frown. "I'm sorry. I didn't know."

"No, it's okay. It's hard. So hard," I admit.

"How's he handling it?"

"Not well. I'm pretty sure he hates me." I rearrange the pillows on the couch again so I can avoid looking at her.

"He doesn't hate you."

"No, I'm pretty sure he does."

"When's the last time you talked?"

"He called me a couple of weeks ago. It was short. Formalities." I shrug.

"Well, if he called you, he surely doesn't hate you." I sit down next to Jess on the couch and fold my hands into my lap. Thank goodness the Oxy has kicked in and I'm no longer shaking or nauseous.

"I made the biggest mistake taking this job," I admit to my friend.

"No, Linds, don't say that. It's scary and new and you're navigating this alone. Be proud of your accomplishments."

"Would you leave Gabe for a job across the country?"

She laughs quietly. "I kind of did that, remember? Circumstances were a little different, I'm going to assume, but we made it."

"I'm not holding my breath that we'll be as lucky as you and Gabe," I acknowledge. "In fact, I'm pretty sure we'll never recover from this." I lean my head onto Jess' shoulder and close my eyes.

"Don't give up," she whispers quietly as a tear slides down my cheek.

Jess and I sit at a small table on top of one of the hotels in downtown Phoenix that has a restaurant that spins, giving us a three-hundred-and-sixty-degree view of the Valley of the Sun. It's gorgeous and offers amazing views of the mountains, downtown Phoenix, and the stunning orange and pink sunsets that have graced the skies lately. We toast to our friendship and eat an amazing dinner. Well, Jess ate and I picked at a piece of grilled salmon.

"So tell me about the wedding," I ask Jess as I sip on my Appletini. She spins the simple, yet large princess-cut diamond around her ring finger. "It's going to be small. Just our families and close friends. You'll be invited." She smiles and sips on her drink. "I think we're looking at March. March in California is beautiful. It'll be in Santa Barbara for sure."

"Beach wedding?"

"God, no. Gabe's family would kill us if we didn't get married in a church." She rolls her eyes, but a smile tugs at the corner of her lips. I know she'd do anything Gabe asked her to. "They're Mexican, strict Catholics." She laughs.

We order one last round of drinks before we decide to head back to the condo. We giggle and loop our arms together as we balance on each other and walk back the four blocks to my condo. Even at nine o'clock in the evening, the Phoenix heat stings my face. We reach the twenty-second floor of my building and walk past Jonah's condo and I can hear the music blaring through the door and into the hallway.

"Is your neighbor always that loud?"

"Only when he's being a dick." I insert the key into my door and push it open.

"Ladies," Jonah's voice echoes through the tiled hallway. I step inside the condo quickly, doing my best to avoid him. I look back over my shoulder and see that Jess has stopped in the hall and is shaking hands with Jonah. He turns his head and peeks into the condo, but I look away, avoiding eye contact with him. They spend a minute chatting before Jess finally comes inside and closes the door.

"That is your neighbor?" Jess giggles.

"That's him," I say sarcastically.

"He's hot, and he invited us over later."

"Jess. You're engaged. You're not allowed to think other guys are hot. And we're not going over there."

She rolls her eyes and laughs. "Uh, yeah... I'm allowed to

look, and it might be fun. We should stop by."

"We'll see," I mumble as I pull the cork from the bottle of wine that was chilling while we went to dinner.

Jess and I spend the next few hours indulging in wine and reminiscing. For the first time in weeks, my heart is happy. In between glasses of wine, Jess and I make progress on cleaning the living room and kitchen. While I grab the sheets from the dryer, Jess carries her bags to the bedroom and I meet her there with an arm full of clean sheets and pillowcases.

I toss the sheets into the middle of the bed while Jess kicks piles of my clothes into one large pile in the corner.

"Good God, woman." She laughs at me as the stack of dirty clothes continues to grow.

"I know. I need to get to the dry cleaners and wash some clothes."

"We're going to start tackling this tomorrow." She laughs and shakes her head. I see her reach down and pick something off the floor as I begin making the bed with the freshly washed sheets.

"Lindsay," she says quietly as she approaches me.

"Yeah." I turn my head toward her as I tuck sheets under one side of the mattress. She stands holding a condom wrapper. I stop what I'm doing and stand up, brushing the hair out of my face that's fallen from my messy bun. She watches me with contemplative eyes.

"Here." She places the wrapper in my hand. "You might want to toss that." I nod and close my fingers around the wrapper. Jess goes back to quietly piling my clothes and tossing my shoes into the closet, before she starts unpacking her overnight bag. The giggling and laughter is gone, replaced by an uncomfortable air of sadness.

"All done," I let Jess know as I pull the down comforter back onto the bed. "At least I washed the sheets," I say, cracking a joke. Jess smiles at me and stops unpacking her bag. She has a small pile of clothes on the nightstand. She walks over to me and pulls me into a hug.

"I know you miss him, Linds. I can see it. But please be careful. I don't know what you're doing, but don't do anything you'll regret."

I nod, swallowing the lump in my throat. "I already have," I whisper. There is a loud commotion out in the living room and some whoops and hollers. "What the hell is that?" I grumble, jumping up from the bed and running toward the living room.

"Who is that?" Jess asks as I move toward the door.

"Take one guess?" I snap. "Guys, didn't your mothers teach you it's rude to just let yourself into someone's home?" Dominic stands at my refrigerator with the door open and his head stuck inside. I met Dominic in the hallway as he was knocking on Jonah's door one afternoon, and two other guys I remember seeing at Jonah's stand at the kitchen island and talk to each other animatedly. All three turn to look at me as I approach.

"Hey, beautiful," Dominic says as he shuts the refrigerator door and strides over to me. I glance over my shoulder and find Jess leaning against the bedroom doorjamb with her arms folded across her chest, assessing the situation. "Jonah said he invited you and your friend," he nods at Jess, "to come over. We came to personally walk you there—you know, make sure you get there safe and all." He winks at me and a smile crawls across his face that makes my stomach turn.

"It's next door. I think we'll be fine." Dominic smiles at me and moves closer—way too close.

"I brought you a little incentive." He pulls a baggie from his front pocket and dangles it in front of my face. I snatch it as quickly as I can to hide it, but he pulls it right back out of my hand. It's a baggie full of pills.

"Put it away," I snarl at him through clenched teeth.

"Everything okay?" Jess asks as she comes into the living room, leaving the safety of the bedroom behind.

"Everything's fine," I tell her, giving Dominic *the look*, the one that says get the hell out of here.

"Everything's great!" Dominic says, shoving the baggie of pills into his front pocket as he leans around me to address Jess. "We'll see you in just a little bit. Right, Lindsay?" He tips his head to the side and licks his lips. I look back at Jess and she shrugs.

"Yeah, we'll stop by for just a few minutes."

Leaning in, Dominic whispers in my ear, "You're cute when you're pissed. Find me and they're yours, sweetheart. My treat." With a wink and a devilish smile, he steps away from me and turns toward the door. "Let's go, guys. The ladies will be over in just a bit."

The door shuts behind the guys as they leave, and I look at Jess. "We don't have to go if you don't want to."

"No, let's just stop by. It'll be fun," she says with a smile.

"Are you sure?"

"Yes. It'll be fun."

After a quick change of clothes, Jess and I head next door. "Anytime you're ready to leave, just say something or give me a look," I inform her as we stand outside Jonah's door. We can hear voices inside along with music.

"Deal."

I push the doorbell and wait for Jonah or anyone to answer the door. The door opens and Jonah stands just inside, holding a bottle of beer. He steps aside and opens the door further, welcoming us.

"Lindsay." He tilts his head and looks at me funny.

"Hi, Jonah. You met Jess earlier," I reintroduce her as we step into his condo. I've never been inside his place; I've only seen it from the open doorway. It's the typical bachelor pad with exposed brick walls, wood floors, black leather sofa and loveseat, and an entertainment system that rivals that of a movie theater.

"We did meet. I'm glad you guys stopped by," he says, bringing me back to the present.

"We're not staying long. Just wanted to make an appearance." I scan the room, looking for Dominic. I find him in a corner of the living room, pressing a woman against the wall, his lips to her neck, all while managing a bottle of beer in one of his hands—classy.

"Everyone, this is Lindsay and Jess. Jess and Lindsay, this is everyone," Jonah announces as he shuts the door. "What can I get you to drink? We've got beer, wine, vodka…"

"Vodka cranberry," I say, looking to Jess.

"Water for now. I'll have something else in a little while," Jess answers with a smile.

"Vodka cranberry and a water coming up," Jonah repeats. Jess walks into the living room where people stand in small circles, talking. She walks right up to a group of two girls and introduces herself, immediately making herself comfortable in a sea of strangers. I envy her confidence. Working in a profession where I talk to strangers every day, I'm uncomfortable here in a room with strange people I've never met.

"Having fun with Jess?" Jonah asks as he drops some ice into a glass.

"Yeah. I've really missed her."

"She's gorgeous," he says as he tips the bottle of vodka and pours a small amount into the glass before he hesitates.

"She is."

"So are you, Lindsay."

I let out a long sigh. "Jonah, can we please not do this right now."

"Do what? I can't tell you you're beautiful?" He sets the bottle of vodka on the island and turns toward me quickly. His large hands grip each side of my head.

"Look at me, Lindsay." His voice is commanding and his brown eyes search mine. "Last night wasn't a one-time deal for me," he whispers as he presses his soft lips to my jaw. With slow kisses, his lips travel up my jaw to the sensitive spot just behind my ear. He sucks lightly on my ear lobe and I feel my head fall back, giving him more access to my neck. "I will be doing that to you again," he mumbles against my neck.

"There won't be an again," I say gently, pushing him away.

"What's going on over here?" the husky male voice says and begins laughing. Jonah steps back and I rub the spot on my neck that he was nibbling on.

"Just welcoming our guests," Jonah says as he stirs the cranberry juice in my drink. "Dominic, have you met my next-door neighbor, Lindsay?"

"Actually, it's pretty funny. I was at her place earlier..." He laughs as if it's funny. Jonah visibly tenses up when Dominic says that.

"We met in the hallway one day," I interrupt him. "He was knocking on your door and you weren't home. I was just getting home from work. We talked for just a few minutes in the hall, and that's how we met." My answers are short and direct.

"What she said." He laughs and takes a long drag on a cigarette. "We exchanged phone numbers, we're 'friends.'" He makes with air quotes. The smoke swirls from his mouth and hangs heavy over the kitchen island. I swat it away from my face, and Jonah looks suspiciously at Dominic.

"So you went to her place today? And you two exchanged phone numbers?" he questions him and looks at me.

"Just stopped by and invited her to the party. Don't worry, man. I'm not going to move in on your old lady." He pulls a shot glass off the kitchen island and fills it with Jack Daniel's and tosses it back, smacking his lips when he's finished. "But it worked, didn't it? Got your girl here." He winks at me and saunters away back to the girl who is still leaning against the wall.

"Stay away from him, Lindsay," Jonah orders. He stares at Dominic as he walks away. His glare is icy and cold. "He's bad news."

"Yeah, of course. I mean, he's your friend…"

"He's not my friend. He's Jason's friend. I don't like that punk. Delete his number from your phone." I nod at him as he hands me my drink. Opening the refrigerator, he pulls out a bottle of water for Jess and walks it over to her where she still stands talking to two girls she walked up to minutes ago. Just then, there is a loud noise and glass shatters when a girl who was dancing drops her glass, shattering it on the wood floor. Jonah is visibly annoyed as he walks to the hall closet and pulls out a broom and dust pan.

Jonah sweeps up the glass as people continue to dance around him, making it difficult for him to clean up. I turn around and quietly flip the latch on the sliding patio door and step out onto his balcony, closing the door behind me. It's still miserably hot as I lean on the edge of the railing and prop my chin on my hand, watching the cars drive on the street twenty-two stories below.

I can make out the stars in the clear sky and the crescent moon sits high in the sky. Jonah's patio curves around to the other side of his condo and there are patio doors into the master bedroom and the living room. The living room door slides open and Dominic steps out onto the dark patio.

"There you are," he says, the cigarette from earlier still hanging from his lips. I don't say anything in return as he walks closer and leans on the railing next to me. "I was surprised to get a text from you," he says and flicks the butt of his cigarette off the balcony. I watch the red ember fade as it falls to the street below. His hand reaches into his front pocket and he pulls out the baggie of pills and holds them out to me.

"I could only get fifty," he says, "but I should be able to get more later this week."

"Fifty is great for now," I say, reaching for the baggie.

"Hey now," he says as we both tug at the plastic bag that holds the pills I need.

"What do I owe you?" His bright blue eyes fix on me as he thinks. "Money isn't an issue," I tell him as I yank the bag from his hand.

"I told you earlier: this is my treat. Plus, maybe it's not money I want," he says, rubbing his hand on my shoulder.

"Dom." Jonah's voice is firm and the patio door slams shut as he steps out. I quickly shove the baggie of pills into the front pocket of my shorts and take a step back from Dominic.

"What's up, man?" Dominic asks Jonah as he approaches.

"What's going on out here?" Jonah is glaring at Dominic and I tentatively step back. Dominic pulls out another cigarette and rests it between his teeth.

"Not much. Just talking to Lindsayyyyyy." He drags out the end of my name. "You've got yourself a cute little thing." He winks at me.

"Fuck off, Dom. Stay away from her."

Dom laughs as he pulls out a lighter and flicks it, the flame roaring to life as he lights his cigarette. Jonah breathes heavily, balling his fists. His chest rises and falls dramatically.

"That girl you brought is inside looking for you."

"Yeah, better get back inside." He never takes his haunting blue eyes off of me. "Nice talking to you," he says, tilting his head to the side. "Nice talking business with you." He saunters away with a cocky attitude.

"You okay?"

"God, why do you always think I'm in trouble or that something's wrong?" I lash out at Jonah. "I'm fine."

"Lindsay, calm down. Jesus. I saw Dom's hand on your shoulder and you looked uncomfortable."

"I'm fine. I'm going to get Jess and we're going to head back to my place. Thanks for having us over." I try to push past him, but his long arm grabs me at my elbow, stopping me.

"What did he mean 'talking business' with you? Is he where you're getting your pills from? So help me God, Lindsay, if it's him… I'll fucking kill him." My heart races as I watch Jonah's face become angrier. He snatches my drink from my hand and dumps it into a potted plant that sits on the balcony. "And don't fucking mix alcohol and pills, do you understand me?" His eyes soften, going from anger to concern.

"Let go of me," I say through gritted teeth as I yank my arm out of his grasp. "Thanks for having us over." My tone is snarky. I just want to get out of here. I enter the condo and immediately find Jess.

"Hey," she says as I walk up to her.

"Let's go." I walk past her and wait for her at the front door. She says goodbye to the girls she was speaking with earlier and, as we leave, I see Jonah watching us with a scowl on his face. "Sorry, wasn't in the mood to hang out," I tell Jess as we leave.

"It's fine. I came to spend time with you, not your neighbors." She bumps her shoulder against mine. "Let's have some more wine and just catch up."

"I'd like that," I admit. Jess heads straight for the small wine fridge that's built into the kitchen island and pulls out another bottle while I head to the bedroom to change. I close the bedroom door behind me and pull the baggie of pills from my front pocket. I take out two and set them on my tongue while I hide the baggie under a book in the drawer of my nightstand. I lean over the bathroom sink and drink some water directly from the tap.

Using the pads of my fingers, I wipe what I think is eyeliner from underneath my eyes, but soon realize that it's dark circles and not make-up. I can hear Jess rummaging around out in the kitchen and I pull my hair into a messy bun and join her. She's popping microwave popcorn and pouring two glasses of chilled white wine.

"You haven't changed a bit." I laugh as I walk through the living room and pull one of the wine glasses off the kitchen island.

"Why do you say that?" She smiles.

"You're still obsessed with microwave popcorn." She used to eat it all the time when we interned together in North Carolina.

"And wine," she interjects.

"That too." I laugh.

"Where is there a large bowl?" she asks as she flings open cupboard doors.

"I'm not sure. Check the cabinets beneath the island."

"How do you not know where you have a bowl?"

"I never cook," I say, sipping on my wine. I sit on the

barstool that's at the kitchen island and tuck one leg underneath, the other one swinging from the stool.

"Lindsay, be honest with me. When is the last time you ate something? And don't say tonight, because you didn't take one bite of that salmon. I watched you." She stands up and sets a large, plastic bowl on the granite counter. Her eyes soften when she looks at me. I should go on the defensive, but her eyes are concerned and I'm just so thankful I have someone here with me.

"I eat," I say, looking away from her.

"What do you eat and when? Lindsay, you've lost so much weight since I've seen you last. And yes, that was a long time ago, but you're too skinny." I nod my head and swallow tightly. "I'm worried about you." I turn and look at her. "Look at this place. Lindsay, you always have everything immaculate. You never left anything less than perfect; you were borderline OCD." I shrug and watch her as she walks around the island and stands next to me.

"Talk to me," she says quietly. I lift the wine glass and press it against my lips. I take a large drink of the wine and set it on the counter in front of me.

"Everything has gone to hell," I stutter. Jess leans against the island and pushes herself up on the counter. She sits in front of me and crosses her legs. "I just don't care about anything anymore."

"I'm all ears; let's work this out." She offers me a tight smile.

"Jess, there's nothing to work out. I've fucked up everything."

"What have you fucked up?"

"My career, Matt... just everything."

"Start from the beginning." She leans over and pulls her glass of wine to her. "We've got all night and then some." I watch Jess

149

as she settles in, on top of my cold granite counter, making herself at home. Her long, brown, wavy hair hangs loose over her shoulders and her long, tan legs twist into a knot as she sits cross-legged on my counter.

"Wait!" she says, hopping off the counter and walking over to the microwave, pulling out the bag of freshly popped popcorn. She pulls at the edges of the paper bag it's popped in and dumps the popcorn into a bowl. She walks back around and resumes her cross-legged position on the kitchen island with the bowl of popcorn tucked neatly in her lap.

"Okay, go. From the beginning and don't leave *anything* out." She raises her eyebrows at me in warning. I take another sip of wine and then a deep breath. My palms are sweating and I can feel my emotions teetering on the edge of a steep cliff, waiting to spill over. My chin quivers lightly as I begin.

"Matt and I quietly started seeing each other about two years ago, but you knew that." I get lost momentarily in the memories of our first date, our first kiss… so many firsts together. "We never really dated; we just kind of settled into each other's lives and never left. Our relationship progressed quickly, but everything about it was *right*. From the beginning we were inseparable. We both had our careers and our personal lives were great. I found my mom." I take a quick sip of wine and let it slide down my throat. "That is another story, for another time." Jess nods and pulls a handful of popcorn from the bowl. "We didn't announce we were together or seeing each other until just a couple of months ago."

"Why?" Jess asks, scrunching her eyebrows in confusion.

"Because he's Landon's best friend and ex-partner at work, and it was just weird. Plus, it became the worst kept secret in the history of relationships." I roll my eyes.

"I'm marrying my best friend's older brother. I get it." She smiles at me. "Go on."

"Anyway, Jack, my agent had been pressing me to take a job outside of WXZI. He kept telling me I'm better than the small market and that I belong in a top twenty market. So he started looking, quietly putting out feelers. Less than a week later, I had this offer on the table." I sit up a little straighter and set my wine glass on the counter. Jess leans over and tops it off with the open bottle that is sitting next to her.

"Jess, you know I love my job. I couldn't imagine doing anything else…"

"But…"

"But, everything just happened so fast. I made irrational decisions based on what I thought I wanted or needed, and I destroyed everything in taking this job. I lost Matt, now I've fucked up this job because of some pretentious bitch-hole." I clear my throat. "Everything I've loved has or is slipping through my fingers."

"Back up. What happened with Matt?"

"Everything," I mumble. Rubbing my head, I continue, "I remember the look on his face when he heard me tell Jack that I'd take this job in Phoenix. It wasn't even anger; it was pure sadness and devastation. I'd chosen a job over him. He would have never chosen anything over me. I destroyed him in a matter of seconds. Who does that to the one person that means more to them than anyone else in the world? Me."

"Shit, Linds," Jess says quietly.

"He hates me."

"He doesn't hate you. He's hurt, but he doesn't hate you. How long is the contract for?"

"One year." Jess tops off her glass of wine and hands me

mine. "Let me ask you something, Jess. When you moved home, why didn't you work in TV?"

"Just wasn't something I was passionate about anymore," she admits. "But you love it, don't you?"

"I used to. But I don't love it more than I love Matt."

"So then why did you take the job?"

"Because I've always done what's expected of me, what I should do. As you know, my life was no bed of roses growing up, so I always played it safe and set goals to achieve. This was on my list of goals, so I took the job. For once, I did something that I thought might make me happy."

"But this goal isn't making you happy."

"It's not." I shake my head and feel a tear fall from my eye and roll down my cheek. I swat it away and sip some more wine.

"So you haven't been eating, or taking care of yourself or your place." Jess looks around at my filthy condo. I shake my head.

"You have to eat, Linds."

"I know," I mumble.

"You don't look healthy."

I snort. "Well, according to the bitch-hole Amanda, I'm a fat cow."

"And you're really going to listen to her? Newsrooms around the country are filled with crazy-ass women trying to compete with one another, calling each other fat or ugly. Come on, Lindsay; you're smarter than that."

"She found my weak spot. I used to be anorexic in college," I admit. "My life was such a mess back then, Jess. What I put in my mouth, or the lack thereof, was the only thing I could control. It was the only thing that made me feel powerful. It's so easy to fall back into that trap when your life is spiraling out of control."

"You need help, Linds." Jess sets the bowl of popcorn on the island and slides off. "Let me help you. We'll start by getting this place cleaned up and look for some local resources to help you with the eating disorder." She places her hand on my forearm. More tears spill from my eyes and, this time, I don't bother to chase them away—I let them fall. Jess wraps her long arms around my neck and hugs me while I cry.

"I'm sorry you came to spend time with me this weekend and, here I am, a total mess," I say, pulling myself together.

"I wouldn't want to be anywhere else other than with my friend right now."

Jess and I spend the next few hours reminiscing and drinking more wine. I notice the three empty bottles on the kitchen island and find myself nearly dozing off. "I'm going to call it a night," I say with a yawn and stretch my arms over my head.

"I'm going to finish cleaning up out here," Jess says as she turns on the kitchen sink. I stumble back to the bedroom, my eyes heavy and my head dizzy. I feel light-headed, I'm sure due to a combination of the wine and Oxy. I pull open the nightstand and feel around for the baggie. Pulling it from under the book, I try to open the top of the baggie through blurred vision, but before I do, I feel myself falling.

# CHAPTER 16

## Matt

"A royal flush," I say with a straight face as I set my cards down on the felt table.

"Bullshit," I hear Landon say as he leans in to inspect my hand. "Bastard," I hear as I see cards fly across the table! I reach in and pull the chips over to my side of the table and laugh.

"I've never in my life had a royal flush," I say, stacking the poker chips.

"How in the hell did you manage that?" Landon asks as he collects the loose cards. His cell phone rings in his pocket. "Shit," he grumbles. "Better not be work. I need a couple of hours sleep tonight." I glance at my phone and can't believe that it's two-thirty in the morning. We've been playing poker for over five hours straight. Landon looks at his phone and back at me then back to his screen.

"Who is it?" I ask, putting the chips in the heavy metal case.

"Jess," he says, confused. The phone stops ringing.

"Jess?" I blurt out. "What is she doing calling you?" He

shrugs and swallows hard, still looking at the missed call on his phone. The phone begins ringing again and he looks at me before swiping the answer icon and pushing himself away from the table to take the phone call. The other guys and I all watch him as he walks over to the other side of the game room.

"What happened?" I hear him say as he runs his hand across his jaw. "Jesus Christ," he mumbles into the phone. "How far away is he?" He paces the game room, glancing quickly at me. "Let him decide. Don't leave her until he gets there and call an ambulance if anything changes before he arrives." I jump up and move toward him. He watches me, then looks at the watch on his left wrist. "I'll be on the first flight in the morning," he says as he shoves the phone back in his front pocket.

I jump in quickly. "Man, you cannot go running to her rescue. Don't fall into this trap, Landon. She's been gone for two years. Your entire life is falling into place..." I start preaching to him. I know how hard he took it when Jess left to move back home to California. It took him a long time to get over her and he is finally happy and engaged to Reagan. I won't let him screw this up.

"It's not Jess," he says quietly.

"Then why is she calling you?" I set the metal case of poker chips on top of his wooden bar.

"It's Lindsay."

"Lindsay's calling you from Jess' phone?" Now I'm confused.

"No. Jess is with Lindsay. Something happened to Lindsay." He's lost in thought and my adrenaline kicks in.

"What happened to her?"

"Jess found her in her room. Looks like she fell and hit her head on her nightstand, but she found a baggie full of pills next to her."

"What kind of pills?"

"Jess doesn't know, but she's afraid to call an ambulance because she's afraid that they're illegal, and that if this is made public, it will destroy Lindsay's career."

"Fuck her career." I'm so angry right now. "She needs to call an ambulance." I start yelling orders to Landon. "How many times on patrol have we seen this? Anything can happen to someone on pills. Dammit, Landon, call her back and tell her to call an ambulance. NOW!"

"Gabe is on his way; he was about ten minutes away when she called him. He's a firefighter or EMT. She's going to let him make the call, then she's going to call me back." I've seen Landon in many situations throughout our friendship and this is the first time I've seen him truly shaken—scared.

"What is all the yelling about? It's almost three in the morning," Reagan says, tying the belt on her robe as she walks tiredly into the game room. Her hair is a mess, as we've obviously woken her up. "Some of us have to work in the morning and be coherent enough to treat patients."

I look away from her and back to Landon. "I'm going with you; it's not up for discussion." He swallows and nods his head before walking toward Reagan.

"It's Lindsay," Landon tells Reagan, pulling her into a hug. "Something's happened and we're waiting to get more details." Landon begins telling Reagan the little information that we know and the other guys leave quietly, telling us to keep them updated. Time stands still as we wait to hear from Jess. Landon stares at the screen of his phone, willing it to ring, and Reagan has retreated to the kitchen to make coffee.

"Hear anything yet?" Reagan asks as she carries two large mugs of steaming coffee.

"Not yet," I say as Landon remains silent and shakes his head.

"Don't panic, guys," Reagan says quietly.

"She said Gabe was ten minutes away and it's been over twenty minutes since she called," Landon says, setting the mug of coffee on the bar. Just then, Landon's phone rings and vibrates all at the same time.

"It's her," he says before answering. "Jess?" I notice his hand shaking as he raises the phone to his ear.

"Mmm hmm, okay. Okay. Thank you." He pulls the phone away from his ear and ends the call. "They called an ambulance. Gabe said she has a pretty decent head laceration and most likely a concussion. Her pulse was weak, not terrible, but she's dehydrated and he's concerned about the pills and how many she took."

"What pills was she taking?" Reagan asks from the sofa, where she sits bundled under a blanket.

"She wasn't taking anything I was aware of. She finished her pain meds when she completed rehab months ago," I inform them as I grab my phone and keys from the bar.

"Go pack," Reagan says, pushing the blanket off of her. "I'll book you two tickets and text you with the details. I'll drop you off at the airport." She walks over and hugs Landon before leaving us.

"What the fuck is going on?" Landon asks me.

"I wish I knew," I reply numbly.

Four and a half hours later, Landon and I are on a flight to Phoenix. Five hours after that, we land in Phoenix. One hour later, Landon and I are walking into Good Samaritan Hospital in downtown Phoenix. Jess has texted Landon the floor information as Lindsay hasn't yet been placed into a room. We ride the elevator to the second floor and exit. The hallways are white and sterile, exactly like every other hospital. We walk the long corridor until we get to a centrally located desk where three other hallways connect.

"Lindsay Christianson," Landon announces at the desk. The nurse checks her computer before turning back to Landon.

"We're just getting her settled into a room. You can take a seat in the waiting room down the hall and a doctor will be in to speak with you before you can see her," she says with a short smile. We walk down the hall where the nurse directed us and open the door. Jess sits sleeping, curled up in a ball with her head resting on the shoulder of whom I presume is Gabe, her fiancé.

Gabe looks up and nods at both of us before gently waking Jess. Her green eyes pop open and she jumps up quickly from the chair and walks to Landon. He immediately pulls her into a hug and she starts crying against his chest. Landon comforts her, shushing her and rubbing her back. I chance a look at Gabe, who looks uncomfortable and quickly stands up.

"I'll let you all catch up. I'm going to get some coffee," he announces and slips out of the waiting room, leaving the three of us alone. Jess finally lets go of Landon and pulls tissues from the Kleenex box on a table to wipe her eyes.

"Hi, Matt," she says, giving me a quick hug. I didn't get the chance to spend a lot of time with Jess when she was in North Carolina, but she looks exactly like I remember her. Landon reaches out to Jess' wet cheek and I can't help but notice how, even though it's been two years, he's just as caring with her now as he was back in North Carolina. This is a side of Landon we rarely see.

"So tell me everything," Landon encourages Jess as we all sit down together. She takes a deep, cleansing breath, folds her hands in her lap, and lays out the last twenty-four hours in gory detail.

"When I got to her condo about two-thirty yesterday, the place was a disaster. Just so out of character of the Lindsay I remember," she starts. "I brushed it off, knowing that she's busy with her new job and just getting settled, but immediately, something just didn't seem *right*. You know what I mean?"

"She's the poster child for OCD," I remark and Landon nods in agreement before Jess continues. "Another thing that I noticed right away was how skinny she was and how tired she looked." Landon buries his head in his hands.

"Fuck, she used to starve herself in college," he mumbles, his face still buried. It's killing me as I'm listening to Lindsay's past and present collide, knowing I wasn't there to help her when she needed it. My heart thrums as I think back to her telling me she was leaving for Phoenix. What an asshole I was for acting the way I did. I was selfish. Maybe if I had been more accepting, if we had tried to make it work long distance, she wouldn't be in the hospital today.

"I know what you're thinking," Landon says, looking at me. "There was nothing you could have done or I could have done. There is nothing anyone could have done. I thought she was better and past that," he says quietly.

"Go on," Landon tells Jess.

"I didn't know about her anorexia either," Jess admits. "We went to dinner and she had a couple of drinks, but just picked at her dinner. She didn't eat. When we got back to the condo, her next door neighbor, Jonah, stopped us and invited us over to a party at his place. I thanked him for the invitation and we went inside and started picking up her room and making the bed when a couple of guys showed up from the party."

"Did she know them?"

"I think so. She was talking quietly with one of them when I left the bedroom to see what was going on." Landon and I look at each other. "Anyway, we go next door, but just for a little bit, maybe twenty minutes. I was talking to a couple of girls and, all of the sudden, Lindsay was upset and wanted to leave."

"Did she say what upset her?"

"No, just that she was ready to go home. So we did. When we got home, we opened some wine, and she finally told me about how miserable her job has been, her anorexia, you." She looks at me with sad eyes. "She misses you so much and thinks you hate her."

"I don't hate her; I could never," I say quietly.

"That's what I told her." She inhales sharply. "So we had a couple of bottles of wine and were talking, when she suddenly got up and said she needed to go to bed. I decided I'd clean up the kitchen and that's when I heard the thump. I went to check on her and that's where I found her, bleeding from the head on the floor with the baggie of pills next to her."

"Do you know what the pills are?" Landon asks Jess.

"No. I showed Gabe and he thinks they're Oxy. He runs into it a lot on his calls," she says.

"She was on Oxy after the car accident," I remind Landon.

"Yeah, but she was off that a long time ago."

"I know. Did she mention taking the pain meds to you?" I ask out of curiosity.

"I didn't know anything about the pills," she says, turning around to see who is entering the waiting room. It's Gabe with a cardboard carrier full of coffees. He sets the tray on the small end table that sits between us while Jess continues.

"I immediately checked her vitals. She was breathing. The cut on her forehead was deep, so I grabbed a washcloth and the phone. I panicked. I know what being in the public eye is like, so I hesitated on calling an ambulance when I knew she wasn't in imminent danger, so that's when I called Gabe. I told him how I found Lindsay, the pills, the wine and, fortunately, he was about ten minutes away at a sports bar." Landon looks at Gabe, who is sitting next to Jess, holding her hand.

"She needed an ambulance," Gabe cuts in. "She was in pretty bad shape. Her breathing was labored and, with the head injury and unknown substance mixed with alcohol, she needed to be transported, and fast."

"I appreciate it," Landon says.

"We haven't heard much since we arrived," Gabe says, pulling a coffee from the tray.

"The nurse said that they were putting her in a room and a doctor would come and find us here," Landon sighs.

Jess hands out the remaining coffees and we all sit in silence, absorbing everything we've just learned. Silent prayers and unknown answers linger in the stale air between us.

"Christianson. Lindsay Christianson," the doctor announces as he pushes open the door to the waiting room.

"Yes," Landon says as we all stand up to greet him. The young doctor, who looks to be in his late twenties, looks between all four of us.

"Are you all immediate family?"

"Yes," Landon answers without hesitating.

"Very well. I'm Doctor Jorgenson. I've been treating Ms. Christianson. She's stable for the time being and we've just placed her in a room. She's going to be with us for a few days." He clears his throat. "We have her intubated to keep her airway open. She has severe respiratory depression. Most likely a side effect of the narcotics she has been taking. She has had a CT scan due to the head injury and she appears to have a mild concussion, no fractures or bleeding, though, which is positive. A plastic surgeon has already stitched up the laceration on her forehead and we're running an IV with saline and Narcan."

"Narcan?" I ask.

The doctor nods his head. "We ran a blood toxicology report and, along with an elevated blood alcohol level, there were significant amounts of Oxycodone or OxyContin in her bloodstream. The Narcan helps counter the effects of the Oxycodone and also helps with the respiratory depression."

"When can we see her?" Landon asks.

"Well, she's still not awake. Once she is, we'll need to evaluate her. You won't be able to see her for at least another four to six hours, most likely the latter." We all stand in silence for a few moments and look at each other.

"Thank you, Dr. Jorgenson," Landon says as he leaves quietly.

"So now what?" Jess asks.

"We wait," I pipe in.

"We have to think beyond this, you guys. What happens when she leaves the hospital? She needs help," Jess says.

"She does," Landon agrees.

"We talked about her getting help for the anorexia and she was optimistic about it, but I didn't know about the pills at that time."

"Jess, did she tell you why she hates work so much?" I'm so curious. This was supposed to be the opportunity of a lifetime for her and to see the effects of her job push her to pills and starvation saddens me.

She takes a deep breath. "She did. Before I tell you the whole story, let me tell you this. Wilmington was a piece of cake. Everyone at WXZI got along. It was a small station where we were essentially a family. It's not like that in most markets and at most television stations. It's a dog-eat-dog, competitive business where people will stab their own grandmother in the back to get ahead. I've heard the stories. Fortunately, I left the business before I got to experience any of this. This is exactly what greeted Lindsay here in Phoenix. From the sounds of it, there is one woman in particular who has it out for her."

"Shit," I grumble and slouch back in my chair.

"Anyway, Lindsay has been killing it here. I was checking out the social media feed on the news station's page and everyone loves her. Every comment was so positive. Lindsay told me she was putting together a story earlier this week and somehow it disappeared from the server along with the SIM card carrying the raw footage. Lindsay can't prove it was the girl she works with, but…"

"Why would someone mess with her? I don't understand," I question Jess.

"Jealousy, plain and simple. Lindsay mentioned that the news director was giving her the anchor position at weekend desk. The normal anchor is out of town on vacation and Lindsay has proven herself since she's been here. Then the missing story happened, and the news director pulled the weekend anchor slot out from underneath her."

"Jesus Christ," Landon says.

"It gets worse, guys. When the news director pulled the opportunity out from under her, Lindsay lashed out at the girl who everyone believes sabotaged her story and deleted the SIM card."

"What do you mean by 'lashed out'?" Gabe asks.

"She pushed her against a wall and verbally threatened her in front of other employees. Lindsay said the news director mentioned she was lucky no charges were being pressed."

"I'm done. I've heard enough." I jump up. "I need to get into her condo. I'm searching that place for more pills. I need something to focus on until she wakes up."

"Do you think that's a good idea?" Jess asks. "I mean, that's her personal stuff."

"I understand what you're saying, Jess, but right now, the only thing that matters to me is that she doesn't have access to use pills once she gets out of here."

"So what happens when we all leave? You all are going back to North Carolina, and Gabe and I have to go home to California. What happens then?" The room falls silent while we ponder Jess' words. "We have to convince her to get help, you guys—not just for the pills," she says quietly.

"You're right, Jess," Landon says. "But I'm with Matt on this. We're going to the condo to make sure there are no pills. But what concerns me more is where she's getting them."

"Do you have the keys to her place?" I ask Jess, who looks hesitantly at Gabe. He nods his head at her and squeezes her hand.

"I have them," she admits.

"Let's go, then. There is no point in us sitting here for another four to six hours," Landon says, pushing himself up from the chair. Jess sends Gabe back to his hotel to get some rest, telling him she'll meet him later. We leave quietly, none of us really speaking to each other. I see the worry on Landon's face, and the exhaustion on Jess' and, inside, I feel mostly sad. Sad that I wasn't here to help her, sad that she fell back into a lifestyle that she depended on before me, but mostly sad because she was alone and lost.

Landon, Jess, and I weave through the busy Phoenix streets to Lindsay's downtown condo. We park on the street in front of Lindsay's condo at a parking meter and step out into the torrid Phoenix air. Jess has the keys to Lindsay's condo in her hand and leads us through the upscale lobby to the elevators. There is a sense of uneasiness as we all step through the threshold and into Lindsay's condo. It feels as if we're invading her privacy, and we are—except we're doing it to save her.

"Jesus," Landon mutters as he looks around the condo.

"It's mostly just clutter," Jess tells us. "I've already cleaned the kitchen and we started on her bedroom. I've got a giant pile of clothes that need to go to the dry cleaners, and then she has about twelve loads of just normal laundry. I'll get started on that while you two search for pills." I stand and look around the modern condo and try to envision Lindsay's life here, without me. Everything in the condo is new; the furniture, the décor, her life—there are no traces of me or her old life anywhere except, for the clothes that are scattered on the floor.

"I'll start in the kitchen," Landon says as he opens cupboards and drawers.

"Search, and search well, but do not make a mess. I just got that kitchen put back in order," Jess says, carrying a load of clothes in a laundry basket from what I presume is Lindsay's room. I stand numb as I battle the conflicting emotions swirling around inside of me—sadness, hurt, and anger.

"I'll start in the bedroom," I say as I sidestep pillows and a remote control that lie on the floor. I step into the master bedroom and I immediately smell her. The light scent of her perfume hangs in the air or on her clothes that sit in sorted piles on the floor. There is a picture of Landon, Lindsay, and their mom, Josie, on her nightstand.

I walk across the room and pull the long, white sheer curtains open to let the sunlight in. Everything in the room is white; the curtains, the bedding, even the large rug that the bed sits on. The oversized wood furniture is white washed and looks exactly like something Lindsay would like. I pull open the top drawer of the chest that sits against the wall and look for any traces of pills. I search drawer after drawer and find nothing. The first nightstand is empty, clearly not the side of the bed she sleeps on, so I move to the other. Inside the drawer is a book she must be reading, as she has a page dog-eared, a small notebook, a pen, and a small box of condoms.

"What the fuck," I mumble to myself as I pick up and open the box. I remember her buying this box of condoms when she was sick and on antibiotics, but we never used them. I count nine condoms from a ten-count box. My stomach flips and my heart sinks. I put the box back in the drawer and close it, hard. The lamp that sits on the table shakes and eventually falls over, crashing to the wood floor.

"Matt," Jess asks quietly from behind me. "Are you okay? Did you find pills?" I turn quickly and find her leaning against the doorframe.

"Did she mention she was seeing anybody?" I don't know why I ask. I honest to God think it's best not to know the answer to that question, but somewhere deep inside, I need to know.

"She didn't say anything about seeing anyone." She walks toward me tentatively. "Did you find something?" I stare at the piles of clothes, shoes, and purses on the floor of her bedroom and lose myself in thoughts of her with another man. I nod my head.

"Yeah, a box of condoms—one's missing." Jess' eyes open wide and she purses her lips, but she doesn't say anything, "And this picture of her and some guy drinking wine." I fling the picture at Jess, who catches it and glances at it briefly. Her eyes widen in what I presume is recognition.

"Matt, none of us can be upset about anything we find. We're nosing around through her personal items, and I know it's for good reason, but it's still her personal stuff," she says with sympathy in her eyes. "I did things with someone," she looks over her shoulder and out into the living room where Landon is searching the media stand, "when I wasn't with Gabe. I can't confirm she did anything, but you can't be angry with her. You're not together."

"I am angry, Jess. I'm fucking irate," I scream at her. "She let another man touch her."

"We don't know that." She raises her voice back at me.

"What's going on?" Landon asks, stepping into the bedroom.

"I need some fresh air, that's what's going on," I say, pushing past both of them.

I spend the next hour sitting on a lounge chair, sweating my ass off on Lindsay's patio. It's amazing how quickly the decisions you've been struggling to make come to you when you're angry. I beat myself up for not agreeing to come with Lindsay when she asked me, but instead, I rejected her pleas and she left anyway—alone.

I peel my sweaty body off the thick-cushioned chair and into the retreat of the air-conditioned condo. Landon and Jess sit on the couch talking while Jess folds a pile of clothes, setting them on the coffee table in front of her.

"Hey," Landon says as I close the patio door behind me. Both Jess and Landon watch me hesitantly.

"Hey," I reply somberly.

"You okay, man?" Landon asks.

"Been better; not gonna lie."

"Matt, she loves you," Jess says. "We talked about it. This entire decision was based on her needing to do something just once in her life for herself. She set career goals for herself and you know she's one to give everything she has once she's set her mind on something. She didn't realize it was going to destroy everything she loved. She hates her job, she hates Phoenix—she hates herself."

I nod my head before turning to Landon. "I'm going to grab my bag from the car and catch a cab to the airport. It's probably best that you and Jess talk to her without me." I clench my jaw and choke back my emotions.

"Matt, you have to see her," Jess begs me. "Don't leave without seeing her."

"Honestly, Jess, I've seen enough. She has clearly moved on. You two and whatever his name is—the guy in the picture—can take care of her," I say quietly before walking away—for good.

# CHAPTER 17

## *Lindsay*

I wake up and try to talk, but am suddenly scared when I realize where I am—in a hospital, alone, with a tube down my throat. As I try to remember how I got here, a doctor and nurse finally come in to remove my breathing tube and answer all the questions that have been going through my head. My fingers brush against the large bandage on my forehead, but it's the throbbing headache that really gets my attention. It's a combination of feeling like I've been hit in the head with a baseball bat and the worst hangover I've ever had. They quietly disappear with promise of returning soon and I let the gravity of my situation finally settle in.

I rest my arm on a pillow to keep the IV from tugging at the delicate skin on my arm. It's then I feel the warm tears form in my eyes and slide down my cheeks, pooling in my hair, which rests on the foam hospital pillow. I roll onto my side and sob for everything I've done to get me to this point. My stomach aches with hunger and turns with disgust all at the same time. This is truly my rock bottom.

I hear the door to my room squeak open, but I don't bother to look. I close my eyes and chew on my bottom lip as I hear the footsteps slowly approach my bed.

"She doesn't even look like herself." I hear the familiar voice. My brother. My protector. The only person who understands and fully accepts what a mess I am.

"Lan?" I ask quietly, turning toward his voice. He stands next to Jess with his arm around her shoulders and they both look down at me. Jess' eyes are full of unshed tears and Landon looks tired.

"I'm here," he says, releasing Jess and leaning down to hug me. I roll onto my back and wrap my arms around his neck tightly and begin to sob again. Aside from Matt, Landon is my safe place. He's always looked out for me and, no matter what, he was there for me—always. "Shh… I'm here," he says again as I cry into his shoulder.

"When did you get here?" I ask between sobs.

"This morning. Jess called me last night." It's so strange to see him standing next to Jess again. There was a time when all I wanted was them to work through whatever it was they were going through. I wanted Jess for my sister. I believe that everything in life happens the way it's supposed to, and I cannot wait for him to marry Reagan. Jess is happy with Gabe, and regardless of the fact that she's not my sister by blood or marriage, she will always be my sister through friendship.

"Why didn't you let us know how bad things were?" he asks me, finally relaxing his grip on me and releasing me from his hug.

"I didn't want you to worry," I admit. "I made this decision and I had to live with the consequences."

"I will always worry about you," he says, tousling my hair. "That's what family is for. To lean on each other in the hard times." He sighs. "Lindsay, if there is one thing I learned about us early on, it's that life is always going to throw us a curveball. Nothing will ever come easy for you and me. That's just how the universe works for us. But if there is one thing you can ever trust or believe in, it's that, no matter what, I will always be here for you. Always."

Jess stands behind Landon, who is sitting on the edge of my bed, holding my hand. She wipes tears from her eyes as she listens to Landon.

"I'm so sorry, you guys," I tell them, my lip trembling. "I thought I had it under control in the beginning. They just helped take the edge off," I say, my voice trailing off. "But then, I started using them to numb the pain."

Jess sits in the chair next to the bed and Landon stays sitting on the edge of my bed. We all sit in silence until Jess addresses the elephant in the room.

"Lindsay, you have to get help."

"I know. I was planning on it before you even said anything." It's so hard to admit you have a problem, especially to the people you love the most.

"I've never been so afraid of losing you," Jess chokes out. "You scared me so bad last night, Linds."

"I'm so sorry," I tell her through the falling tears. "I'm so sorry you had to see that."

"I'm so thankful I did, Lindsay. I kept thinking what if this had happened when no one was around to help you?" Jess warns. I nod. She's right. I'm very lucky I wasn't alone. The door opens again and a lab technician and a nurse enter. Landon leans in and presses a kiss to my cheek.

"I'm going to take Jess and get her something to eat. We'll be back in just a bit."

"I'm not going anywhere," I sigh, showing him my arm, which is attached to the IV stand.

Four vials of blood drawn, two additional nurses, and two doctors later, Landon and Jess return. Landon carries a tray of hospital food and sets it on the bedside table next to me.

"How do you feel about chicken broth, Jello, and apple juice?" Landon quips.

"Like they're trying to starve me," I tease.

"Bad joke, Linds," Landon grumbles, and I roll my eyes. Jess sits at the end of my bed and watches me as I take a sip from the small, plastic container of apple juice. Surprisingly, the cool, sweet juice tastes like heaven. In three swallows, I finish the juice and see Jess crack a small smile.

"So, it looks like I have to stay another day or two," I casually mention. "They're making me see a psychologist before they'll release me."

"Good," Jess interrupts me. "Sometimes, talking to a neutral third party helps you see things and evaluate things without prejudice. I still talk with a counselor for some of the issues I am working through." She looks at Landon, whose eyes drop from hers to the floor.

"When are you leaving?" I ask Landon, my voice shaking a bit. I clear my throat, trying to regain my composure. The thought of everyone leaving all at the same time has me suddenly shaken.

"Whenever you want me to," Landon says. "I'll stay as long as you need me." I turn to Jess, who sits at the end of my bed, her long hair tied up in a messy ponytail. Her bright green eyes pop against her tan skin and dark hair. She's truly beautiful, inside and out.

"When do you have to leave?" I ask Jess. Her eyes shift to Landon, who looks back at her and nods.

"We're headed back tomorrow," she says quietly. "It's just better if I'm out of the way. You and Landon have a lot…"

"To figure out," I interrupt her. "I know. In fact, I've made a few decisions already." Landon watches me carefully, letting me take my time to speak. Jess sits quietly and focuses all of her attention on me.

"I'm going home. I'm leaving the job. Phoenix. Everything. I'm coming home and getting myself into treatment. When I took this job in Phoenix, I thought I was finally doing something for myself, accomplishing goals I had set, yet little did I realize I was only hurting myself. I was leaving the things that truly make me happy—my family, Matt, North Carolina. I was fleeing from the things that keep me grounded for a career that was sucking the life out of me. I want to go home to the things that make me truly happy, but in order for that to happen, I know I need help first."

Jess looks at Landon again and they share a look. "Why do you two keep looking at each other like that?"

"Go ahead." He nods at Jess. She takes a deep breath and slides up closer on the edge of my bed before she begins.

"Linds, Matt was here."

"What do you mean *was*?"

"He left. He went back to North Carolina."

"Okay…" I say, prodding for more information, when Landon jumps in.

"We went to your condo to make sure there were no more pills. When we were there, he saw something that upset him—

enough that he decided it was best he didn't come to see you here."

"What did he see?" I ask frantically. I can't think of anything at my place that would upset him. Landon shrugs and Jess sits with her eyes downcast.

"What did he see, Jess?"

"It doesn't matter. We just thought you should know he was here and why he's not now. We didn't want you blindsided…"

"What did he see?" I scream at both of them. The blood pressure cuff attached to my left arm begins inflating and I rip the stupid thing off my arm.

"The condoms," Jess whispers. "He counted them. And a picture of you and Jonah."

"I need to be alone right now," I tell both of them angrily. Landon reaches out to help Jess off the bed.

"We'll be just down the hall," Landon tells me. I roll over into the fetal position again and cry myself to sleep.

"Lindsay, wake up." I hear Jess' voice urging me awake. My eyes flutter and adjust to the dark room, the only lights coming from the monitors attached to me. "I'm so sorry to wake you up," she whispers and sits down in the chair next to me. My entire body aches as I roll onto my back and look at the dark ceiling. Anger roils through me as I remember what Jess told me earlier.

"I just wanted to come in and say goodbye," she says quietly.

"Bye," I snap at her.

"Lindsay, I'm so sorry…"

"Sorry isn't going to help me," I burst out.

"I didn't want…"

"Get out of here," I snarl.

"Lindsay!" Landon yells at her from the door. "Stop it."

Jess stands up from the chair she was sitting in and the light from the hallway allows me to see the tears in her eyes. "I'm sorry," she mumbles before walking toward Landon and disappearing outside the door with him. The door snaps shut, but I can see both of them through the long, glass window that encases the door on one side. Landon stands, comforting her. A brief wave of guilt washes over me, but it disappears just as quickly when I see him hugging her and her head buried in his chest.

"Bitch," I mutter to myself and roll back onto my side so I don't have to see them together. I'm hardly comfortable in this miserable bed and, within seconds, the door flies open, the light flickers on, and Landon darts across the room to my bed.

"Don't you ever talk to her like that again," he yells at me. "You're acting like a selfish little brat." The vein in his neck throbs as he stares at me. His jaw muscles flex as he grinds his teeth in anger.

"I'm dropping Jess off to Gabe, then I'm going to get some sleep. I'll be back in the morning." His heavy footsteps lead him back to the door, where he flicks off the light once again and leaves me alone in the dark. Sadly, I feel nothing when he yells at me. I'm just thankful they're both gone.

I wake to sounds of a food tray being slid onto my bedside table. There is a kink in my neck from the way I slept and my mouth is insanely dry. "Morning," the young girl says as she pulls the cover off a plate of scrambled eggs. "Scrambled eggs, applesauce, and grape juice," she says, smiling at me. My stomach turns when she lists today's breakfast. I've been nauseous since I drank the apple juice yesterday. I push the incline button on the bed and raise myself to a seated position. It's the first time I've sat up since I've been in here.

A nurse comes to check my vitals and tells me that today they will let me shower. I push the scrambled eggs around the plate with the fork, but attempt a couple of bites of the applesauce. My stomach growls and I finally take a couple of bites of egg. I catch Landon out of the corner of my eye as he stands in the doorway of the room, waiting for the nurse to finish and leave. He steps aside as she leaves and he comes in, closing the door behind him.

"Hey," he says as he stands at the foot of the bed.

"Hey," I repeat, not making eye contact with him. I take another bite of eggs before picking up the cover and placing it back on the plate. I shove the bedside table away and recline back in the bed just a bit.

"So you're not going to talk to me?" Landon asks.

"What do you want me to say?" I finally look at him.

"Let's start with how you're feeling this morning." He turns his head to the side in a cocky manner.

I sigh, knowing that Landon isn't going to leave me alone, so I may as well just get over my attitude with him. "I'm feeling okay. They are letting me shower later, so I'm sure I'll feel even better after that."

"Good. When are you meeting with the psychologist?"

"Tomorrow. Depending on the outcome of that meeting, I might be able to leave. At least that's what the nurse said."

"Are you still planning to leave Phoenix?" he asks hesitantly.

"Plans are still the same." I nod my head. "Well, parts of the plan are." I swallow hard when I think about Matt and the conversation I owe him when I get home. But first and foremost, I have a lot of loose ends to wrap up in the next two days.

"Lan? Two questions."

"Go for it," he says.

"Did Jess and Gabe leave yet?"

He inhales sharply, then sighs. "Yeah, they left last night. Jess was pretty upset and Gabe just wanted to get her home." I close my eyes momentarily as guilt settles in when I think of how I handled the situation with her last night. It's not her fault that Matt left, but I know my reactions and my words implied it was.

"Okay. Can you bring me my laptop and cellphone from the condo?" I ask him my final question.

"Yeah, sure."

With one last night in the hospital before they discharge me tomorrow, hopefully, I decide that I'm the only one that can get my life back.

I step into Landon's rental car and lean back against the headrest, closing my eyes as he drives me back to my condo. I mentally make a list of everything I will need back in North Carolina. I've made phone calls to Jack, my agent, who was, for the first time in his life, a man of very few words. I explained my entire situation and, surprisingly, he was encouraging and supportive. I've left a voicemail for Rob and sent a text to Mike.

Stepping into the condo, I'm shocked to see how clean it is. I set my keys on the kitchen island and look around. "I didn't realize how bad it had gotten until I see it now," I muster.

"This was all Jess," he says. A giant stack of dry cleaning hangs from a wardrobe rack just outside my bedroom door. Every dress and pantsuit has been cleaned and carefully arranged on the rack. I thumb through the hangers and look at Landon.

"Jess?" I ask. He nods.

Piles of clean laundry sit folded on the foot of my bed. Jess made my bed for the first time since the day I moved in. The bathroom has been cleaned and the counter full of cosmetics and lotions have been arranged neatly and orderly. I look at Landon, who has been following me from room to room and my eyes tear up when I think about how terribly I treated Jess. My friend single handedly was piecing my life, the way she remembered it, back together.

I walk to my bed and sit down, my legs dangling over the edge. My toes brush the wood floor below as I turn to look at Landon. "Do you think she will forgive me?"

He takes a few steps toward me and sits down on the bed next to me, careful not to tip over the neatly folded piles of clothes. "I don't know. But what I do know is that you're the only person who can right your wrongs." I let the words sink in and think about everything I need to do. I rest my head on my brother's shoulder, much like I did when we were kids. He reaches his arm around me and holds me, whispering promises that everything will be fine.

I tape the last box and shove the remaining clothes into the large suitcase I plan to bring with me. The doorbell rings and Landon abruptly looks up from his phone in concern. I walk to the door and look through the peephole to find Mike and Javier standing on the other side of the door. I turn the lock and open the door just as Mike scoops me up into a giant hug.

"Sweet girl," he says in a low voice, "what in the world is going on?" He sets me back on my feet and I lean in to Javier, giving him a quick hug.

"Mike, Javier, this is my brother, Landon." Landon stands up from the couch and shakes each of their hands.

"I got your texts and I'm trying to piece everything together," Mike says. Javier sits down opposite of Landon and strikes up a conversation. I pull Mike over to the kitchen island, where we sit, and I fill him in on everything.

"Why didn't you tell me?" he asks as he holds my hand. "I knew you weren't happy here, but pills, Lindsay?"

"I know," I say shamefully. "I've talked to Rob, and Jack, my agent, is working to get me out of my contract."

"You know you don't just walk away from a contract like that without consequences." He grimaces.

"Oh, I know. It's very unlikely I'll ever work in this business again," I say humbly. "My name will always be tarnished."

"You're too good to walk away, sweetheart."

"It's just a job. I need to focus on getting my life in order. The rest will happen as it's meant to be."

"You're wiser than I thought you were." He leans from his stool and gives me another hug. "So these are the boxes you need me to send?" He taps the top of the brown box addressed to Landon's house.

"Just these two. Here is a spare key to the condo. If I need anything else, I'll call you. The lease is paid through the end of the year, so I'll figure out what I'm doing once

I get through treatment."

"I'm proud of you, you know."

"Thanks, Mike. You've been a great friend to me."

We say our goodbyes and Landon looks at the watch on his wrist. "We need to get going." I nod and pull my purse from the kitchen counter. He wheels my large suitcase and I pull a smaller one.

"You ready?" he asks.

"Yeah," I say quietly. Walking past Jonah's door, I pause. "Can you wait by the elevator? I need to do something really quick." He looks at me cautiously. "I'm just going to say goodbye to someone; that's all."

"You have two minutes, Lindsay. We have to get to the airport." I knock on Jonah's door as I watch Landon pull my suitcase down the hall. I wait a few seconds before I knock again. He's not answering. I knock one last time before I begin to walk away with my suitcase and guilt the size of Texas hanging over me. As we pull out of the parking garage and onto the busy Phoenix street, I press my forehead against the window and watch as life around me goes on. A tear slips from my eye not because I'm sad to leave, but because I'm sad I failed. I failed at something that I was sure was going to be good for my career and, eventually, my personal life. As Landon turns the corner, I catch a glimpse of Jonah on the street corner. He raises his hand slightly and offers half of a wave. I close my eyes and pretend I don't see him because, as usual, it's easier to pretend things and people that matter really don't.

Stepping out of the airport, into the humid North Carolina air, brings a sense of peace, an aura of calm through me. *"Home,"* I whisper when that moist air hits my face. It's seven in the morning, and even though the air is cool, you can feel the impending heat waiting to make its presence known. I inhale deeply, taking the heavy, humid air into my lungs. I stand outside the airport with my small suitcase while Landon waits at the baggage carousel for my other bag. I lean against a concrete pillar and feel a small smile tug at my lips when I see Reagan's SUV pull up to the curb. She pulls her sunglasses off her face and places them on top of her head before she opens her door and walks around the front of the car.

"Lindsay," she says with a giant smile and open arms. I leave my bag on the curb as I meet her with a giant hug. The automatic glass doors slide open and Landon exits with my suitcase and his bag. Reagan releases me and jogs over to him. Landon pulls her into a giant hug and kisses her for longer than is really necessary in public. I roll my eyes and laugh. I realize it's the first time I've laughed in weeks—a real genuine laugh and it feels good.

Landon loads the luggage and I climb into the back seat of the SUV. The ride to Landon and Reagan's house is quiet. We pull into the large, paved driveway and Reagan kills the engine. An enormous set of concrete steps lead up to the front door of their new house.

"I've got the guest room on the main floor all set up for you," she says, looking over her shoulder.

"Thanks," I respond.

"Go get some rest. We'll get your bags. You've been flying all night. We'll catch up this afternoon." I smile at her and step out of the car. I count each of the twelve steps up to their large front door as I ascend them and am winded from just that small flight of stairs. Landon holds the door open and I step into their beautiful home. It's modern, yet comfortable.

"Down here." Landon gestures down the long hallway just inside their front door. "Last door on the left. There is a bathroom in your room. I'll set your bags outside the door."

I nod my head and kick off my shoes, letting my bare feet pad down the wooden hallway floor. I slow to look at the pictures Reagan has hung in the hallway, and immediately, my heart races when I see a picture of the four us—Landon, Reagan, Matt and me—at Landon and Reagan's engagement party. Landon is on the end with Reagan next to him. I'm next to Reagan and Matt is on the other end. My head is tipped back and I'm laughing at something. *Always laughing,* I think to myself. I want to be that girl again. Matt's head is turned and he's looking at me with a huge smile on his face. Exactly how I remember him. I smile at the memory of us four, and tear up, knowing it will never be like that again.

"You okay?" Landon asks, pulling me from my thoughts.

"Yeah, I will be." I smile and bat away the tears from under my eyes.

"Lan?" I say, turning around to look at him. "Thank you for coming to Phoenix and bringing me home."

"You're welcome," he whispers. I disappear into the bedroom and immediately jump into bed.

Sleep came immediately. I didn't dream, I slept—hard. I wake up slowly to sweat rolling down my temples. With a shaky hand, I reach up and feel the trickle of sweat as it travels around the bandage on my forehead and into my hair. I sit up slowly to get my bearings. Sliding off the bed, I bury my toes in the thick carpeting of the bedroom floor. I walk carefully, noticing my dizziness, to the attached bathroom.

I stand in front of the mirror and gently pull away the bandage from my forehead. There are approximately eight small stitches that stretch across the giant lump where my forehead met the bedside table in my bedroom. The skin is various shades of purple and pink, and I pull my long hair back behind my head and twist it around itself into a makeshift bun so I can rinse my face. My fingers tremor as I pull the water from the faucet toward my face carefully. Most of the water spills back into the sink, and I repeat the process four or five times—enough times to get some water all over my face. I pull the hand towel from the towel rack and pat my face dry.

I finally take in the bedroom that Reagan and Landon are letting me stay in while I figure out what I'm doing after rehab and where my life will take me. The room is cozy and comfortable and perfect for me. My favorite item is the large chaise lounge in the corner with a light that hangs over it. *A perfect place to read*, I think to myself. I pull my suitcases into the room and set aside some clean clothes to change into, placing the remaining clothes in the dresser. I slip into a navy blue sundress that used to fit, but now hangs awkwardly large on my body.

I find Landon and Reagan sitting at the small table in the breakfast nook, talking over glasses of iced tea. Reagan smiles when she sees me. "Feel better?" she asks.

"I do. I slept so well. What time is it anyway?"

"After four in the afternoon. You slept all day."

"Guess I needed the rest," I say with a shrug.

"Can I get you something to eat or drink?" Reagan asks, standing up from the small table.

"Iced tea sounds great; I'm not sure about food," I say, scrunching my nose. I don't even know what to ask for to eat. Nothing sounds appetizing, but I know I need to begin eating small amounts of food. I sit down in the chair next to Landon and notice him staring out the window into the backyard. The late afternoon sun is beginning its descent in the sky.

Reagan sets down a glass of tea in front of me, along with a plate of assorted cheeses, yogurt, fresh fruit, a granola bar, some wheat crackers, and some cut-up vegetables. My eyes must have widened in horror because she begins laughing.

"I don't expect you to eat all of that." She giggles. "But you have to eat something. I just didn't know what you'd like, or what your stomach could handle, so just pick at what you want." Landon laughs through his nose before sipping on his iced tea.

"So what are your plans?" he asks cautiously.

"I'm checking into rehab tomorrow," I tell him as I tear the foil cover off the container of strawberry yogurt. Reagan sets a spoon down in front of me as she joins us back at the table. "And I'll play it by ear from there, I guess." I spoon a small bite of the cool yogurt into my mouth and let it settle on my tongue. It tastes good and feels refreshing as it slides down my throat. I notice my hand shaking as I set the spoon down to rest on the edge of the plate. "A lot of it will be dependent on how long my treatment is, I guess. A lot is up in the air."

"I think that's a great start, Linds," Reagan says with a sincere smile. "And you are welcome to stay here as long as you want and or need to."

"Well, considering your wedding is just around the corner, I plan to be gone by then. Just what you want to come home to after your honeymoon is Landon's baby sister in your house." I wink at her.

"Lindsay, we mean it. You're welcome to stay here as long as you need us. You'll always be welcome here," Landon says seriously. I feel my throat tightening, but I'm able to choke out another grateful "Thank you" without completely falling apart. I swallow another spoonful of yogurt and set down the spoon. "There is one thing. Can I borrow one of your cars tonight? There is something I have to do before I check in tomorrow." Reagan looks cautiously at Landon before turning to me.

"Of course. You can take my car whenever you need it."

"I don't know how I'll ever repay you both," I say quietly.

"Get better, Linds. That's how you can repay us. Just get better," Landon says as he reaches across the table and squeezes my hand.

# CHAPTER 18

## Matt

I set my large suitcase by the front door alongside the backpack. My keys, passport, and wallet all sit on the sofa table so that I don't forget anything. I glance at the clock that hangs on the living room wall. It reads eight twenty-eight p.m. Melissa said she'd be here around eight thirty. I pull a beer from the refrigerator and twist off the top just as the doorbell rings.

"Doors open," I holler from the kitchen. I hear the door squeak open. "In the kitchen," I say, pressing the cool bottle to my lips. Her footsteps echo off the wood floor and suddenly stop before she gets to the kitchen. I step around the kitchen island and stop dead in my tracks when I see Lindsay standing in my living room. She has stopped in front of the empty shelf that used to hold all of our pictures. Two nights ago, in anger, I removed all of the pictures and the shelf sits with empty frames. I'll always hold the memories in my heart, but I couldn't stand the constant reminder of what used to be.

My heart races when I see her—a battle of emotions, anger,

and relief. She stares at the empty shelf until I get her attention, "Lindsay?" She quickly wipes under her eyes and I see her chin trembling.

"Hi," she is barely able to squeak out. "I'm sorry to come by unannounced, but I was afraid you wouldn't see me," she says, twisting her fingers around each other nervously. I don't say anything, but stand and look at the stranger standing in front of me—skinny and lost.

"What are you doing here?" I ask. "In North Carolina, I mean."

"I flew back with Landon," she says quietly. Her oversized purse hangs from her bony shoulder. "I'm going to check myself into a rehab program tomorrow."

"Here in Wilmington?" I ask, setting the beer bottle on the kitchen island. She shakes her head.

"Outside of Raleigh," she says quietly. "Did I catch you at a bad time? I see there is luggage by the front door."

"Yes. I mean, no. I'm leaving for Europe tomorrow morning, early." I don't mean to sound vague, but I'm caught off guard that she's actually standing in front of me. She nods quickly.

"I won't take much of your time, but do you have a couple of minutes to talk? There're a few things I need to tell you." I watch the frail girl standing before me and sadness overcomes me for how sick she looks and how quickly we've become strangers.

"I have a couple of minutes. Someone is coming over and…"

"I won't take long. I promise," she cuts me off.

"Okay, let's go out on the back patio."

"Can I set this on the counter?" she asks, pulling her purse from her shoulder. I actually almost laugh at the question. She used to live here. This was her house, her space. Now she's asking permission to set her purse on my counter.

"Yeah." I pull the sliding glass door open and step onto the large patio. This was one of our favorite spots. We'd sit in the plush patio furniture for hours and talk and look for shooting stars. She told me the first time she ever saw a shooting star was with me. I'll never forget that night; the smile on her face when she saw that flash of light shoot across the sky.

I sit down in the chair I always used to sit in, and she takes her spot across from me. She bobs her knees nervously and folds her hands in her lap. I glance inside, waiting for Melissa to come, then back to Lindsay. She looks terrified and jittery, but I won't rush her. She raises her chin confidently and takes a deep breath before she begins.

"Jess told me you came to Phoenix, but you left. Why did you come to Phoenix?"

"I thought you had something to tell me, Lindsay, not question me about my trip to Phoenix." I realize quickly what an asshole I sound like, but I can't talk about Phoenix right now.

"You're right. I'm sorry." She immediately backs down. Her eyes fall to her folded hands and I suddenly realize she isn't the Lindsay I ever knew. The old Lindsay would have told me to fuck off and answer her question.

"I did come to Phoenix and I did leave. It was just more than I could take," I admit, sounding like a coward. "I'm not going to lie. It's really hard seeing you like this, right now." I gesture to her sitting in front of me. I take a quick drink of the beer I have in my hand, realizing that I look like a giant dick sitting here drinking a beer when Lindsay's battling her own addiction demons. I reach over the edge of the patio and dump the beer onto the grass below.

"Matt, I'm so sorry."

"Sorry for what, Linds? Leaving? Pills? Starving yourself?" My voice becomes louder. "Fucking someone else?" Her eyes find mine, filling with tears. She doesn't say anything; she listens to me lash out and she takes it. I hate seeing her like this. I hate that she won't deny what I've just thrown at her.

"I'm sorry for all of it," she whispers. "I know nothing I say will change anything that I've done, but before I leave tomorrow, I needed to apologize to you."

"Feel better?" I snap at her and toss the beer bottle across the backyard.

She shakes her head. "No, I don't. I didn't come here to make you angry, and I can see I've upset you, so I'll leave." She stands up quickly, her legs wobbling under her.

"It's not anger, Lindsay. It's fear. I'm so fucking scared I'm going to lose you—and not just lose you to someone else, but *really* lose you… problem is, I already have."

The air hangs heavy between us. Her face looks tired. Her normally bright eyes are dull, and dark circles have made their home beneath them. "Seeing you like this scares the shit out of me." My voice becomes softer. "How much do you weigh?"

"Don't you know it's not polite to ask a girl how much she weighs?" She smirks, trying to lighten the mood, a glimpse of the old Lindsay.

"Now is not the time for jokes, Lindsay. How much do you weigh? Don't tell me you don't know." She stands quietly, contemplating. She has no reason to tell me anything; she came here to apologize and she has.

"Last time I checked, I was ninety-six pounds."

I nod and feel my lips curl in anger. "And the pills?"

"What about them?"

"What were they and where'd you get them?" I know the first answer, but I want to know where she was getting them.

"Oxy. I've been using them since the accident a couple of years ago. I was off them completely until I moved to Phoenix."

"Why'd you start using them again?" My jaw muscles flex and I can hear my teeth grinding against each other.

"They were an easy fix to help numb everything that I was feeling. I felt so guilty for leaving you." Her voice cracks. "The guilt, my sucky job, the pressure to be successful and skinny and beautiful… I like how they helped me feel numb—I felt nothing when I used them."

"Where were you getting them?"

"Doesn't matter." She looks away from me.

"Where were you getting them? They are a controlled substance, Lindsay. I know you're not getting them from a doctor—the baggie Jess found next to you had enough pills to tranquilize eight horses." She shrugs timidly. Her hands are shaking and her chin trembles.

"My next-door neighbor has a friend…" I roll my eyes. Of course she was getting them from a street dealer. Fuck.

"That preppy little fuck that lives next door to you? I saw him in the hallway when I left. You're getting them from a street dealer?"

"Don't blame Jonah. He's been trying to help me."

"What else has Jonah been helping you with?" I raise my voice again and I smack the arm of the chair I'm sitting in. She flinches and backs away. "Never mind; don't answer that."

"I'm sorry, Matt," she says again, and all I can do is nod my head. "I never wanted to hurt you—ever."

"You did, Lindsay. You fucking destroyed me," I admit like a pussy. "From the day I met you, I was madly in love with you. I never in a million years thought you'd leave me—let alone let another man touch you." I stare off into the dark backyard while she stands silently watching me.

Her breaths come deep and harsh. Her tiny body shakes as she tries to speak. "I will always love you, Matt, but it kills me to know you're not happy. I need you to be happy," she sobs.

"The thing about love, Lindsay, is that when you love someone, you put all of their needs above your own. I need you healthy—mentally and physically. That is the only way I'll ever be happy. I need to know you're safe. So it looks like we're stuck in a vicious little cycle here." Her eyes blink rapidly. "You know I'll always love you, but you made your choice and it wasn't me. You never have to question my love for you—ever. But you need to learn to love yourself. No one is perfect, Lindsay—you never will be. That's what I always loved about you—all your flaws and all your scars, but you need to learn to love them too. You left me to find yourself, your career—and now that's what I'm doing—finding myself." Her chin trembles and tears fall from her downcast eyes onto her sunken cheeks. "You should probably go."

She walks quickly to the patio door and into the kitchen. She pauses and looks around the kitchen while she grabs her purse from the counter. I follow her through the kitchen and into the living room at the exact time that Melissa walks through the front door. *Shit.*

"Sorry I'm late," Melissa says loudly, almost running directly into Lindsay as she's leaving. The women both stand stunned, looking at each other for mere seconds, registering each other's presence.

"Lindsay," Melissa says just above a whisper. "Good to see you."

"You too, Melissa," Lindsay chokes out before looking back over her shoulder at me, tears streaming down her face. She steps around Melissa quickly and disappears out the front door. Melissa remains still, stunned just as I was when I saw Lindsay.

"I didn't know she was going to be here. Is she okay?" Melissa asks as I stand planted in front of the large window and watch as Lindsay sits in Reagan's SUV parked in the driveway, her head resting on the steering wheel.

"I didn't know she was going to be here either."

"She didn't look good," Melissa says, an observation which instantly pisses me off, but I shove the anger down and just get to business.

"Here's the house key." I reach for the single key that sits on the sofa table just inside the front door. "Just set the mail on the kitchen counter, and that's the only plant I have." I point to the houseplant that Reagan gave me to breathe some life into this house. "Give it a little water once a week." I turn just in time to see the red taillights of Reagan's SUV disappear down the street. I turn back to Melissa. "Any questions?"

"No."

"Good. I'll message you once I'm back for the key. Thanks again for watching the house." I know I'm being short, but I want her gone.

"You're welcome," she says, quietly leaving me alone. I sit on the couch and stare at the packed suitcase and backpack and second-guess my trip to Europe.

# CHAPTER 19

## *Lindsay*

A million memories and a million more things I should have said, or apologized for, flash through my head as I drive back to Landon and Reagan's house. I should never have stopped by Matt's unannounced, nor do I have any right to be hurt or angry at seeing Melissa at his house—but I am. My heart aches.

I pull into Reagan and Landon's long, paved driveway and immediately see my mom's car. I had planned to go talk to her in the morning on my way to Raleigh. Pulling the car into the garage, I kill the engine and spend a moment collecting myself. My cheeks are spotted red from crying and there is no hiding the dark circles that have taken up permanent residence under my eyes. "Fuck it," I mumble and step down from the SUV.

Reagan meets me at the door with a sympathetic look on her face. "I tried to get her to leave," she says, and I shake my head.

"Thanks. I may as well get this over with tonight too."

"How'd it go with Matt?" If my splotchy face and red eyes aren't indication enough, I politely answer.

"Not good," I mumble and step out of my sandals. "Did you know he's seeing Melissa?" I ask her. "A little heads up might have been nice." I realize my tone is sharp and accusing.

"I don't think they're seeing each other. I know they've been hiking once in a while, but Lindsay, don't jump to conclusions."

"Well, she just showed up at his house, in a dress, at nine o'clock in the evening. Hardly hiking attire," I say as I walk past her and into the living room where my mom sits on a couch talking to Landon. I feel guilty for snapping at Reagan.

My mother gasps when she sees me, her hand flying up to cover her mouth, then her heart. She jumps up from the couch and pulls me to her. "Lindsay," she says her voice breaking.

"Hi, Mom."

"What is going on? Are you sick? You're so skinny. Oh my god," she gasps again and holds on to my upper arms, standing back to inspect me further.

"I was going to stop by tomorrow, Mom."

"Tomorrow? I wasn't going to wait until tomorrow to see you. You've been avoiding my calls, and when Reagan told me Landon flew to Phoenix, I knew something was going on." I glance at Reagan and narrow my eyes at her. She mouths *"sorry"* to me and scurries away into the kitchen. I give Landon the *"don't you dare leave"* look and he sits back down in his chair as I take a seat next to my mom on the couch.

"What is going on, Lindsay?" my mom asks in a hushed tone.

"I came home to get help," I say quietly. I've learned that admitting my problems to my family and close friends, whom you're supposed to love and trust the most, is harder than admitting them to a complete stranger. That's because those that love you will be the ones let down by your mistakes—and the most likely to judge you.

"Help for what?"

"I have a lot going on, Mom."

"Well, I know. You're always so busy. I hardly even saw you when you were here..."

"No, Mom. I have a lot of issues I need to seek help for. Anorexia being one of them and addiction to prescription pills being another." My admission is quiet, shameful. She inhales sharply.

"Lindsay," she cries.

"I've been on a collision course for a long time. In college, I was anorexic and used recreational drugs to numb the emotional pain I dealt with from my childhood."

"That's my fault," she musters as she wipes tears from her eyes. "I blame myself for everything you two went through." I look at Landon, who sits watching us, his chin resting on his steepled fingers. He remains silent but focused while I continue my story.

"I was able to get it together in college. I stopped using, started eating better, and was feeling really good, but I never really dealt with the issues from my past. I buried them. I never learned how to cope when things got hard." I pause, looking at Landon, who still remains silent. "I dove into my internship and career, and then Matt I got together, and everything felt perfect. I honestly thought I couldn't be any happier."

"What happened, Lindsay?" She reaches out and grabs my hand. Reagan comes into the room quietly and sits on the arm of the chair that Landon is sitting in. She wraps her arm around him and he pulls her into him.

"Life happened. The car accident with Reagan happened and I still blame myself for that. I was reckless. I knew better than to drive in a storm like that."

"It's not your fault," Reagan says quietly. "I never blamed you for that—ever. You need to stop blaming yourself."

"That's easier said than done." I take a deep breath. "They gave me OxyContin for the pain when I was in the hospital—and it was heaven in a little prescription bottle. I didn't feel anything. It didn't just numb the physical pain from the wreck, but it numbed the hurt inside too." My mom pulls tissues from her purse and wipes her eyes and nose.

"I weaned myself off those, though, but there was still something inside of me—something that felt empty. I don't know what it was—I'm still not sure," I admit. "But when Jack offered me that job in Phoenix, something clicked. Something came alive inside of me, a hunger that I used to feel, and I knew I needed to go for it. All the while, another piece of me, the piece that needed Matt, died. I realized very quickly, when I got to Phoenix, that it was Matt that was important to me, not the job."

"Oh, Lindsay." My mom squeezes my hand.

"I still had some Oxy left from the accident and I just started taking it to numb myself. Numb myself for hurting Matt. Numb myself from the pressures of the job in Phoenix. Numb the voices that were always telling me I wasn't good enough, pretty enough, skinny enough. Then, when those pills were gone, I turned to an illegal street dealer to get more." Embarrassment washes over me at the admission I'd become one of those people who is so desperate for a high, I'd turned to the streets to get my fix.

Reagan wipes tears from her eyes and Landon sits, his jaw muscles flexing. "There was nothing any of you could have done," I say. I know Landon is placing blame on himself. He always has. He was always my protector, but this time, it's up to me to save myself. "So I used the pills and stopped eating. My demons from college paid me another visit and, instead of shutting the door on them, I invited them in."

We all sit quietly, no one saying anything. "So tomorrow, I'm checking myself into rehab and finally getting the help I should have gotten a long time ago," I say quietly. "I need to get my life back, at least as much of it as I can."

I wake up with a raging headache, a combination of not having Oxy for the last four days and crying so much. The pressure in my head is killing me and my hands shake violently as I try to splash water on my face. I open the medicine cabinet to look for aspirin and it's been cleaned out. I pull my hair into a ponytail and walk to the kitchen. Reagan stands at the large island with a mug of coffee, staring out onto the back patio.

"Got any more coffee?" I ask, startling her. "Sorry." I laugh quietly.

"Yeah, let me get you a mug. Still take it with light cream?"

"I do."

"You're up early," she says while pulling down a large mug from the cupboard. I watch her steady hand as she fills the mug with steaming coffee from the coffee pot. She sets the creamer and a spoon in front of me along with the mug.

"I couldn't sleep. Bad headache and nerves, I guess. Speaking of headaches, do you have any aspirin?" I blow the steam from the top of the mug and press the mug to my lips.

"I do, but I called the rehab yesterday for any instructions and they don't want you to have anything. Not even aspirin." I nod my head and pray that the coffee helps with the pounding going on inside my head. Reagan keeps looking behind me, out onto the patio, and I finally turn around to see what she's looking at. Landon and Matt sit outside at a patio table, drinking coffee.

"I thought he was leaving this morning?" I say, turning back to Reagan.

"He is. We didn't expect him to come by, but he said he needed to talk to Landon about something."

"What do you think it's about?" I ask curiously. They both sit outside, leaning forward, deep in conversation, serious expressions on their faces.

Reagan shrugs. "I think it's work related." I stand momentarily watching them talk to each other with concerned looks on their faces.

"I'm going to take this to my room and make sure I have everything packed," I tell her, raising the mug of coffee. After last night and already having a shaky morning, I'm not in the right state of mind to talk to Matt. "I'll be ready in about thirty minutes." I walk through the large open living room, careful not to spill the mug of coffee. Back in my room, I open the wood shutters and sit on the chaise lounge, looking out into the open backyard. I take a couple of minutes to enjoy the coffee and close my eyes, willing the headache to go away before I start packing. I grab clean clothes and head into the bathroom for a quick shower.

I wash myself quickly and get changed into a pair of faded, torn-up jeans and a t-shirt that used to be tight on me, which now hangs off my shoulders. I tuck my wavy hair under an old Atlanta Braves baseball hat that used to be Matt's, and put on some silver hoop earrings. *You can do this, Lindsay,* I whisper to myself.

I shove the last stack of clothes into my suitcase and zip it up. I take a look around the room and close the door behind me. I pull the suitcase down the hall and leave it next to the front door.

It's almost seven and we have a two-hour drive, so I go in search of Reagan, who has offered to drive me. I'm glad it's her and not Landon. I'm not sure I could say goodbye to him. I see her on the patio with Landon and Matt. I hesitate before opening the door to the patio and sticking my head out.

"I'm all set," I say quietly, and all three of them turn to look at me. Reagan jumps up from her seat and heads towards me, so I step back inside and open the door for her. "Let me just get my purse and we'll head out."

I pull myself back inside the house and close the door. I walk toward the front door and wait for Reagan, when Landon and Matt come walking over. Matt has his hands shoved into the front pockets of his jeans and his head down. He stands back further into the living room while Landon walks over and pulls me into a hug, his embrace so tight I can hardly breathe. In this moment, I become that scared little girl that he used to hold when our world was crumbling around us and I break down and sob. I cry because I'm scared—I'm scared I won't be strong enough. "Don't cry, Linds." Landon tries to comfort me.

"I'm so scared." My voice shakes as I tell him.

"The hardest part is over," he says softly. I pull out of his embrace and wipe the tears from under my eyes. I notice Matt has stepped back even further, allowing Landon and me some privacy. "I'll take your suitcase to the car. Call when you get there and every chance you can, okay?"

"Okay," I promise, nodding. Reagan comes down the hall with her purse in hand.

"Ready?"

"Yeah," I sigh as she opens the front door and walks out. I glance over to Matt, whose head is still down and his hands are still stuffed in his pockets. "Have a great trip, Matt," I say quietly and step through the front door and onto the steps. I'm about halfway down the steps when I hear his somber voice.

"Linds?" I stop and turn around, meeting his dark brown eyes. He looks at his old hat that I'm wearing, then his eyes meet mine.

"Yeah?"

"Good luck." I can feel myself on the verge of another round of tears, so I nod my head and whisper a quiet "Thanks" before turning around and taking the rest of the steps down to the waiting SUV. Landon closes the car door and leans in the window.

"I mean it, Lindsay. Call."

"I will, I promise." Reagan puts the car in drive and we take off for Raleigh.

Reagan drops me off and we say our goodbyes quickly to keep from crying. We were both awkwardly silent on the two-hour drive with our emotions simmering at the surface. As a doctor, she's familiar with the rehabilitation process and told me what I could expect. She was spot on. The first hour was check-in and paperwork followed by a luggage inspection, and then a thorough physical and mental evaluation. To say I'm already exhausted and it's not even noon would be an understatement.

I am finally assigned a room and follow the counselor down a long hallway to the last door on the left to meet my roommate, Samantha. She's young, nineteen, and from a small town just outside of Wilmington. She's pretty in a unique, plain kind of way, with long, jet-black hair and gray eyes. She's quiet and keeps her nose tucked into a book while I unpack.

There is a regimented schedule here that we must follow and it's now lunchtime. Samantha walks me to the cafeteria, where there is a limited variety of food choices, but since I'm not only being treated for drug addiction, I have a special diet prescribed by the nutritionist. A tray labeled with my name sits waiting for me, taking the guessing out of what I would have chosen. We sit at a small, round table and eat quietly when Samantha finally opens up.

"I've seen you on TV," she says quietly, her gray eyes scanning the cafeteria to see if anyone is watching us. I turn to see what or who she's looking at. No one is paying us any attention. In fact, I think there are less than twenty of us total in this rehab center. I smile at her and nod my head.

"Seems like a lifetime ago."

"You're not on TV anymore?"

I shake my head from side to side. "Not anymore."

"You were really good. I almost didn't recognize you, though, when you walked in. You've gotten really skinny."

"Part of the reason why I'm here," I admit. "That, and pills."

She smiles a crooked little smile. "I did whatever I could get my hands on. Pills, booze, smack…" My eyes widen in disbelief. "For a preacher's daughter, I didn't say no to anything." I remain quiet and eat slowly. I decide to change the subject. I'm not sure I want to learn everything about Samantha on my first day here.

"So what do you read? I saw your nose stuck in that book all morning while I was unpacking."

"I love romance." she smiles. "I love when the girl gets the guy or the guy gets the girl. I want that someday. Someone who will fight for me." I swallow hard when I think of Matt and how I actually had that, but I was selfish and let it go.

"Get yourself better, Samantha, and you will. You'll find someone deserving of you," I tell her. Her eyes shift downward and she picks at the sandwich on her tray. We finish our lunch in silence before heading back to our room, where I lie down for a nap. Samantha heads off to the lounge, where there is a television and most of the residents gather after lunch. I'm not in the mood to mingle or be social today.

Rehab is exactly what Reagan said it would be. We now have a group therapy session, where I get to introduce myself as the new girl and tell everyone my "story." I'm surprised at how comfortable I am admitting my demons to a group of strangers. However, they are here for many of the same reasons, so I know there is no judgment. They watch me intently, everyone sympathetic to my story. Samantha is in my group and sits quietly, her fingers playing with the seam of her dark blue jeans. There are eight people in my group session. All of us are battling drug or alcohol addiction and a few of us, me included, are the lucky ones with an extra little something trying to bring us down—for me, it's anorexia; for another girl, it's OCD.

I watch each person speak as they tell their story. And while our stories are not the same, and we're so different due to our ages, our genders, our looks, our nationalities, or our socioeconomic statuses, we're all the same—we all have struggles, we all want to get better. Our session ends and we're free for the remainder of the afternoon and evening. Dinner, social time, and phone calls are on the agenda for the evening. Since it's also my first day, I have to check in with the staff physician before dinner.

Samantha sits on her bed, reading, and occasionally glances at me while I finish unpacking. I make a mental note to ask her more about her books, to see if I can get her talking. The rest of the day passes quickly. I actually do a decent job of finishing my dinner of chicken breast, steamed vegetables, fresh fruit, yogurt, and a dinner roll. I'm so uncomfortably full it's hard to walk. I visit the staff physician, who takes my vitals and monitors me for signs of withdrawal. Most of that happened back at the hospital, which I'm thankful for. He notes my shaky hands and starts me on vitamins to replace what I've been depriving my body of. All in all, it is an uneventful first day.

I shower and get ready for bed before I find the small, private rooms to make phone calls. We were allowed to bring cellphones and laptops to check email, but they strongly encourage us to focus on rehabilitating ourselves, so I gladly handed mine over. I walk into the small room that has a chair and a side table with the phone sitting on it. I close the glass door behind me. Everything here is semi-private; there are lots of glass doors and cameras everywhere. I pick up the receiver and dial Landon's cell phone. Three rings later, he finally picks up.

"Hi, Lan," I say with a smile.

"Linds, how are you?"

Just the sound of his voice is immediately comforting. "I'm good. Just spent most of the day getting settled, eating, and had my first group therapy session."

"How was that?"

"Actually, pretty good," I respond.

"And did you eat?"

"I did. Enough to make you proud." I laugh quietly.

"Atta girl. I was actually planning to come up Friday night to visit you if that's okay with you?"

"Yeah, of course."

"I wanted to give you a few days to settle in. Of course, Mom wants to come with me if that's okay."

"Yeah, I'd love that. In fact, before you say anything else, I need to ask you something. It's something that's important, so please consider it." My palms sweat as I anticipate what his response might be.

"Okay…" he says hesitantly.

"My therapist would like to do a family session. You, me, and Mom." He's quiet for longer than usual, which has set off the red flags. "I know what you're thinking, Landon…"

"I'll do it," he cuts me off. "I know Mom will too." I breathe a heavy sigh of relief.

"Thank you."

"I'd do anything for you, Lindsay. I want you healthy."

"I want to be healthy too. Okay, I'll call tomorrow night and I can't wait to see you Friday. Tell Reagan thank you again for bringing me. And, Lan? I love you."

"I love you too, baby sister." I smile and hang up the phone, ready to go to bed.

I actually sleep fairly well for being in a new environment with a roommate that might be part vampire. She doesn't sleep. Ever. She just reads and reads and reads. She has a stack of at least forty books on top of her small chest of drawers and, each time I see her, she's reading a different one. I wake before the staff wakes us, which gives me some time to get to know Samantha a bit better, if she'll talk to me.

"What are you reading?" I ask her, startling her. She jumps and I feel bad. "Sorry," I mumble as I roll onto my side to face her.

"Another romance novel," she says quickly before I lose her in the pages of her book again.

"Any you'd recommend?"

"There's an entire stack over there that I've finished." She nods her head toward her dresser. "The ones on the right are available. Help yourself." I sit up groggily and eye the stack of books.

"Thanks. I'll take a look." I stretch my arms above my head and yawn, finally dragging myself out of bed. "Day two," I whisper to myself and grab my clothes and toiletries to get ready for the day.

The rest of the week is uneventful, more of the individual therapy, group therapy, medical check-ins, drug screens, quiet time, journaling, and eating. I never look at the scale when they weigh me, but the staff doctor is happy with the progress that he's seeing. I've noticed my skin and hair are beginning to look healthier and, every day, my clothes fit just a little differently. Landon and my mom are coming today, which has me in a great mood and nervous all at the same time. I always seem to be a jumble of emotions.

There is a lot of down time at rehab and I find myself getting lonely quite easily. I've been trying to get to know Samantha more, but she's more interested in her books than socializing with me, so I spend a good deal of my time journaling and making lists. Lists of things I need to do, people I need to see, and places I must visit.

Time seems to stand still as I wait for Landon and my mom to arrive. While I wait in the lounge for word of their arrival, I'm conflicted. I'm excited to see them and nervous as hell for family therapy—our family is the poster family for "fucked up." I'm pulled from my thoughts when Samantha pops her head into the lounge to let me know I have visitors in the reception area. I nearly sprint down the long hall, where I see Landon standing, leaning against the reception desk. They're still searching my mom's purse when Landon turns to see me coming. I jump into his arms and he pulls me in for a tight hug.

"Linds," he says, squeezing the air from my lungs. Finally setting me down, he smiles at me while tousling my hair. "You're looking good, kiddo."

"Thanks. I'm feeling really good."

They're still pulling crap out of my mom's purse in search of anything she might be trying to smuggle in. Landon laughs and pulls me aside. "They do a better search here than we do at the police department," he jokes and wraps his arm around my shoulder as we wait for them to clear my mom. Haphazardly throwing her belongings back into her giant handbag, she rushes over to me and pulls me into an embrace. While she hugs me, her hand rubs gently up and down my back in a comforting motion. This is the first time I remember her ever comforting me. My therapist, David, arrives, interrupting our little reunion, and he guides us down the hall to his office, where there are three chairs set up in a semi-circle. His chair is centered in front of our chairs so he can lead the discussion.

Landon flashes me an uncomfortable look, but we all sit down and turn our attention to David. David cuts right to the chase. We have an hour session scheduled and he's not about to waste a minute of that time. "Josie. Landon," he acknowledges both of them. "Thank you for agreeing to meet. I believe that the family therapy is going to be a critical piece of Lindsay's recovery," he begins. "Lindsay has given me some background, from her perspective, of what her childhood was like." He pauses and looks at the notebook placed on his lap before he continues. "But I'd like her to share with both of you what she shared with me."

I blink back the tears that are stinging my eyes and swallow hard against my dry throat. Landon shifts in his chair and leans forward, resting his forearms on his legs, his head cast downward towards his feet, and his hands pressed together. The muscles in his forearms flex as he presses his hands together. My mom sits eerily still, her body turned slightly in my direction and her attention focused solely on me. With a deep breath, I start from the beginning. Not skipping out on details, or feelings, I explain to my mom that her abandoning Landon and me when we were nothing short of toddlers will always have a lifelong effect on me.

I cry when I look at Landon, my big brother, and tell him how I don't know what I would have done without him. He's not only my brother, but he was my mother, my father—he was everything to me—he raised me. Everyone in the room listens quietly, with no anger or judgment and it allows me just to bleed the resentment, the hurt, and the sadness I've been holding on to for over twenty years. I had forgiven my mother a long time ago, but I never communicated to her what her leaving really did to me.

The room is quiet while everyone processes what I've said. Landon shifts in his chair and my mom wipes tears from under her eyes. She weeps quietly, listening to me speak. My intentions were not to cause pain, but to move forward from pain. My mom clears her throat and speaks up before David offers her a chance to talk. I can see he's happy with her level of engagement.

"I know what I did was wrong, and I pray every single night that you and Landon," she turns her head to look at him. His eyes are fixed on her and he's fully paying attention to what she's saying, "will forgive me. The one regret in life I will always have is that I didn't take you with me, but at the time, I thought I was protecting you, when I should have known better. For the rest of my life, I won't know the damage that leaving you behind did, but I see glimpses of it every day and it kills me." Her lip quivers and her chin trembles. I can't contain my tears, and I've stopped trying to. I want to feel. I want to hurt, and I want to move on.

"Landon, the abuse you endured at the hands of your father was my fault. I was your mother. I should have protected you, but instead, I left you to care for your sister, and fend off abuse from your father." Landon works his jaw muscles while my mom addresses him. "Lindsay forgave me a long time ago, but I worry that I'll die without you forgiving me. Part of me is okay with that, because maybe I don't deserve forgiveness, but you deserve to know how very sorry I am," she sobs.

Landon clears his throat and bobs his knee up and down. "I don't speak a lot about my feelings." He shrugs. "I guess I've learned over the years how to bottle them and keep them in. I had other ways of releasing my anger," he shifts his eyes to mine quickly, then back to David, "that were less destructive than Lindsay's."

"I'd like to explore that," David says. Landon lets out a burst of laughter.

"Not with my sister and mom in the room." He chuckles, bringing the mood down just a bit. I know what he's referencing—his non-committal sex over the years—but our mom is unaware of that. "Anyway, I wouldn't be here in this room, sitting next to you, Mom, if I hadn't forgiven you. I may not have told you those exact words, but letting you back into my life was my way of forgiving and forging a new relationship with you." Mom dabs her tears with a tissue and nods at Landon.

"And Lindsay," he says quietly, his voice cracking with emotion. "There is nothing, absolutely nothing in this world that you could do that is unforgivable. When we had no one, it was you and me. And yes, there were times you had no idea you were helping me, but you were. Without you, I wouldn't be here. I'd be dead. I need you happy, but most importantly, I need you healthy," he says quietly.

David spends a few minutes talking about communication and healing before releasing us. We walk quietly through the hall and I show them my room, the lounge, the facilities, and we catch up on everything happening back in Wilmington.

Time flies and before I know it, visiting hours are over. I feel guilty that they drove all this way and now they still have a two-hour drive back home. We say our goodbyes and I retreat back to my room, exhausted. As I close my eyes, I whisper a prayer and fall into an easy slumber.

# CHAPTER 20

## *Lindsay*

My time at rehab is winding down with only one day left. I'm armed with books and journals and a list of things I have to do to right my wrongs, to move forward and help me heal. This is my biggest fear, facing the people I've hurt with my behaviors and asking forgiveness. I said goodbye to Samantha a week ago when she was released. She finally opened up to me a bit and, as a parting gift, left me thirty-seven romance novels that I promised her I'd read and pass along. I've made my way through two of them and, surprisingly, have found a new love and escape in reading. I've added the other thirty-five books to my to-read list to have completed by the end of the year, along with a whole host of other things I plan to do for myself.

My therapist and physicians have cleared me for discharge, happy with the progress I've made over the last thirty days. Tonight, I begin the task of packing my belongings, as Landon is picking me up in the morning. I have one last individual therapy session in the morning and then I'm free to leave. I've agreed to continue therapy back in Wilmington and I know this will help me transition back to regular life. I laugh when I think of *regular life*. What is regular life for me? That has yet to be seen, but I'm excited to find out. As I crawl into bed tonight, I have a content heart and a peaceful mind, but I'm definitely ready to go home.

I walk into David's office two minutes to the hour for my last individual therapy session. *Early as always*, I think to myself. Something that has never changed with me is that I take pride in being on time and being respectful of other's time. I guess there are some things ingrained in a person that can never really be conquered. I know that addiction won't be one of them. I take a seat in the chair I always sit in and cross my legs, patiently waiting for him to acknowledge me.

"Lindsay." He smiles at me, looking up from his notepad.

"Hey, David," I greet him in response.

"So it's our last day together."

"It is."

"How are you feeling?"

"About?" I inquire.

"Everything. Leaving, your treatment, your plans. Do you have any new anxieties since we spoke yesterday?"

I smile and don't hesitate like I normally do before answering. "I don't. For the first time in a long time, I'm totally fine with not having a plan. I'm going to go home and work on some things I've been journaling about. I'm going to help my brother and sister-in-law with their wedding, and I'm going to travel a little bit." He smiles at me.

"Here is the name of the therapist I've referred you to in Wilmington. She's a phenomenal doctor and great friend. You'll be in excellent care with her." I take the business card he hands to me and set it in my lap.

"I do have one last question for you, David. Is it possible to forgive yourself for hurting others, even if they don't forgive you? I mean, sometimes you hurt people so badly they can't find it within themselves to forgive you. Is it possible to forgive yourself for the hurt you've caused when they won't let it go?"

He thinks tentatively. "Lindsay, that's a deep question, but the answer is yes. You can't control anyone else's feelings, emotions, or thoughts. You can only control your behavior and your actions. If you do your best to make amends with someone and they choose to not forgive, that should not inhibit your own self-forgiveness."

I take in what David is saying and smile. "Does that make sense?" he asks.

"It does. I just think that this will be the hardest thing for me to accept."

"That others won't forgive you?"

I nod my head. "Yeah. Some of the damage I've done is pretty unforgiveable."

"Lindsay, there is nothing, and I mean nothing, that is unforgivable."

"Thanks, David."

I glance at the business card he gave me while he shuffles a few more papers around. "Here are follow-up instructions and information for your nutritionist. Please schedule an appointment with your physician at home as well."

"I will."

"Lindsay," he says quietly, setting his notebook down on his wood desk. "I never want to tell a person it was great having them here, because I know the journey that got you here was devastating. But you have so much promise. I know you will be successful in this recovery and I have so much faith in you." He leans back in his large, leather desk chair and pulls the wire-framed glasses from his face. "I want you to believe that too."

I take a deep, cleansing breath and feel a smile spread across my face. "I think I actually do believe that. Thank you for everything."

"You have my email. Keep in touch. I'd love to hear how you're doing."

I push myself up from my chair and leave David's office with a sense of hope. Gathering my final belongings, I wheel my suitcase down the hall to the main reception desk where Landon is waiting for me, leaning against a wall while talking on his phone. He hangs up quickly and rushes over to help me with my bag while I sign out of the treatment facility.

The late summer air still hangs with humidity, but it doesn't feel heavy. I no longer feel weighed down. "Ready?" he asks, lifting my suitcase into the back of his car.

"Ready!"

We arrive home to an empty house. Reagan is at the hospital, delivering a baby, and the house is quiet. I spend several hours doing laundry and getting settled back into my brother's house. Landon insisted that I stay with them until I figure out what I'm doing or where I'm going to land permanently. Money isn't an issue. I have more money than I know what to do with sitting in a trust fund from when my father was killed. Landon gave me his portion—I guess that was his way of finally freeing himself of anything related to our father. I believe Landon wants me here at his house so that he can watch over me to make sure my recovery stays on track.

I stack the books from Samantha neatly on a bookshelf in my room and shove the large suitcase in the closet just as Landon peeks in the door.

"All settled?"

"Pretty much," I say, brushing a loose strand of hair off my forehead, tucking it behind my ear.

"Good. Wanna do something with me?" He has a cocky grin on his face.

"I don't know. I don't like the look you have on your face right now," I say, standing with my hands on my hips.

"Come on; it'll be fun. Change into shorts. It's warm out." He shuts the door quickly, not allowing me time to question him further. I change into a pair of knee-length khaki shorts and a bright yellow tank top and slide on a pair of brown leather sandals. I pull my long hair back into a ponytail and grab my purse on the way out of the bedroom.

"Let's go," Landon urges me as he waits for me by the front door.

"Where are we going?" I ask as I close the front door behind me.

"Golfing." He smiles.

I glance at him out of the corner of my eye.

"I hate golf."

"You used to love golfing with me."

"I was seventeen and liked *who* you were golfing with, not the actual sport of golf."

"You used me for my friends?" He feigns hurt, then starts laughing. I can't help but laugh in return. "It'll be fun. A little brother-sister bonding, plus Reagan won't ever golf with me."

"I don't blame her," I balk. "Don't you usually go with Matt?" It's funny how his name just falls from my lips so naturally, yet it still stings so much.

"Yeah, he's still in Europe. Extended his trip, I guess." He shrugs. "So you get to golf with me today." He turns the car into the parking lot of a golf course that is attached to their community. "Perks of buying this house; it comes with a golf membership."

"Swanky." I roll my eyes at him in mock disgust and he laughs at me. Landon puts my old set of golf clubs in the back of the cart next to his while I change into my old golf shoes. I can't believe they still fit.

"You know, the good thing about golf shoes is that they're so hideous, they never really go out of style," I tease him. "Who knew a pink Nike swoosh could stand the test of time?"

"This isn't a fashion show, Linds. We've got some serious golfing to do, and I need to kick your ass doing it."

"Really?" I smirk. "Well, game on. Last I remember, you've got a terrible slice." He mumbles something under his breath while sliding into the golf cart. I laugh out loud, knowing that I hit a sore spot with him. We spend the afternoon on a nearly empty course. It's nice to spend time with Landon and just enjoy the last days of summer. It's warm, but the sun feels good on my face and I tilt my head back and soak up the rays while Landon gets ready to tee off on the eighteenth hole. It won't be more than a few weeks before the days start cooling down.

He swings and hits the ball perfectly. "Nice shot," I commend him as we get into the cart. "This was really fun today.

Thanks for dragging my sorry ass out here." I lean over and bump his shoulder with mine. "Maybe we can do this again sometime."

"I'd like that." He turns his head and smiles at me.

"So what, only a few more weeks until the wedding? I can't believe how fast that's snuck up on us. What are you guys doing for the bachelor party?" I raise my eyebrows and look over the top of my sunglasses at him.

"I'm not sure yet. Matt's planning it, and since he's not home yet, I honestly don't know what the plans are."

"Ah, well, he'll make sure it's perfect," I say quietly. "He's a good friend to you. I don't want things to be weird with you two because of me."

He sighs as we park the cart and get out on the green. "It's hard for it not to be weird Lindsay, but I want you to know something. You are my family, my blood. He is my friend. You will always come first. The nice thing is, with Matt, I know he'd never make me choose. He'll always be my friend." He smiles a crooked smile at me. "Now let's wrap this up so I can officially call myself the winner."

"You're only three strokes ahead of me. Anything can happen." I laugh at him.

We finish the game with Landon being victorious. "This just feeds your ego," I say, shoving my putter into the golf bag.

"I hate losing," he smirks. "Even to my baby sister."

"Jerk," I grumble in a kidding manner and he laughs at me.

Arriving home, we find Reagan in the kitchen, cooking dinner.

The smell is amazing. The entire house smells like fresh pasta sauce.

"Smells delicious," Landon says as we walk into the kitchen. He walks over to Reagan and presses a kiss to her cheek while she stirs a huge pot of homemade marinara sauce.

"How was golf?" she asks, looking at me with a smile.

"I won," Landon says. "That's all that matters." He winks at me while popping an olive off the relish tray into his mouth.

"Precisely why I won't golf with him," she says, setting the large, wooden spoon on the spoon rest. "He's too competitive."

"I actually had fun," I admit. "The weather was gorgeous and I haven't golfed in years."

"I'm glad you two got to spend some time together," she says sincerely.

The kitchen table in the breakfast nook is set with three place settings. There is a large garden salad on the table and Reagan carries over a large platter of fresh ravioli covered in her homemade marinara sauce. It smells divine. Landon carries three glasses of ice water to the table and places one glass at each place setting. Normally, there would be bottles of wine on the table, but they are noticeably absent tonight. Looking at all the food is overwhelming and, even though my stomach growls in hunger, part of me wants to skip dinner.

I've come so far, and actually feel good, so I force myself to sit down at the table, placing a napkin in my lap and taking a hearty helping of the garden salad. Reagan is a diligent cook and goes all out for every meal. The salad is full of mixed greens, onions, tomatoes, hearts of palm, and banana peppers.

"You know, just because I'm not drinking, doesn't mean you can't have wine," I say as I pick up the platter of ravioli. I spoon two of the large ravioli onto my plate. "I don't want my sobriety to hinder your lifestyle."

It's awkwardly quiet for a moment before Reagan pipes in, "Lindsay, we will always support you and your sobriety. It's your first day back in *this* reality." She motions around the room. "There will always be temptation and, on your first day out of rehab, I'm not going to set that temptation in front of your face." She takes the platter of pasta from me and scoops some onto her plate before passing it to Landon. "Will there be a time when we'll drink in front of you again? I'm sure there will be, but it will be when we know you're comfortable with that, not your first day home. Plus, I won't be drinking any wine for at least nine months so…"

"What?" I ask, dropping my fork.

"I won't be drinking for…"

"No, I heard you. Are you serious?" She nods and smiles at me. "Oh my god." I jump up from my seat and run around the table, throwing myself at her. She opens her arms and pulls me into a hug. "I'm so happy for you," I whisper. Pulling myself away, I turn to Landon. "Why didn't you tell me this afternoon?" I swat his arm before leaning down to give him a congratulatory hug.

"We wanted to tell you together."

"I can't believe I'm going to be an aunt," I say, taking my seat at the table again. "Wait, have you told Mom?"

"No!" Landon pipes in quickly.

"We're not going to tell anyone until after the wedding," Reagan says. "I'm very early in the pregnancy, only about five weeks along. Anything could happen between now and the wedding."

"Nothing's going to happen," Landon says, looking out the corner of his eye at Reagan. "We want the focus to be on the wedding, not the baby—but we wanted to tell you."

"Okay, personal question," I say, taking a drink of water quickly. "Were you trying to get pregnant?" Landon laughs quietly and shakes his head from side to side.

"No," Reagan answers. "Well, let's put it this way. We weren't trying to get pregnant, but we weren't doing anything to prevent it either. It just happened really fast. We thought it would happen after the wedding, not before."

"Holy crap," I mutter. "I'm so happy for you both."

"Thanks," Landon says, shoving a ravioli into his mouth. "It's a little surreal, honestly."

"How are you feeling?" I ask Reagan.

"Actually pretty good, so far. My boobs hurt like hell, and I'm really tired, but that's to be expected. I've just been trying to make sure I rest and eat well. By the time we get married, I'll be starting my second trimester, so I should be feeling great by then."

"Good. So this is a good segue into something else I wanted to talk to you about." I set my fork down and look between the two of them.

"I don't have any immediate plans for work. I have to talk to Jack, but I'm pretty sure I ruined my broadcasting career when I broke the contract in Phoenix. I'm a liability at this point, and everyone talks. No one is going to want to hire me back in the business. So while I figure out what I'm going to do with my life, I was thinking of taking some time off to just help you with wedding plans, travel a little bit, and just figure things out."

"I think that sounds like a really sensible idea," Reagan says. "Take your time easing back into life, Lindsay. You always worked too hard. If we're being honest with each other, I was really nervous you were going to dive right back into work and I was worried about the pressure of the business and how it would affect you."

I nod my head. Reagan is right. I worked too much and placed too much value on my career and not enough importance on the things that really did matter to me.

"That's a valid concern." I smile at her. "And I know you said I could stay here as long as I like, but my goal is to be out by the time you get back from your honeymoon."

Landon looks to Reagan, then back to me. "Reagan and I already discussed this, Lindsay. There is no need to rush out of here. You're welcome to stay for as long as you want."

"Well, if I can't find a job, you may have to hire me to be your nanny," I tease.

We spend the next hour enjoying dinner and just catching up. It feels so good to laugh and be happy again. I help Reagan clean up after dinner, washing and drying the dishes before calling it an early night. I'm tired and ready for a little quiet time. In rehab, I learned to appreciate some alone time, time to think, time to plan, time to journal—time to focus on myself.

I shower and change into a pair of silk pajamas, leaving my long hair wet and loose. I stand in front of the giant bookshelf in my bedroom and pull down one of Samantha's books. I lose myself in the romance novel for the next three hours and love every minute of it. I soak up the words that leap from the pages and let myself feel the emotions of the journey happening in front of me. I can understand now why Samantha loved reading and I can't wait to delve into the rest of the books she left me—a gift she didn't realize I'd love so much.

Crawling into bed, I lie on my side and look at the muted moonlight that peeks through the slats on the wood shutters and whisper long, overdue prayers for all the blessings I have and for new beginnings. Every night, when I close my eyes, I relive the pain I've caused and the people I've hurt. I know the sins I've committed against the person I love the most are unforgiven, and that's my cross to bear.

# CHAPTER 21

## Matt

I'm in a daze as I watch the baggage carousel spin in circles as I wait for my suitcase. The flights back to the U.S. were long and, after spending a month in Europe, I am glad to be home.

"Hey, brother," Landon says from behind me. He shakes my hand and fist bumps me when I turn around to greet him. "Good to have you back."

"It's good to be back," I admit. While traveling alone was an adventure and I got to see everything I wanted to, there were definitely times it was lonely. Everywhere I went, I imagined Lindsay with me, loving the architecture, the wine, the culture.

"You're looking a little like Grizzly Adams. Do they not sell razors in Europe?" Landon jokes about the beard I've let grow out while away. I laugh and shake my head. "I hardly recognize you."

"Decided to do something different," I tell him.

"I'm just giving you a hard time." He smacks my shoulder. "How many bags are we waiting on?"

"Just one. That one, right there," I say just as the large, black suitcase comes into sight. I lean over and pull it from the metal carousel. Landon grabs my backpack and we walk toward the elevators to the parking garage.

"So how was Europe?"

"Good, but exhausting," I admit. "I'm glad I went, though. Had a lot of time to think and just kind of sort out my life, you know?" Landon nods his head as we load my bags into the back of Reagan's SUV. "How've you been, man?"

"Great, actually. Work has been crazy. We finally busted the kid over at the high school that's been dealing the heroin…"

"Oh yeah? Good to hear."

"It's been a busy couple of weeks. Lindsay's finally home." He drops that in nonchalantly.

"How's she doing?" I'm dying to know but don't want to sound overly anxious.

He lets out a long sigh before actually speaking. "She's actually doing really, really well. She looks fantastic. She's put on weight and is ready to move forward. She's got doctors and therapists lined up here until she figures out where she's going."

"She's going to leave again?" My heart skips a beat and my stomach drops.

"I don't know. She's taking the next couple of months off to just kind of figure out her life. She said she wants to move out and have a plan by the time we get back from the honeymoon."

"Well, where else would she go? Back to Phoenix?"

"Nah, Phoenix is a done deal. She really hasn't said. I think she's leaving her options open." I swallow hard against my dry throat. I don't know why this upsets me—the possibility of her leaving again. "I'm just glad she's getting better," he admits quietly.

"Me too."

The rest of the ride to my house is quiet. I'm lost in my thoughts of Lindsay, and I am exhausted from the trip. Landon pulls into my driveway just as Melissa pulls up in front of my house. "Looks like someone is excited to see you." He waves to her as she gets out of her car. I lay my head back against the seat rest, inhaling a deep breath.

"It's not what it looks like."

"I vaguely remember that used to be my line." This makes me laugh and I open my car door and walk around the back of the SUV. Pulling my luggage down from the car, I give a short wave to Landon as he wags his eyebrows and offers me a smirk. I flip him the middle finger and I can see him laughing as he backs out of my driveway. Melissa meets me and waits on the front step with a smile on her face.

"Hey, stranger," she drawls.

"Hey, Melissa."

"I was just coming over to water your plant and tidy everything up before you got home. Wasn't sure what time you'd be here." She inserts my house key into the door, disables the alarm, and holds the door open for me, like this is where she belongs. I toss my suitcase and backpack into the corner and kick off my tennis shoes.

"I've got it," I politely tell her. "I really appreciate you taking care of the place and getting my mail. I'm completely exhausted right now, but maybe we can catch up sometime this week?" I hope I don't sound like a complete ass, but I really just want a shower and a long nap.

"Yeah, sure, of course." She shakes her head a little, visibly upset. I hate nothing more than hurting people and I instantly feel guilty for putting her off.

"Maybe we can hike on Sunday and grab breakfast afterwards," I offer quickly in an attempt to ward off any hurt feelings. A small smile tugs at her lips.

"That sounds nice."

"I'll text you. Thanks again. I really appreciate it." She quietly leaves and I breathe a sigh of relief.

I immediately jump back into work upon my return from Europe. Staying busy helps keep my mind from wandering into dangerous places; however, it still wanders every night before I go to sleep. I wonder if I'll ever not wonder where Lindsay is, who she's with, who's holding her, or if I'll ever hear her laugh again? I still see her smile when I close my eyes, and feel her arm lying across my chest in the middle of the night. Every morning, when I sit and have coffee, I swear I hear her in my bedroom, getting ready for the day. I promised myself in Europe I'd let Lindsay's ghost go, but maybe I'm just not ready yet.

My phone rings loudly from the table in the living room and I jog over to get it, Melissa's name flashes across the screen. I hit ignore and set the phone back down, turning on the TV to ESPN. I sip coffee and catch up on the sports highlights before checking my voice messages. I turn the speakerphone on and listen to the message while I gather my belongings for work.

*"Matt, I have to cancel our hike for this weekend. I have to watch my nephew for my sister. Was thinking maybe we could grab a movie on Friday night instead? They're playing the original* Star Wars *at that old theater downtown that they recently refurbished. I thought it might be fun to go. Let me know if you're interested."*

The phone disconnects itself at the end of the message. I pick it up and shove it into my pocket as I head out the door for work. Thirty minutes later, I'm dressed and headed into our pre-shift meeting. Our sergeant provides us with updates and our detectives alert us to which people they're looking for, or what information they'd like us to listen out for.

I stand in the back of the small room, leaning against the wall. I'm still riding solo, and totally okay with that. My beat is typically quiet, although, at times, a partner to talk to might make the shift go by faster. Landon quietly enters the room and leans against the back wall next to me.

"What's up, man?" he whispers, but watches the sergeant giving his updates.

"Not much. Back to the grind."

"I know. I can't believe you're not taking a few more days off just to relax."

"Nah, no need to."

"Hey, Friday poker at my house. You in?"

"Ah, I can't. I just told Melissa I'd go to the movies with her," I whisper. He looks at me out of the corner of his eye, and I shrug. "Don't ask. She can't hike on Sunday, so she invited me to the movies."

"Next week, then?"

"Deal."

"Take care, man."

"You too." He pushes himself off the wall and slides out the side door. My first shift back is actually busy—a welcome change from the norm. I find myself across the street from the theater Melissa wants to go to Friday night where a new Starbucks has recently opened. It's big and bright and full of tables and unique work spaces. It's bustling with people for ten o'clock on a

Thursday evening. As I wait for my order, I take in the enormity of the place. Tables ranging in all different sizes from small, two-person tables, all the way to larger family-style tables that hold up to twelve people. Each table has power outlets so people can work and access the wi-fi all while getting their caffeine fix.

It's there, while waiting for my coffee, that I see her, tucked away at a small table in the corner, almost hidden from view. Her back is pressed up against an exposed brick wall and she rests her chin in her hand, staring out the window. A laptop is open in front of her, but she's not working. She's lost in her thoughts. She looks so different from when I last saw her. Her face has filled back out, and her normally wavy hair is straight today. Her lips are pursed as she stares out the glass window and I'd give anything to sit down and talk to her, to know what she's thinking.

"Sir."

I notice a large bottle of water and a paperback book sitting next to her laptop.

"Sir?" the young male voice says louder.

"Oh, sorry," I say, pulling my attention back to the young man behind the counter.

"Here's your drink," he says, sliding the cup of iced coffee across the counter at me. I pull out my wallet and a ten-dollar bill.

"See that girl back in the corner? The blonde in the navy tank top with the yellow scarf?"

"Yeah, she'd be hard to miss," he says. I give him a snide look. Even the teen boys notice Lindsay's beauty.

"Can you make her a grande skinny vanilla latte, no foam, extra hot?"

"Yeah, I'd be glad to."

"Keep the change. Oh, and if she asks, don't tell her it was me. Just tell her someone was thinking of her."

"You got it."

I weave through the display cases that hold glass coffee mugs and bags of coffee beans and push through the glass doors. I stand out on the street next to my squad car, leaning against the hood and just watch her through the window. Her blue eyes that were dull the last time I saw her are bright again. The dark circles under her eyes are gone and her cheeks are fuller. She's still thin, but she looks good. My heart still races just looking at her.

The boy from behind the counter saunters up, wearing his green apron and a big smile on his face. She turns her head to look at him and smiles. Words are exchanged and she accepts the paper cup of coffee. I see her turn the cup to see what it is that's been given to her and she jumps up from the table, craning her neck as she looks around the coffee shop.

A smile pulls at my lips when I figure she must know it's me. I can't imagine anyone else knowing her coffee order. My radio alerts me to a call, and I push myself off the hood of my car and slide into the driver's seat. I respond to dispatch, but before I leave, taking one last look at Lindsay, who is still standing next to her table and staring at the cup of coffee in her hand—a smile on her face.

# CHAPTER 22

## *Lindsay*

One of my new favorite things to do is sit on the back patio of Landon and Reagan's house every morning with a giant mug of coffee and watch the sun come up. It peeks just over the horizon and signals a new day; its ascent into the sky every morning marks another day to learn and love and *live*. I've been home from treatment for over a month and spend the days reconnecting with my family and helping Reagan with the wedding tasks.

The sliding glass door opens and Landon steps onto the patio. I'm huddled under a large blanket. The mornings are cool and the air is getting more brisk every passing day.

"Hey," he says, closing the door behind him. He takes a seat in the large chair next to me.

"Hey, are you just getting home?" His clothes are wrinkled and he has dark circles under his bloodshot eyes.

"Yeah. Had an exciting night." He winks at me. "You're up early."

"I am. I like getting up early. I like watching the sun rise. It's kind of my *thing* now." I smile at him and sip from the steaming mug of coffee. We sit in silence and watch the orange sky become brighter. A few leaves on some of the trees are just starting to turn in color and the dew looks frosty on the green grass. Fall is my favorite time of year.

"Can you believe you're getting married in a little over a week, and going to be a dad in six months?" I ask, taking another sip of my coffee.

"I'm ready," he says quietly. He turns to look at me and, for the first time, I see how much my brother has changed.

"I know you are, and I'm glad," I tell him.

"Life just has a funny way of falling into place when it's the right time."

I snort and roll my eyes. "For you."

"It'll happen for you too when the time is right, Linds. Believe that." He stands up and opens the door to go back in the house. "Oh, I tried calling you last night. Your voice mailbox is full."

"I haven't turned my phone on since I left for rehab."

"Lindsay, do you realize how long ago that was?"

"I haven't had a reason to turn it on." I shrug.

"Charge it and turn it on."

"Yeah, yeah." I wave him off.

"Do it!" he mouths through the glass door. He's so bossy.

I spend the day running errands with Reagan. We've met and finalized all the details with the florist, the church, the bakery, and the caterer. We've picked up programs from the printer and settled the final payment with the pianist and violinist for the wedding. The wedding details are officially done. To celebrate, Reagan pulls into a small bistro that overlooks the beach to treat me to lunch.

"They have amazing sandwiches and salads here," she says.

"Did you finally get your appetite back?" I ask, stepping out of the car and closing the door behind me.

"I did. That nausea was brutal," she said.

"Well, you don't look pregnant, so I think your secret will be safe until after the wedding." I giggle.

"I have one last fitting on Wednesday with the seamstress and I'm so nervous. She said not to worry, but Lindsay, my dress is skintight and fitted."

"You'll be fine. You don't even have a bump."

"A lot can change in a few days." She laughs. "Trust me. I've seen it all!"

We take a seat on the outdoor patio and I order a bowl of chicken noodle soup and Reagan orders a salad. We both tip our heads back into the late afternoon sun, soaking in the last few rays of the day.

"Feels so good," I mumble.

"I thought you hated the heat. Landon told me stories of you bitching that you thought you were living in hell when you were in Phoenix."

I can't help but laugh. "Let's just say Phoenix is an entirely different kind of heat that you never hope to experience." She laughs and shakes her head at me. Speaking of Phoenix," I say, sitting up and clearing my throat. "I need to make a trip back there to settle a few loose ends."

"Do you think that's a good idea?" she asks me, genuinely concerned. She unwraps her silverware, sets it on the table, and sips from her iced tea.

"It is. I have to make a few amends, wrap things up at the condo, and I need to get to California too. I have to see Jess."

"Lindsay, I'm just worried..."

"Don't be," I cut her off. "I need to do this and I'm ready. I've given this a lot of thought and it just seems like now is the right time."

"Okay," she whispers. "But Landon told me you haven't turned on your phone."

"I haven't. I will tonight. It's charging."

"You cannot leave without us being able to reach you, Lindsay."

"You're already sounding like a mom, Rea," I joke with her.

"We love you, Lindsay. All of us, and we're just worried about you."

"I love you guys too, and I appreciate your concerns, but I need to do this."

"I know."

"I don't know how I'll ever be able to repay you for everything you've done for me."

"Babysitting. You'll pay us back in babysitting." She laughs.

"Deal. I think I can handle that." Our server delivers our food and we enjoy lunch together, just laughing and having a nice afternoon. "Can you do me one more favor?" I ask Reagan as she pushes her plate away.

"Of course. What do you need?"

"Will you take me to get a car after lunch?"

"Yeah, sure. I mean, you can use ours. We're going to be gone for two weeks after the wedding. There's no need for you to rush and buy a car."

I shake my head. "No, I'm ready for this too. I want to get a car and I hope to find a place of my own so that when you get back, I'm all settled."

Her tone becomes more serious. "Are you going to stay here? I mean, stay in North Carolina?"

"Here or nearby. The furthest I'd go would be Charlotte or Raleigh."

"Those are hours away, Linds."

"I know. It just depends on where I can find a job. I'm going to start looking when I get back."

"When are you leaving?"

"I was thinking about Sunday."

She gasps. "Does Landon know?"

"No. Because he's going to want to go with me. I need to do this on my own, Reagan."

She nods her head. "I understand. But you have to tell him and turn on your phone."

"Turning it on as soon as we get home from buying a car!"

"Whose car is that in the driveway?" Landon hollers as he slams the front door behind him.

"Welcome home, honey!" I holler back as I flip through the pages of my *Shape* magazine.

"Who's here?" he asks as he walks into the kitchen and kisses the top of my head. I'm sitting at the large kitchen island, enjoying an iced tea, reading articles, and getting healthy eating ideas.

"No one. The car is mine."

"You went and bought a car?"

"Yeah. Reagan took me. Why do you look so wounded?"

"That was kind of *our* thing to do together."

"The only time you went with me, you embarrassed me. Matt went with me the last time I bought a car. And this time, I went with Reagan. It was a fairly painless process," I admit and turn another page in the magazine. He scoffs and pulls a cup out of the cabinet, pouring himself a glass of iced tea. My cell phone sits on the counter in front of me. I've yet to turn it on, but it's fully charged. He's eyeing it and looks at me.

"Did you turn it on?"

"Not yet."

"You're not turning it on to piss me off, aren't you?"

"Maybe."

"You're just as annoying as always, you know that, right?"

"Yep."

"Turn it on, Lindsay. I like to know how to get ahold of you, especially now that you're driving again."

"I was driving before."

"In our cars, so we always knew where you were going."

"I'm not twelve, Landon."

"Just turn the phone on so we can get ahold of you, please, and stop being so difficult."

I roll my eyes at my overprotective brother, but I push the power button on the top and watch as the screen comes to life. I set it back on the counter and drink my tea. The phone begins to buzz and hum and chirp and vibrate. The damn thing looks like it's having a seizure.

"Jesus Christ," he says, laughing at it as it bounces around the counter.

"This is why I left it off." I laugh. I rest my hand over the phone and hold it in place and look up at Landon, who's leaning back against the kitchen island. "Hey, Lan?"

"Yeah."

"I'm leaving on Sunday for just a few days."

"Where to?"

"I need to go wrap up some loose ends and hopefully

make some amends." His blue eyes grow slightly larger.

"No way in hell you're going to Phoenix alone," he says, rubbing the side of his face.

"I am. I'm ready and strong enough and I *need* to do this. I have to go pack up a few things and I need to go back to the station and talk to Rob. I have to apologize for my behavior and just have closure there."

"I don't think it's a good idea," he voices his concern.

"Then, I'm flying to California. I need to talk to Jess. She's my best friend and I miss her, but a phone call isn't going to cut it. I need to see her and apologize." He nods his head.

"Okay," he says quietly. "But that fucking phone stays on and charged the entire time."

"It will be, I promise."

"I don't like this, Lindsay. But I trust you."

"Thank you, Landon."

He grumbles something as he walks away and I finally swipe the screen on my phone to see all the voice messages, emails, and text messages that I've successfully ignored for the last two and half months.

I sit on the patio with a notepad jotting down each and every phone call that I have to return. Most of the messages are from my agent, Jack, who I'm sure has all but given up on me. There were four messages from Jonah, begging and pleading with me to return his calls, and then there were a few surprises—Elaine, my old boss at WXZI here in Wilmington, and even one from Jess. I plan to speak to Jonah and Jess in person, so I don't immediately call them back.

My finger hovers over Jack's name in my contact list and I hesitantly tap it, pressing the phone to my ear. My heart thrums nervously as the phone begins ringing.

"Jack O'Toole," his gruff voice answers.

"Hey, Jack. It's Lindsay." There is a moment of silence while he registers who's calling.

"How are you?" he immediately asks.

"I'm doing well. I'm sorry I haven't returned your calls sooner. I finally turned on my phone today for the first time since I left Phoenix." He mumbles something inaudible and I can hear the tension in his voice. "I just wanted to call to tell you that I know I screwed up, Jack. I know you put your neck on the line to get me that job in Phoenix." There is a deep sigh on the phone and the rustling of papers in the background. "I also understand that I broke my contract and I'm not calling you to ask you for any favors. I'm simply calling you to say I'm sorry."

"I'm sorry too, Lindsay. I know I pressured you to take that job in Phoenix and I knew you had reservations. I was selfish for pushing you, but I truly believed in your talent—I still do."

"I'm headed back to Phoenix to clean out the condo, and I would like to stop by and apologize to Rob, unless you feel that it would be a bad idea."

"No, I think that's an excellent idea. He's been asking about you."

"Good. I'm headed there Sunday. I'll make sure to stop by, probably on Monday. One last question, Jack. Do you have any idea why Elaine is calling me?" He grumbles again.

"Just call her, Lindsay. Today!" he barks at me before disconnecting the call. Since he's still barking orders, I'm going to assume he hasn't fired me as a client. I shake my head in confusion and cross his name off the list on my notepad.

I spend a few minutes calling and pushing out next week's doctor and therapy appointments to the following week when I return from the west coast. I pull out my laptop and log in to American Airlines to book a ticket to Phoenix and spend a few minutes returning the insane amount of emails staring at me from my inbox.

I close the screen on my laptop and pick up my cell phone, searching for Elaine's name in my contacts and press her name. She answers on the second ring—prompt as always.

"Lindsay Christianson, about damn time you called me back." She laughs. Her laugh is more of a cackle. She is the tiniest person I've ever met, but her personality and voice are huge.

"Hi, Elaine. I'm so sorry it's taken me so long to return your calls. I finally turned on my phone today after it's been off for months—it's a really long story," I blurt out, trying to explain my lack of response without going into detail.

"No need to explain. Jack's filled me in. Let me cut to the chase. I have something I'd like to talk to you about. In person."

"Sure, um… I'm headed to Phoenix on Sunday to wrap up a few loose ends, and I'm planning to return Friday afternoon, but my brother is getting married, and I have the rehearsal and dinner Friday night."

"Tonight, Lindsay. I know it's last minute, but meet me for coffee tonight."

"I can do that. Do you know the new Starbucks down on Main?"

"I know exactly where it's at. Meet me there at seven."

"I will."

"Perfect. See you there." I hang up, anxious to see what she wants to talk to me about, but more importantly, I only have an hour and a half to shower, clean up, and get there. Hurrying to my room, I pull a black three-quarter sleeve, button-down dress out of the closet along with a pair of open-toe wedges. It's not too dressy, not too casual. I shower and style my hair into long, loose waves and actually put on make-up for the first time in months. I feel good and I'm happy with how I look. Grabbing my clutch and the keys to my new car, I head out the door by six thirty so I have time to park and be on time.

I push the heavy glass door open to the smell of freshly brewed coffee. The smell of coffee hangs heavy in the air and I inhale deeply, taking in the aroma I love so much. I see Elaine waving at me from a table in the center of the coffee shop with her cell phone pressed to her ear. She's in a dark pantsuit with large-framed black-rimmed glasses. She's insanely trendy for her age, and I can't help but smile at her. As I approach, she stands up on her tiptoes and pulls me into a hug while finishing up her phone call.

"Lindsay," she says, shoving her phone into her large handbag before she loops the straps over the corner of her chair. "It's so good to see you."

"So good to see you too. How are you?"

"I'm good. Busy as ever. Still single." She raises an eyebrow and laughs. Elaine is the epitome of workaholic. She's lived her entire life in the news business and made it her priority. While part of me respects her work ethic and commitment to her career, part of me is sad for her. "I bet you're wondering why I asked you to meet me?"

"I am," I answer her curiously.

"You know Jack and I go way back. I was so disappointed to lose you to Phoenix, Lindsay, but I understood it. Trust me. I understood why you'd take that opportunity," she says with an animated sigh. I nod and listen intently and let her continue. "Jack and I had lunch and he briefly mentioned you weren't in Phoenix any longer. Of course, I pressed him for details, but he was very respectful and just said I needed to talk to you. Of course, everyone in this business talks. I made two phone calls and heard a few variations of what happened there." She tilts her head at me. I clear my throat and lace my fingers together on the table in front of me nervously. "I don't know exactly what happened there, Lindsay, and quite frankly, I don't care. You are talented beyond belief and you have a gift for telling a story. You were a part of the WXZI family for years, and I'd love to have you back if you want to come back."

"You're offering me a job?" I mumble.

"Of course I am. We need you. Our ratings have tanked, and I blame it on you leaving." She winks at me and I laugh at her.

"Elaine, I don't know what to say."

"Say you'll come back."

"I have to think more about it. Something I promised myself is that I wasn't going to jump back into a career that consumed me. And I'm not going to lie, WXZI consumed me. There's a lot that Jack probably hasn't told you…"

"Whatever you want, Lindsay. We'll make it work. Just tell me you'll come back," she interrupts me.

"I thought for sure I would be blacklisted from broadcast journalism," I say with a laugh.

"Oh, I'm sure there'll be questions about my sanity in hiring you after what went down in Phoenix, but you know me well enough to know I don't give a rat's ass what people think." I love her feisty personality and her no-nonsense attitude. "Just take a few days and think about it."

"I will."

She stands up and pulls her purse off the back of her chair. "I'm really glad you're home, Lindsay. We've all missed you."

"It's good to be home," I admit. Elaine's phone rings and, with a brisk wave, she disappears into the line of bodies waiting to order coffee while I remain seated, contemplating her offer. I smile and look around the Starbucks that is buzzing with people and positive energy. *Good things happen here,* I think to myself as I easily make a decision about the job offer. I grab a coffee to go as I run through the mental checklist of things I have to pack for my trip to Arizona and California.

# CHAPTER 23

## *Lindsay*

I waited a day to call Elaine and accept the position, so long as they were willing to work with me on keeping reasonable hours and were flexible with some of the appointments I'd like to maintain with my therapist and nutritionist. She didn't hesitate and we agreed that I'd start in two-weeks, which gives me time to get through Landon and Reagan's wedding and find a place to live. I search online for apartments while I wait to board my flight to Phoenix and I've found a couple of places that are close to the beach, yet still convenient to downtown. I spend the entire flight reading another book from Samantha and making a list of things to do when I get back to Wilmington.

My nerves finally settle in when I land in Phoenix. I'm blasted by heat once again when I step off the plane and into the jetway. Does it ever cool down here? I walk through the massive airport and exit to find Mike and Javier waiting for me. Mike is holding a piece of cardboard that has "Christianson" written in bold black letters. I laugh out loud and run over to him, jumping into his hug.

"Look. At. You," he says, squeezing me. Javier picks up my suitcase, which fell over when I jumped into Mike's arms. "You look amazing."

"I feel amazing," I tell him as he sets me back onto my feet.

"Welcome back," Javier says, giving me a quick hug.

"Thank you both for picking me up. I really appreciate it." Mike scoffs at me.

"Not a chance I was letting you sneak back into town without spending time with you." We start walking toward the elevators that will take us to the parking garage. "I can't believe you're leaving us for good, though." He sticks out his bottom lip in a pouty motion. "But I understand; we all do."

"I'm going to go into the office and talk to Rob tomorrow. I'm nervous."

"Don't be," he says kindly. "He's been asking if I've heard from you."

"I just don't want to see Amanda."

"Don't even think about that witch."

"Hard not to," I say, settling into the back seat of Javier's car.

The ride to the condo is full of laughs and catching up. I only begin to get nervous when we pull into the attached parking garage. I pull the keycard from my purse and hand it to Javier, who swipes it and the metal gate opens, allowing us to enter. Jack made arrangements for my leased Lexus to be returned, so Javier pulls into the empty spot for my condo.

Anxiety sets in as we ride quietly in the elevator to the twenty-second floor. Mike notices and gently pulls my hand into his, giving it a light squeeze. Javier carries my luggage and I hold the key to my condo in my hand. The elevator doors slide open and we step out into the quiet hallway. Mike nudges me, urging me to walk down the hall toward my door. My feet carry me down the narrow hall to the door, where I insert the key and twist it. I push the door open and step inside the darkened condo.

All the curtains had been pulled tightly closed over the floor-length windows and the air conditioning had been turned off, making the condo warm with heavy, dank air.

"Where's the thermostat?" Javier asks, setting my suitcase on the floor just inside the door.

"On the wall next to the master bedroom." I point toward the wall with the open door. Javier crosses the living room and starts pushing buttons on the keypad of the thermostat.

"Let's open this place up," Mike says, reaching for the long rod that hangs from all of the curtains. He pushes the long curtains open, securing them behind the finials on the wall. "That's better."

The warm afternoon sun pours into the condo and casts an amber glow throughout. The air conditioning kicks on and cool air starts filling the room. Javier carries my suitcase to the bedroom and I sit on the couch, quietly taking in the surroundings of the condo for the first time all over again. There are boxes packed and taped shut sitting on the kitchen island.

"I'll ship those," Mike says when he sees me eyeing them. "The only thing I didn't pack was your dresser. It just seemed too personal to have me rummaging through your intimates." He winks at me. "Your closet is packed in most of those tall boxes." He gestures toward the large wardrobe boxes. "If you pack up your dresser while you're here, I'll have all the boxes picked up and sent at the same time."

"Mike." I turn to look at him. "Thank you for everything."

"It's really no problem at all. I'm just glad you're feeling better."

"Mike, let's give Lindsay some time to get settled," Javier interjects. "I'm sure she's tired from the flight and might like some time to be alone." He raises his eyebrows and encourages Mike to get up.

"Call me if you need anything," Mike says, standing up. "And let me know when you're on your way over to the station tomorrow. I'll meet you in the reception area. I'm sure your access badge has been shut off."

"I will. Thank you both—for everything," I tell them as they leave. Javier nods at me as he closes the door behind them. I stretch out on the long couch with a throw pillow propped under my head and stare out the window at the afternoon sun that has just begun to set.

I jerk awake suddenly at the loud banging. It takes me a moment to remember that I'm in my condo in Phoenix. The moonlight illuminates the dark condo and I stumble into the kitchen to flip on some lights. The banging continues and I realize someone is out in the hall, knocking on Jonah's door. I'm unable to see anyone through the peephole and I turn the deadbolt lock on my door just as a precaution. I eye the stack of empty boxes in the corner and grab one as I head into the bedroom to pack up the last remaining items to be shipped back to North Carolina.

I set the box on the floor next to my bed and begin with the nightstand. I pull the drawer open and eye the contents. A book, some pictures, a notebook and pen, and the open box of condoms. I pull each condom out of the large box and count all nine of them. I walk them to the bathroom garbage and throw them in the trash along with the box they came in. I tie up the trash bag and toss it out the door and into the living room before moving on to the small toiletry closet in the bathroom. Emptying that closet of the handful of items that were in there, I tape the box closed and carry it to the kitchen, adding it to the pile of boxes all set to ship.

I pack one more box of clothing from my dresser before taking a quick shower and crawling into bed for the evening. My stomach twists with anxiety when I think about talking to Rob at the TV station tomorrow morning and cleaning out my desk—closing the door on that job and moving forward to my new life back in Wilmington.

As I lie in the dark, the mirror on my wall begins to shake from the beat of the bass next door and I lie sleepless, much like I did my first night in Phoenix; the irony. I push the sheet off of me and swing my legs over the side of the bed. I reach for my cellphone and swipe the screen. Pushing the contacts button, I scroll to Jonah's name and push the call button. Reaching over, I turn on the bedside lamp that sits on the nightstand while the phone rings. After the fourth ring, I get sent to voicemail. I end the call and set the phone back on my nightstand while I contemplate whether to go knock on his door.

My cellphone begins vibrating and I reach for it as Jonah's name flashes across the screen.

"Hello?" I answer quietly. Loud music and screaming voices fill the line in the background.

"Lindsay." His voice is cool, his attitude clipped. "You called?"

"Hi, Jonah." He doesn't respond. I can hear the music clearly through the phone as I sit deciding what to say to him. "Think you can turn the music down? I'm trying to sleep."

"Where are you?" he asks quickly.

"In my bed." With no other words said, the line goes dead. Suddenly, the mirror stops shaking, the music is shut off, and I lay my head back down on my pillow. I leave on the lamp on my nightstand and close my eyes. Not even five minutes later, there is a loud rap on my door and I take a deep breath, knowing that it's Jonah.

I walk through the dark living room, careful to avoid the coffee table and end tables as I make my way to the front door. I peek through the peephole and see Jonah with his forehead resting against my door. I flip the deadbolt, unlocking the door, and turn the handle. Jonah stands on wobbly legs as I pull the door open and braces himself against the doorframe. He smells of alcohol and nicotine.

"Jonah," I say as he smiles at me and stumbles.

"You're here."

"I am. You're drunk."

"I am. Can I come in?"

"No. I have an early appointment in the morning and I have to get to bed." He looks over my shoulder and sees the boxes stacked on and next to the kitchen island.

"You're moving?"

I nod quickly. "I am, back to North Carolina."

"No, Lindsay, wait…"

"Jonah," I cut him off. "We'll talk tomorrow." I place my hand on his chest to help steady him, but to also keep him from coming into my condo. "I promise. As soon as I'm back from my meeting, I'll stop by. You need to sleep—and shower," I say. The odor of alcohol is seeping from his skin.

"Can I sleep here?" He leans into me and I push back on him.

"No." My answer is firm and direct. "We'll talk tomorrow."

"Don't shut me out, Lindsay," he says quietly.

"Jonah," I say, my voice strong in warning. "We'll talk tomorrow." I step back and shut the door, turning the deadbolt. I stand momentarily, waiting to hear him shuffle next door, but I don't hear him leave. I retreat back to my bedroom, shutting off the light and crawling under the covers. I lay awake most of the night, a million thoughts swirling through my busy mind. I vaguely remember closing my eyes and drifting off to sleep just as the sun is beginning to rise.

My eyes flutter open to the sun bleeding through the sheer curtains of my room. I jump out of bed and quickly shower and dry my hair. I step into a multi-colored cotton shift dress and a pair of wedge heels. Nice enough for a meeting with Rob, but comfortable enough to pack up my desk at the same time. I spend a few minutes applying make-up and running a large curling iron through my already wavy hair. Satisfied with how I look, I feel good—confident.

Grabbing my cell phone and purse, I pound out a quick text message to Mike, letting him know I'm picking up coffees on my way to the office and I need his order. Pulling the door open, I find Jonah sitting in the hallway, his legs propped up and bent at the knees. His head is resting against the wall and his eyes are red and bloodshot.

"Jonah," I say, shutting the door behind me and locking it. "What are you doing out here?"

"Waiting for you." He swallows hard and I watch his Adam's apple jump slightly in his neck.

"I told you I had an appointment this morning and I would talk to you when I got back."

"You can't leave," he says quietly. I sigh and bend down next to him.

"Go rest. I promise to come over in a couple of hours. Come on." I tug on his arm, coaxing him to stand up. He pushes himself upward and leans against the wall to balance himself. "Go shower. I'll be over as soon as I'm done with my appointment." He nods and walks alongside me to his condo as I walk to the elevator. I press the call button and wait while Jonah leans against his door, staring at me.

"You're beautiful," he says with his hand on the door handle.

"Thank you," I reply quietly. "You're a mess," I joke with him, but I smile in return as I step into the elevator.

"No doubt," I hear him say as the elevator doors close behind me.

Thirty minutes later, I'm standing in the lobby of the TV station, holding two cups of coffee and wearing a nervous smile on my face. The large, wooden door opens and Mike finally greets me, pulling his cup of coffee from my hand.

"Morning," he says, pressing an air kiss next to my cheek.

"Morning," I respond and follow him through the door and down the hallway back to the offices. My heart races as Rob's office comes into view.

"He knows you're coming. I told him after the morning production meeting," Mike says. "I've got a box in your cube. When you're through in Rob's office, meet me there," he says with a smile. "Don't be nervous. He's excited to see you."

"I look like I'm going to barf, don't I?"

"Yes," he says with a laugh. "Just go get it over with." With his encouragement, I stride over to the glass door and knock twice. Rob looks up from his desk and a smile stretches across his bearded face. He waves me in and I turn the handle on his office door.

"Lindsay," he says excitedly.

"Hi, Rob."

"So good to see you. You look great." I shut the door behind me and stand nervously juggling my coffee from one hand to the other and back again. "Please sit down."

I set the cup of coffee on Rob's desk as I sit down and straighten out my dress and cross my legs. Once I'm situated I take a quick sip of the coffee in hopes to calm the uneasiness in my voice.

"Thanks for seeing me."

"I'm really glad you came by. How are you doing?" He sits in his leather chair, his hands folded neatly in his lap.

"I'm doing really, really well. Thank you for asking."

"You look happy."

"I am. I didn't realize how miserable I was until it was too late. Rob, I owe you an apology. You took a chance on me and I let you down. A part of me was excited for this opportunity, but another part of me was absolutely miserable leaving North Carolina. I was trying to prove myself to you and Jack and I was self-destructing at the same time." He holds up his hand to stop me.

"Lindsay. You have the talent to make it in a market this size. Your ability to tell a story is like very few others I've seen. You're young and you're ambitious, but I knew your heart wasn't here."

"It wasn't," I confirm. "I shouldn't have acted, or should I say, reacted to Amanda the way I did."

He rolls his eyes. "Between you and me, she deserved much worse than what you handed to her. I just couldn't have that happen in the office on my watch," he smirks. "I really do wish nothing but the best for you, and I'm actually really disappointed to see you go."

"I was pretty sure that breaking contract with you was going to tank my career." He shakes his head.

"I told Jack I wouldn't let that happen. Don't get me wrong. It was a pretty big inconvenience explaining your sudden departure, and subsequently finding your replacement, but in the end, everything always works out how it should."

I breathe a huge sigh of relief. "Thank you for everything. I mean it." He nods his head.

"So what are your plans?" he asks.

"Surprisingly, WXZI offered me my position back. I still have to work out all the details, but my priorities have changed and they're willing to work with that." I smile when I think about spending more time focusing on me. Spending days doing things I love other than working every single day for over twelve hours.

"Good." He smiles. "I knew Jack would take care of you."

I stand up from my chair and adjust the purse that hangs from my shoulder and the cup of coffee in my hand.

"Thank you again, Rob."

"Keep in touch, Lindsay. I'm sure our paths will cross again someday."

"I hope they will," I admit honestly. I leave his office, shutting the door behind me. Mike stands in the hall just outside my cube entrance, waiting for me. I glide down the hallway, happy that the burden of talking to Rob is over and went better than I anticipated. Every day, a little weight I've been carrying seems suddenly to lift.

"How'd it go?" Mike asks reluctantly as I duck into my cube.

"Actually, really good. He was great."

"Told you," he smirks.

"You're just like my brother… you always have to be right," I joke with him. I take a box from the floor and set it on my desk, filling it with the two picture frames I have sitting on my desk and a few notebooks. My bottom drawer holds a make-up bag and four pairs of shoes that I always kept at the office as "back-up." I shove all of that into the box and fold the flaps of the box, securing the top.

"That's it?" Mike asks.

I let out a little chuckle. "That's it. I hardly had time to settle in."

"Well, if I find anything else, I'll ship it with all your other boxes."

I sit in my desk chair and swing the chair from side to side slowly. "What did I do to deserve such a good friend?" I ask Mike seriously.

"Good people attract good people, Lindsay. What can I say? We're the best," he smirks.

"I'm going to miss you."

"I'm going to miss you too, Lindsay." I push myself up out of my desk chair and Mike picks up my box. "When are you headed back to North Carolina?" he asks.

"Friday morning. I'm headed to Orange County tomorrow to see my friend, Jess." Mike sets the box down at his desk and walks me to the front reception area of the TV station.

"Give me a hug," he says, pulling me to him. He wraps his arms around me and gives me a good squeeze. "Let me know you've made it back, okay?"

"I will." My throat tightens and I get a little teary saying goodbye to Mike. "Send my love to Javier," I say, my voice cracking.

"Will do," he says, releasing me from his hug. I pull the sunglasses from the top of my head down and put them on. I fake a smile and blow a kiss to Mike as I step out the front doors of the TV station. The walk back to my condo is quick; the office was only five or six blocks away, but I never walked it, I always drove. Today, I take my time returning to the condo, even though the late morning sun burns hot on my face. I notice the little shops and restaurants that I always drove right past, and a small boutique with trendy clothes and jewelry. I stop inside and purchase a necklace for Jess, a peace offering.

By the time I make it back to my condo, the hallway is clear, which means Jonah must safely be inside his. The hall is clear of Jonah, yet the smell of stale booze and cigarettes still hangs in the air. Rather than prolong the inevitable, I knock on his door and wait for him to answer. When he doesn't answer, I knock again and wait. This time, the door opens slowly and Jonah stands in a pair of sweat pants and nothing else. His chest is bare and his hair is messy. I've obviously woken him up.

"I can come back later," I say, taking a step backwards.

"No. Come in," he says, rubbing his eyes. "I've been waiting to talk to you." I inhale sharply when I step through the door and into his condo. His kitchen is a disaster; every countertop surface is covered in liquor bottles, beer cans, and cups half full of god only knows what. My shoes cling to the sticky wood floor as I walk through the living room.

"Sorry about the mess," he says with a little laugh. "When did you get back?" he asks as he motions for me to take a seat on his black leather sofa. I eye the couch suspiciously, choosing to remain standing.

"Yesterday. I'm leaving tomorrow."

"For good?"

"Yeah. I took a job back in Wilmington," I say quietly. We stand in awkward silence as we take in the sight of each other. Under clear and sober eyes, Jonah looks so much younger than I remember. His hair has grown out and patches of facial hair are growing along his jawline. I shift uncomfortably from foot to foot as I ponder the right words to use for what I have to say.

"Jonah, what happened with us…" He sighs loudly and laces his fingers behind his head, his tan chest and muscular stomach on full display right in front of me. "It should never have happened."

"It wasn't just a one-night thing for me," he says quietly.

"I don't know how to say this without upsetting you, so bear with me. Jonah, you've been a great friend to me, but my heart belongs to someone else. What happened with us wasn't love for me."

"So you used me?"

I swallow hard and look directly at him. "I was so messed up. Pills, alcohol, starving myself." I hang my head in disgust at myself and my behaviors. "I think it's fair to say I used you. I used you to try to feel something—anything. I was lonely and wanted to be wanted. The only thing it did was hurt you and make me hate myself."

"Nice," he says sarcastically.

"I'm sorry, Jonah. I never wanted to hurt you. Honestly, you and I are in such different places in our lives. Even if I wasn't in love with someone else, I'm not sure we would have been a good fit together."

"So that's it?" He exhales loudly. "You're sorry, you feel bad… yada yada yada."

"Jonah, please don't be like that."

"Like what? Upset?"

"Yeah."

"Well, I am upset. Goddammit, Lindsay, the last time I saw you, you were driving away with some guy I'd never seen. Do you know how worried I was? I called and left you numerous voicemails and text messages and you never responded. Now all you can say is 'I'm sorry?' He drops his hands from his head and walks over to me, resting his hands on top of my shoulders at the base of my neck. His thumbs rub my neck and he tilts my head back so that I'm looking directly at him. "Give me one more night," he whispers, his voice strained. "I need one more night with you, Lindsay." His eyes are red and his voice pulls with emotion. "Let me show you how I feel."

"I'm sorry, I can't," I whisper. "I'm so sorry."

"So am I." He leans in to kiss me and I pull away from him. His face twists in disgust.

"Are you done?" he asks abruptly, startling me. I nod my head. "Good; you can leave now."

I feel defeated. I didn't expect Jonah to be happy, but I didn't expect him to be so angry. I walk as fast as I can to the door and open it. I look back over my shoulder at him standing in the exact place I left him.

"I'm sorry, Jonah. I hope you can forgive me." He doesn't reply before I shut the door and hurry back to my condo.

I spend the evening on my balcony eating Thai food from a takeout container and watching the city bustling below me. I never took advantage of my patio and the amazing views of Phoenix it had to offer. I watch the sun set and the city lights come to life twenty-two stories below me. Closing up the patio and closing the curtains, I run a bath and spend the next hour soaking in a bubble bath and reading. I have a late morning flight to Orange County and about a ninety-minute drive to Santa Ruiz. I sent a text message to Gabe and he confirmed Jess would be home and he was grateful to hear I was coming. I change into my pajamas and finish reading in bed for another hour, finishing another novel before falling quickly to sleep.

I wake refreshed and ready for California. I wash my face, brush my teeth, and pack my small carry-on suitcase. I box up the last remaining items in a small box and tape it shut. I leave Mike a note on the counter, thanking him again for shipping these boxes back to me. I close all the curtains in the condo and turn the air conditioner off, just as it was when I arrived two days ago. Pulling my suitcase behind me, I juggle my oversized handbag on my shoulder as I close the condo door and lock it, closing yet another chapter in my story.

I wait in the lobby of my building for the cab to arrive and I text Landon to let him know that I'm on my way to California. I glance at my reflection in the mirrored wall and smile with my progress. Even in short cut-off jean shorts and a cream three-quarter sleeve blouse, I can see my curves coming back. My face is fuller and the dark circles from under my eyes are gone. I look refreshed. My hair hangs long and loose and I have chunky gold jewelry on and brown strappy sandals.

I hear a horn honk and see the yellow cab at the curb. Pulling my suitcase, I push the glass doors open and out into the Phoenix heat for the last time. I glance over my shoulder and back at my building just in time to see Jonah running toward me.

"Lindsay," he says, out of breath. The cab driver exits the car and lifts my suitcase, putting it in the trunk.

"Jonah," I say, scrunching my eyebrows together in confusion. This is a far cry from the Jonah I left upset in his condo yesterday.

"I had to see you one last time before you go." Sweat trickles from his hairline and down his temple. I look back at the cab and the driver is back in his seat, tapping his finger on the steering wheel.

"I have to go," I mumble and motion to the cab over my

shoulder. In two strides, Jonah invades my space. He grabs my head with his hands and pulls me into a kiss. Just as quickly as he kisses me, he releases me and steps back. Laughing hysterically, he looks at me, his brown eyes wild, and a giant smile spread across his tan face. "That's because you're beautiful. You'll never be just one night to me. Good luck to you, Lindsay Lou!" And as fast as he ran up to me, he's gone. The cab driver shakes his head as I slide into the back seat, wondering what in the hell just happened.

"Lindsay Lou?" I whisper to myself, questioning the nickname. I pull my phone from my purse and shoot him a text message

*"You're insane."* My phone beeps almost immediately.

*"I am, but I needed to see you smile before you left."*

*"I'm smiling because you're nuts."*

*"I know. Take care of yourself."*

*"You too, Jonah."*

And just like that, I can smile and remember Jonah as a happy memory of my time in Phoenix.

I board the plane in Phoenix and hardly have time to get settled before we start to descend into Orange County, California. It's barely an hour-long flight and even though it's warm in California, it's considerably cooler than Phoenix. I know I'm miles from the ocean, but having grown up near the water, I can still smell it. It's close enough. I spend the next hour getting my rental car and programming Jess and Gabe's address into my navigation system. I merge into the insane California traffic and begin my journey to Santa Ruiz.

Two and half hours later, after I've white knuckled the bumper-to-bumper Southern California traffic and made one stop for the restrooms, I'm pulling into a quaint older neighborhood in Santa Ruiz. I park in front of the address that Gabe sent me and smile when I see the cute bungalow. It's been completely remodeled and almost looks brand new. There is a gorgeous wraparound porch with a giant porch swing and I spot Jess immediately in the swing. She doesn't notice I've pulled up because she's lost in a book.

I kill the engine and step out of the car just in time to see Gabe come out the front door. He smiles at me and that's when Jess looks up from her book. She stands up from the swing and sets her book down behind her. I walk up the driveway and Jess comes down the steps of the porch, meeting me on the sidewalk.

"Lindsay?" she says with a look of disbelief on her face. Her long, brown hair blows in the breeze and her fingers wrap themselves around the end of her long-sleeved t-shirt.

"Hi, Jess." I smile at her.

"What are you doing here?"

"I was hoping to talk to you if that would be okay?" My heart hammers in my chest as I look at my best friend, the one I hurt so badly with my words. She's wearing her poker face, and I can't tell if she's happy or upset to see me.

"Yes, of course. Do you want to come inside? I have water or lemonade…"

"Lemonade would be great." I follow her up the steps of her front porch and onto the wooden patio. Gabe smiles at me as he leans against a large, wooden pillar.

"Nice to see you again, Linds," he says warmly. I reach out and give him a hug.

"Thank you," I whisper in his ear. He nods and gives me a

quick hug back before I release him and follow Jess into the house. Stepping inside, I catch my breath at how beautiful their house is. Real wood floors and gorgeous custom windows all trimmed in custom wood trim and molding. The finishes are all modern and trendy, but the furnishings make the house warm, comfortable, and inviting. I follow Jess into the kitchen, where she's filling two glasses with lemonade.

"Let's go sit out back." She gestures to the back patio. There is a set of French doors off the kitchen that lead us out to a huge wood deck in the backyard. There is built-in seating around the edge of the deck, but a huge patio table sits in the center of the deck and we take a seat at the table. I sink into the oversized plush chairs and enjoy the cool breeze on my face.

"I guess you'd like me to explain what I'm doing here, huh?" I smile at Jess. She nods as she takes a sip of lemonade and swallows. "I came here to apologize, Jess. I am so sorry for how I treated you in Phoenix. I'd love to blame it on the pills, the wine; anything other than me—but I can't. I was a horrible friend and placed blame on you when it should have been on me."

I watch her large, green eyes look me over. She's skeptical, and I don't blame her. "I accept your apology," she says quietly. She relaxes a bit and sits back into her chair. Her face is calm, forgiving.

"That's it? You forgive me just like that?"

She lets out a long sigh before she smiles genuinely at me. "If there was anything your brother taught me while I was in North Carolina, it's that you have to forgive to move forward. We'd all be stuck in a vicious cycle of anger, hate, and resentment if we didn't learn how to forgive others—but most importantly, ourselves."

"He taught you that? Landon? Our Landon?"

She chuckles. "Well, your Landon, not my Landon. But yes, he did." I see her fingers go to her wrist, where she unknowingly rubs her white script tattoo.

"I didn't know he was so deep," I remark and look out into the backyard, where a tire swing hangs from a huge oak tree and rocks from side to side in the breeze.

"I'll always be your friend, Lindsay. Always. That's what friends do. They forgive each other when they hurt one another."

"I needed to hear that," I say, swallowing down a newly formed lump in my throat. We spend the next few minutes in complete silence, comfortable in each other's presence. Birds are chirping, and the sun is beginning to set.

"I should probably get going," I finally say, breaking the silence.

"Where are you going?"

"I'm not exactly sure. I was just going to spend the next couple of days checking out the coast. I've never been to California."

"Stay with us. I'll take you to Santa Barbara and Laguna Beach. Gabe has to work, so I'll be alone anyway. Please stay," she begs.

"Are you sure you don't mind the company?"

"Not at all. We're going to dinner at Gabe's parents' house tonight. You'll get to meet all of the Garcias."

"They won't mind?"

"Are you kidding me? They'll love it. They are the best."

Through the glass doors, I see Gabe standing at the kitchen island with another guy that looks almost identical to him, just a little bulkier and a little taller. Both are drinking a beer and laughing.

"That's Luke," Jess says with a smile. "Gabe's older brother.

He's taken or I might try to set you up with him." She laughs.

I hold up my hands in defense. "I don't need any more man drama, trust me." We both laugh together.

"Is it safe to come out?" Gabe pokes his head out the door, asking Jess and me. Still laughing, she nods and smiles. Gabe and Luke join us at the table and we spend the next hour talking and laughing. My heart thrums with happiness just sitting here with my friend, content and laughing.

Gabe retrieves my suitcase from the car while Jess gets me settled in the guest room before we leave for dinner. It's a short walk three houses down the street to Gabe and Luke's parents' house for dinner. My stomach growls immediately when we step in the door and into the kitchen. I'm not sure what's cooking, but it smells amazing.

"*Mijo, Mija*," Gabe's mom says when we walk in the door. She walks around the L-shaped peninsula and pulls Gabe into a hug. She kisses him on the cheek and he blushes slightly, but he lets her fuss over him. She does the exact same thing to Luke, then Jess. I smile at how loving she is with her two sons and Jess.

"*Mija*, welcome," she says, pulling me into a warm embrace.

"Mom, this is Lindsay, my friend from North Carolina. We worked together when I was in Wilmington. Lindsay, this is Angelica, Gabe's mom, and John, Gabe's father."

"So nice to meet you, Lindsay," Angelica says with a smile. John shakes my hand and quietly disappears into the living room.

"Nice to meet you too. I hope it's okay that I join y'all." Her eyes light up when I say "y'all."

"We have more food than we'll ever eat. We're happy you were able to join us." With that, Gabe pulls two beers from the fridge and hands one to Luke. The guys quickly retreat to the living room where they make themselves comfortable and watch a football game on the TV. Jess grabs an apron and starts helping in the kitchen without any direction from Angelica.

"Is there anything I can do to help you, other than touch the food?" Angelica looks at me and her eyes narrow slightly. "I mean you don't want me touching your food. I'm a horrible cook— terrible, actually—and I ruin anything I touch."

"Then let me teach you," she says kindly. She reaches out and pulls me toward the counter where she has all kinds of fruits and vegetables sitting alongside a cutting board and knife.

"You're going to make the guacamole." She smiles and taps my forearm. Her brown eyes shine under the bright kitchen spotlights.

"I think this is a bad idea," I mumble and she shushes me. She is patient and kind as she shows me how to cut open avocados and how to remove the pit, and then cut the ripe flesh inside the skin into small squares. We each cut up two avocados. She finely dices an onion while she has me pulling cilantro leaves off the stem. In a large bowl, I begin smashing and mixing the avocados and onions while she adds salt and pepper along with the cilantro and diced tomatoes. She finishes it off by squeezing some fresh lime juice into the bowl. With a few more stirs, we have an amazing-looking guacamole.

She pulls a small teaspoon from the drawer. "Taste it," she says as I scoop a small amount onto the spoon. "Does it need more salt?"

"I think it tastes really good."

She scoops a small amount on a spoon for herself and tastes it, nodding in agreement. "It does. Those avocados were perfect," she says, setting the spoon in the sink. She transfers the guacamole to a smaller bowl and hands it to me. "Will you set this on the table and gather the men? We'll be ready to eat in just a minute."

I hadn't noticed that Jess has pulled a huge pan of enchiladas from the oven that are already resting on the dining room table and she's now stirring a huge bowl of Spanish rice. I set the bowl of guacamole in the center of the table and walk to the living room to get the guys. Gabe is lying on a loveseat with his feet propped up on the arm and Luke sits on the couch, his legs stretched out and resting on the coffee table. John sits in his recliner, nodding off while Gabe and Luke talk about the football game.

"Dinner's ready," I announce. Gabe sits up quickly and grabs his beer from the coffee table. Luke swings his leg over to the recliner and nudges John awake. All three men rise and quickly take their places at the dining room table as Angelica places a steaming pot of beans on the table. Jess sits next to Gabe and I sit next to her. There are still two open seats at the table. "Ava and Heather usually take those two seats," John says, pointing to the two open seats. "You're in Adrian's seat."

"Adrian is Ava's ex," Jess says quietly, filling me in. "And Heather is Luke's girlfriend." Angelica takes a seat next to John and reaches out to take his hand. "A blessing," she says quietly and everyone bows their head.

"Thank you, Lord, for the food on our table, our health, our family, and please bless our guest, Lindsay. In Jesus' name."

"Amen," everyone says in unison. The men all dive for different dishes and start plating beans, enchiladas, and rice. I laugh quietly at the chaos that ensues when three grown men are clearly hungry. Plates are passed and, before long, I've been served a plate of shredded beef enchiladas with some rice and beans, along with some fresh guacamole. The sauce that covers the enchiladas is divine, and Angelica informs me that she made it from scratch. *Of course she did.*

We fall into easy conversation, spending the better portion of the next hour laughing and sharing stories. Everyone laughs as Gabe and Luke tell stories that they've encountered on the job as firemen, and I smile when I think about how much it reminds me of Landon and Matt and the stories they'd relive and tell. I've never felt so immediately accepted and welcome before, and I understand how Jess loves this family so much.

Gabe, Jess, and I walk down the dark street back to their house. I shower and hang up a few things in the closet before finding Gabe and Jess on the couch, watching a movie. Jess is curled up in the fetal position, sound asleep, her head resting on Gabe's lap. His hand rests protectively on her back and he's watching the movie.

"Hey," he says, turning down the volume as I take a seat on the sectional.

"Whatcha watching?" I ask quietly, pulling a throw pillow into my lap and resting my hands on top of it.

"*Captain America.*"

"I can see why she fell asleep." I laugh quietly. Gabe shifts carefully to look at me.

"I'm really glad you came to talk to Jess."

"I am too. Thank you for helping me arrange it." He nods and offers me a small smile. "Gabe, I never got the chance to thank you for helping Jess take care of me when I fell apart in

Phoenix. I mean, if you weren't there, I don't know what would have happened."

"Lindsay, we all fall apart. We're human. I'm just glad we were there to help you when it happened."

I take a deep, cleansing breath. "I won't see you before I leave," I whisper. "Take care of her."

"I always will. Travel safe and come visit us soon."

"I will. I really like it here. Your family is amazing. You're really lucky."

"They are," he says. "Goodnight, Lindsay."

I settle into bed and spend the next hour reading before finally falling asleep with another huge weight lifted off of my shoulders.

I scratch the tip of my nose and grumble at the light that's filtering in the large window in the bedroom. I pull the covers up closer to my chin just as I hear Jess start laughing. My eyes fly open and there Jess sits on the bed next to me.

"What are you doing?"

"Waking your ass up."

"Were you tickling my nose?"

"Maybe. Come on. I made breakfast, then we're driving to Laguna Beach for the day." She pulls back the covers and pushes me toward the edge of the bed.

"I'm getting up," I mumble at her as my feet hit the floor. I brush my teeth and quickly change and get ready for the day. Pulling my hair into a ponytail and keeping my makeup simple with just some light eye shadow and lip gloss. I'm all about

California casual in my sundress and wedge sandals.

Jess meets me in the kitchen with a carafe of coffee and a plate of food. The sun is bright and warm this morning, so we decide to eat outside on the patio. I actually enjoy the scrambled eggs, turkey bacon, and cut-up fresh fruit Jess prepared while we talked.

"So Santa Barbara and Laguna Beach," she says with a bright smile. "Two of my favorite places. I can't wait to show you around. There are the neatest little boutiques, and amazing little cafés."

"Sounds like heaven," I admit. "I can't believe that I only have two days left with you."

"I know, but I can't believe you're flying home on Friday, the day of your brother's wedding rehearsal. Maybe you should go on Thursday so you're not so exhausted."

"I needed to take this time for me. Reagan and Landon understood. Plus, I've helped Reagan get everything ready for the wedding. All I have to do is show up."

"I still can't believe he's getting married before me." Jess rolls her eyes sarcastically.

"What if it was you two?" I say seriously, sipping my coffee.

She shakes her head aggressively. "Nope. I love him to death, but we would never have worked. We're both too damaged individually to work as a whole." Jess sips on her coffee and appears lost in her thoughts for a moment. "Plus, it sounds like he found someone perfect for him."

"He really did," I admit. "She's amazing and they make a really great couple."

"I'm happy for him. I really am."

My last two days in California are a whirlwind of shopping, beaches, diners, cafes, coffee shops, and bookstores. My heart skipped a beat when I helped Jess pick out the perfect wedding dress for her wedding next spring, and my heart felt genuine sorrow when I had to hug my friend at the airport and say goodbye.

As I sit at my gate, ready to board my flight back to North Carolina, I'm overcome with emotions. I fight back tears as I think about the forgiveness those I've hurt have shown me and how much I needed it from them. The last person, the person I care about the most, I suspect won't be as forgiving.

As I lose myself in thoughts of talking to Matt, I hear the gate attendant announce that my flight will be delayed. *Shit.*

# CHAPTER 24

## *Lindsay*

Landing in Charlotte, I race to the customer service counter in hopes of rebooking a flight to Wilmington. Unfortunately, the next flight isn't until later this evening, and not only would I miss the rehearsal, but the dinner afterward. I glance at my phone and, if I can get a rental car in the next thirty minutes, I will at least make the rehearsal dinner. I frantically call Reagan and explain my situation.

I whisper a quiet prayer of thanks that my new sister-in-law isn't Bridezilla. She completely remained calm about my impending absence from the wedding rehearsal at the church. I drive as fast as feasibly and legally possible to get to Wilmington in record time. Pulling into the parking lot of the upscale steakhouse where the rehearsal dinner is being held, I realize I look like a mess. I slip into the restaurant restroom and spend a few minutes combing my hair and reapplying my make-up so that I look somewhat presentable.

My palms sweat when I think about seeing many of the

people in attendance for the first time since rehab and my stomach does small flips. After a small pep-talk and one last application of lip gloss, I snake through the sea of tables to the party room located off to the side of the steakhouse. There are eight large, rectangle tables that hold eight people to a table and every spot is taken except for one—next to Matt.

My heart races as my mom waves me over to the table. There is a commotion of sorts while people shuffle and my heart sinks when Matt moves to the end of the table and my mom takes his spot.

"Nice of you to join us, Linds," Landon scoffs jokingly.

"Shut up. I've been through hell and back to get here." He leans in and presses a kiss to my cheek.

"I'm kidding. I love you. I'm just glad you made it back."

"I'm so sorry I missed the rehearsal."

"You didn't miss much. You walk down the aisle and stand next to Reagan. I think you can handle that."

"I think I can." I wink at him.

Reagan and I are the only ones not indulging in wine tonight and we exchange glances in a show of support to each other. Waiters and waitresses fill the center of the tables with a variety of hors d'oeuvres and the room is full of laughter. People are standing about chatting and enjoying themselves. The room is dimly lit, and small candles situated on each table fill the room with a hazy, low light. Reagan is wearing a cream shift dress and looks absolutely stunning with her long, dark brown hair in loose curls and Landon wears a black suit that makes his bright blue eyes stand out.

My mom and Louis are deep in conversation and I sit back and breathe for what feels like the first time today. I glance around the room and see familiar faces, but the only face I'm drawn to is Matt's. His dark brown hair is perfectly styled and he looks peaceful—happy as he laughs with the man he's talking to. He catches me looking at him and offers me a stiff smile before looking away quickly. This is what we've become—strangers that exchange half-hearted smiles.

Dinner is served and, while conversation bustles around me, I retreat within, remaining quiet—a listener, not a talker. I finally understand why Samantha was so introverted. Sometimes, it's easier to withdraw from the reality around you and enjoy the fantasy reality in a fictional novel. I want nothing more than to crawl into bed and read right now.

"Everything okay?" Landon asks quietly as he leans in.

"Yeah. I'm just tired. I think I'm going to take off soon and rest so I'm ready for tomorrow. Oh, before I forget, Jess wanted me to give you this." I pull an envelope from my purse and hand it to him. He reaches for it and stares at his and Reagan's names scrawled on the linen envelope.

"Should I open it here?" he asks tentatively. I shrug.

"I can't imagine it's anything that others shouldn't see." He chuckles.

"Good point." Sliding his finger under the flap, he tears the envelope open and pulls out a white card that has a wedding greeting on the front. I lean in to read it with him. He opens the card and a gift card falls out and into his lap, but we both stay focused on reading the handwriting that's beautifully written.

*"Landon and Reagan,*
*Life has a funny way of bringing people together—but it's the love that two people share that keeps them together. May your life together be full of*

*happiness, health, and infinite blessings. My prayers are with you today as you start your lives together.*

*All my love,*

*Jessica"*

"That was really nice of her," I remark at the note inside the card. Landon seems to re-read it again.

"It was," he says finally, picking up the gift card and placing it back inside the card. "Can you put this in your purse and take it home so I don't lose it?"

"Yeah, of course. I think I'm going to head out now anyway. Is it rude to cut out early since I arrived late?" I laugh guiltily.

"I'm pretty sure everyone will understand. You've had a long day."

"Happy last night as a single man," I say, winking at him. "I'm really, really happy for you."

For as long as I can remember, it was always just Landon and me. In the last year, we've welcomed our mom back into our lives and are building a relationship with her and now we welcome Reagan into the craziness.

"Who thought we'd actually end up with a *real* family?" he asks, taking a sip of water.

"Lan, that's something I always said I wanted. A *real* family, but what I've learned the last few months is that even when it was just you and me, we were a *real* family." He nods. "Okay, I'm going to go before I start crying." I stand up and set my napkin on the table. Pulling my purse onto my shoulder, I lean over and kiss him on the cheek. He stands up quickly and pulls me into an embrace, holding onto me tightly, just like he did when we were kids. It's warm and comforting.

As tears fill my eyes, I glance to Reagan, who is wiping tears from hers. Louis stands up and raises his wine glass. Landon finally releases me as I swat away tears that have slipped onto my cheeks.

"A toast to new beginnings," he says.

"To new beginnings," everyone repeats. I catch at quick glance at Matt, who is watching Landon and me with no emotion on his face.

"I have to go. See you in the morning."

"Night, little sister."

# CHAPTER 25

## Matt

Standing in the vestibule of the church, I watch Landon wipe the sweat from his palms onto his tuxedo jacket.

"You can't be nervous." I laugh at him.

"Hell yeah, I can. I mean, I'm not nervous to get married. I'm nervous about standing in front of all those people. We should have just eloped."

"And deny Reagan the wedding of her dreams? I wouldn't have let you do that to her."

"This is why you're my best friend, Matty. You keep my ass in line." I laugh and shake my head at him.

"Always." I reach out to shake his hand and pull him into a half-hug. "I'm really happy for you two."

"Thanks, man."

The pastor pops his head in the door. "You men ready?"

"Let's do this," Landon says quietly, looking between me and his other groomsman, Rob, Reagan's brother. We file out of the room and into the packed church, taking our positions on the stairs of the altar. Standing quietly, Landon focuses on the huge wooden doors at the back of the church. I notice him taking a couple of deep breaths as he rocks back and forth from foot to foot, flexing and unflexing his hands.

The organ starts playing and, on cue, the doors in the back of the church open, spilling bright sunlight into the dim chapel. Everyone stands up and turns around to look at the back of the church and Landon glances over at me.

"Ready?" I mouth to him, and he nods with a giant smile. Reagan's friend from college and bridesmaid, Lauren, begins her walk down the church aisle. As she nears the altar, I see Lindsay step into view. I hold my breath as she makes the long walk down the aisle. You can see her bright blue eyes first, followed by a giant smile on her face. I've never in my life seen a more beautiful woman. Her skin is tan and her blonde hair hangs in long waves down her back.

Landon and Lindsay share an affectionate smile and it reminds me how special their relationship is. As I look to the back of the church, Reagan steps into view, and I can hear audible gasps. As Reagan reaches the altar on her father's arm, Landon steps down to greet them. I steal a glance at Lindsay, who wipes a tear from her cheek while still wearing a genuine smile.

The ceremony is brief but heartfelt. Vows are exchanged, but I pay little attention as my focus is on Lindsay and how much I truly miss her. My heart aches for her. I make a promise to myself to talk to her tonight—to apologize for not supporting her. I wonder if the outcome for her would have been different had I been more supportive.

With a kiss and the confirmation of husband and wife from the pastor, everyone claps for Landon and Reagan. As happy as I am for my best friend, my heart is hollow without Lindsay. We spend the next hour taking pictures while the rest of the guests wait for us at the reception hall. I keep looking for a brief minute to pull Lindsay aside and say hello, start the conversation, but before I know it, she's in the limo with her mom and stepfather and is gone again.

The reception is a cluster of activity. Greeting and talking to guests while making sure Melissa is not ignored. We agreed to come as friends, but I can imagine how this looks to Lindsay or anyone else, for that matter. It amazes me how fast the evening passes because, in my head, time stands still. I watch Lindsay gracefully move from table to table, catching up with old friends and family. Her smile is warm and inviting, and she genuinely looks happy.

I promise myself I won't leave tonight without talking to her, even though my heart tells me she's moved on.

# CHAPTER 26

## Lindsay

The deejay announces, "Welcome Mr. and Mrs. Landon Christianson." Landon and Reagan take to the wooden dance floor for their first dance as husband and wife to the applause of the crowd. I've never seen my brother so happy, and my heart feels genuine happiness for the first time in a long time.

I lean against the wall with my glass of seltzer water and take in the beautiful ballroom. Everything is elegant and perfect, of course. I'd expect nothing else with Reagan's tastes in style. From silk-covered chairs to enormous bouquets on every table, this is a wedding out of *Modern Bride* magazine.

"They're good together." His voice pulls me from my thoughts. I turn to find Matt leaning against the wall beside me. His tuxedo fits perfectly to his tall, lean body. This is the first time he's talked to me since the day I left for treatment. Even as best man and maid of honor, we've not spoken until now. We stole glances at each other at the rehearsal dinner last night—neither of us brave enough to speak to the other. I should have known it would be Matt to make the first move—I've always been the weaker one.

"They are." I smile and watch my brother and new sister-in-law as they hold each other and dance. "I'm just happy that he's happy," I admit.

"So am I," Matt agrees. "I honestly wasn't sure we'd ever see the day he got married." He chuckles, and I laugh in return.

"I'm not sure anyone thought we'd see this day," I say, twirling the small, red straw in my water. "Seltzer water, with a twist of lime," I tell him as I raise the glass and show him. I'm not sure why I feel the need to let him know what I'm drinking, but I sensed maybe his sudden arrival was to make sure I hadn't fallen off the proverbial wagon and was drinking myself into oblivion at my brother's wedding.

"I'm proud of you, Lindsay." For some reason, this admission, this vote of confidence in me immediately sends tears to my eyes, and my throat tightens. Maybe because I've felt like nothing more than a complete disappointment to everyone and because I feel like I've let down everyone I love.

"Thanks." I'm barely able to squeak out around my constricted throat.

"You look good—healthy."

"I feel good, actually." My responses are short, and the conversation is awkward, but there is a feeling of contentment between us—maybe we'll be able to find ourselves in a place where we can be friends. I look at the crowded ballroom full of friends and new family and I see new beginnings. A smile tugs at the corner of my mouth. We stand quietly and take in the extravagant party around us.

"Matt." I say his name like so many times before to get his attention. This time, there is an unwavering need in my tone. "Do you believe people deserve second chances?" His dark eyes find mine and he contemplates his answer.

"I believe there are some people who deserve an infinite number of chances."

"Why?"

"Because some people are worth that. You're worth that, Lindsay."

I turn to him and smile. His dark brown eyes glisten in the low lights of the reception hall. His face is serious, yet soft. I drop my eyes to my feet and look away, feeling tears threatening to form behind them. Looking up, I spot Melissa in the center of the room, standing next to a large, round table, her red hair pulled up into a twist and her eyes scanning the crowd, presumably looking for Matt.

"I think someone is looking for you." I nod at Melissa. "You should probably go dance with her." I don't know why these words hurt so badly, but they do. Maybe it's my way of telling him it's okay to move on—I've given him my permission to let me go, not that he needed it. It's only fair he does. I made my decision, the biggest mistake I've ever made in walking away from him. My eyes suddenly fill with tears and he makes a move toward me— most likely to comfort me— but he stops. He says nothing, but his eyes speak the words he's not saying. *"I forgive you."* He places his hand on my arm and, for just a moment, my world feels— right.

"Yeah, I should probably go. Don't be a stranger, Linds." He squeezes my arm tenderly before he lets go. I nod my head as he walks away toward a smiling Melissa. I shouldn't watch, but I do. I watch him lean into her, both of his hands on her forearms, whispering in her ear. She smiles and nods, and he presses a kiss to her cheek. She looks to me, then back to him. This is my cue to leave. I wish nothing but the best for Matt, but I'm not strong enough to stand around and watch the man I love in the arms of another woman—a better woman.

I set my glass on the table in front of me and excuse myself from the reception rather abruptly. I say a quick goodbye to my mom and Louis and blow a kiss to Landon when he sees me heading for the exit. He knows this has been hard for me and nods his head in approval of my leaving. With a quick wave to Reagan, I quietly leave.

I shiver as the cool, fall Wilmington air hits my face as I press the door open and step out into the dark night. It's quiet outside, with just the faintest sounds of music escaping through the walls. I pull my car keys from the small handbag and hold on to the old metal railing so I don't fall on these steep stone steps. Heels and a tight, long dress with cobblestone stairs are not a good combination. I almost laugh at myself, wondering what a mess I'd have been if the old Lindsay had sipped a drink or two tonight and tried to navigate these stairs.

"Let me help you." There is his voice again, behind me. I pause momentarily before turning around.

"I'm good. I've got this." I smile in gratitude at him.

"I know you do, Lindsay. You are the strongest woman I know. You can do anything, without anyone's help. You've proven that time and again, but let *me* help you." His voice is full of need—he's almost begging me to let him help me.

"Matt, I'm walking down some stairs to my car. I'll be fine. Go back inside; your date is waiting in there for you." I turn around and begin taking the steps slowly, my fingers wrapped tightly around the cool metal railing. *Now is not the time to fall,* I tell myself, *I've just turned down his offer for help.*

"Melissa's not my date." He says it matter-of-factly. "She's a friend who didn't have anyone to take her to her boss' wedding, and I'm a guy who didn't have a date to my best friend's wedding, so we came together and that's where it ends. That's all it is."

I stop, my back still to him. "Matt, it's okay. You don't owe me any explanations, and I, of all people, will be the last to judge what you do or who you see." I turn and look over my shoulder to find he's closed the distance between us. He's standing two steps above me.

"Lindsay, I need to say this and I need you to hear me." He pauses. I turn around to give him my full attention. My knees shake lightly and I hold on to the railing tighter to steady myself. His jaw works and he shakes one of his hands nervously. His dark brown eyes hone in on mine and never falter. "I love you. I have never stopped loving you. From the first time I spoke to you, to the day you left—my love for you never changed." I see him swallow and he takes a deep breath, exhaling loudly. "I don't know what our futures hold, but every time I try to envision mine, you're a part of it. In my dreams, you're the one I wake up next to every morning, and go to sleep with every night. You're the one rocking my babies to sleep, and holding my hand when I'm an old man. It's always been you. It will always be *you*."

I close my eyes and let the weight of these words sink in. My heart feels as if it might burst, it's beating so wildly. The tears I've been fighting back all night deceive me and fall in streams down my face. My mouth won't form words, so I stand and just cry. I cry for how sorry I am. I cry for how much I've obviously hurt him—and myself. I cry for how much I've wanted, no, *needed* to hear him say this. I cry because this is the future I've always envisioned as well—I just never believed I deserved it.

He takes the last two steps down to meet me and pulls me into his arms. Everything I've ever needed is holding on to me and I make a silent promise to myself I'll never let go of him again.

"I love you too, Matt."

I'm not sure how long we stand holding each other, but I know it is a while. I've finally stopped crying, but I don't want to pull out of his embrace—I'm not ready to let him go yet. When I finally let go, I can see his eyes stained red and his cheeks are wet.

"Can we start over?" he asks, his lip shaking. I manage a short smile while I wipe his cheeks with the palms of my hand.

"I'd like that."

"Me too."

# EPILOGUE

*Two years later*

*Lindsay*

"Your turn," Matt says as he turns down the volume on the baby monitor that sits on the nightstand and nudges me gently with his elbow. Emmy is chatting away in her crib and making all kinds of noises. With one half-open eye, I glance at the clock on the bedside table and see that it's three-thirty in the morning.

Pushing myself out of bed, I pad down the hall quietly to the bedroom where a crib, a changing table, and a rocking chair line the walls of the room. The nightlight plugged into the wall provides just enough light to illuminate the room, not needing to turn on the bright overhead light.

"Em," I whisper. "You're always so chatty and happy, even in the middle of the night." She smiles at me as I reach into the crib and pull her to me. "You're going to wake up your sister with all this noise you're making." I lay her on the changing table and change her wet diaper, her little legs kicking wildly the entire time.

I snap her onesie closed and lean down, pressing a gentle kiss to her forehead. There is nothing better than a smell of a baby.

"Hungry?" I ask her. She smiles at me again. I carry her to the kitchen, where I bounce and sway her gently while we wait for her bottle to warm up in the bottle warmer. I pull a burp cloth from the drawer and lay it across her chest and tuck it under her chin before heading back to the rocking chair in the bedroom.

I prop my feet on the gliding ottoman and position Emmy into the crook of my arm. Her little pink lips wrap around the nipple on the bottle and she immediately begins suckling. Her blue eyes focus on my face and she intently watches me as she inhales her bottle in a matter of minutes.

"I can't believe how fast you ate that." I giggle quietly, pressing another kiss to her cheek. I cannot get enough of this baby girl. Propping her on my chest, I burp her gently, alternating between rubbing circles and gentle taps on her back.

"I like the way a baby looks on you," he says, his voice groggy. Matt stands in nothing but a pair of pajama pants, his shoulder pressed against the door jamb.

"Why are you up? This was my feeding."

"I could hear you talking to Emmy through the monitor and I like watching you with her." He walks across the carpeted floor and leans down, pressing a kiss to my lips. Emmy lets out a giant burp and Matt scrunches his nose in disgust.

"God, for how cute babies are, they sure do smell." I can't help but let out a laugh. He kisses me again quickly before whispering in my ear, "Get her back to sleep so we can practice making a baby." He wags his eyebrows at me.

"I love practicing with you," I say with a smile, still rocking Emmy.

"We've been practicing for a long time," he says with a

noticeable sigh. Matt and I decided to start trying to get pregnant a couple of months ago. We've only been married for six months, but I knew it might take some time, as my body is still adjusting and settling into itself after years of abuse, and there is always a lingering fear for me that maybe a baby isn't in the cards for us. I pray every night that the things I did to my body won't compromise or affect Matt and his dreams.

"Go back to bed. I'll be there in a minute," I whisper as I look at Emmy, whose eyes are getting heavy.

Matt and I are babysitting Emmy and her two-year-old sister, Abigail, or better known as Abby, for the weekend. This is Landon and Reagan's first overnight trip away since Emmy was born—and I love every second of it. Both little girls are stunning with dark hair, blue eyes, and olive skin; a perfect combination of both Landon and Reagan. Abby is the light of her Uncle Matt's eye and she rarely leaves his side. I love watching Matt interact with the girls and my heart thrums with excitement as I think about starting a family with him.

Swaddling Emmy in her blanket, I lay her back in the crib. Her little eyelids almost immediately close. I lean over the railing and watch her little chest rise and fall through the blanket. Closing the bedroom door behind me, I pop my head into the other room, where Abby snuggles a bumblebee pillow pet to her chest and her long, dark hair splays on the pillow. I am the luckiest aunt in the world. Landon and Reagan are blessed with the most beautiful little girls I've ever laid eyes on. Landon loves all of his girls more than anything, and even though his hands are full with the little girls, he insists on trying one more time for a boy. Reagan is hearing nothing of the matter, and I laugh every time I see him with his arms full of little girls dressed in pink and their toys. He always thought he'd have a house full of boys.

I crawl back into bed, pulling up the sheets. Matt instantly rolls over and wraps his arm around me, pulling me into him. He nuzzles his face into the crook of my neck, loudly inhaling the scent of my hair. His hand snakes under the hem of my short nightgown and his fingers trail small circles against my stomach.

"Mrs. Kennedy, do you realize we've been married for one hundred and eighty-three days and almost nine and a half hours."

"I love when you call me Mrs. Kennedy." I press a light kiss to his chest. "And how do you know how many days we've been married?" I wiggle in his arms and manage to turn toward him.

"Because I will never forget one minute that you're mine."

"I've always been yours," I say softly. "Always."

"I know, but every day that I wake up and have you next to me is the best day of my life."

"That might be the sweetest thing you've ever said to me." I push myself up and swing my leg over his waist, straddling him. He pushes my nightgown up and positions my hips directly over him.

"Let's practice," he says with a devious smile pulling me onto him. I've known Matt's been anxious to start a family, but I wanted to settle into married life before jumping into parenthood, and he has been completely understanding and supportive of this. The last year and a half has been a whirlwind for us. The most challenging part for me was getting settled back into my career while finding a delicate balance that supports my priorities of sobriety and putting my family first.

We spend the next thirty minutes making love. I'll never get enough of him. I close my eyes as the clock turns to four seventeen in the morning. Just as I doze off, Emmy starts squealing through the baby monitor. I barely remember muttering "your turn" before feeling Matt crawl out of our bed.

I wake up at six thirty and the bed is empty. The sun is bright, illuminating the room through the skylights. Rubbing my eyes, I push myself up and grab my robe. Walking down the hallway, I can hear the TV on and find Matt sitting on the living room floor with Emmy in her little bouncy chair and Abby sitting between his legs, watching *Sophia the First* while eating a bowl of dry Cheerios. Matt is wearing only a pair of sweatpants, his chest is bare, showing off his tan, muscular skin. His hair is a mess and his face is lightly stubbled with a three-day growth. I've never seen him more handsome than he is right now, surrounded by babies.

"Morning," I say, walking across the living room.

"Princess," Abby says excitedly and points to the TV.

"Yes, Princess Sophia," I tell her and she flashes me a giant, toothy smile. I sit down next to Matt and he leans his head against my shoulder. "You look exhausted."

"I haven't been back to bed," he says quietly. "Em wouldn't sleep. Then, just as I got her settled, Abs woke up." I laugh quietly, wondering if this is what our life could look like.

"Go rest. I'll take over. I'll make some breakfast and wake you up in a few hours." He shakes his head and lightly pulls on one of Abby's long, loose curls.

"We'll sleep after they leave. Landon already sent a text and said they'd be here about eight. He said Reagan is missing the girls."

"That means he's missing the girls."

"Yeah, that's what I figured."

We sit and watch cartoons with Abby and I change Emmy, getting her dressed in a pink jumper. Matt has a bottle waiting when I bring her back to the living room and he feeds her while I start breakfast. Throwing some bacon in the oven to cook, I make pancakes and cut up fresh fruit to make a giant fruit bowl.

Landon and Reagan burst through the door around seven forty-five and Landon scoops Abby off the floor and into his arms. Abby squeals as Landon peppers her with kisses all over her face. The guys tend to the girls while Reagan joins me in the kitchen.

"Could you seriously have married someone any more adorable or sweet?" she says sarcastically. "I mean, my God, my baby looks amazing in that man's arms." She laughs.

"I know," I sigh, looking at Matt feeding Emmy. "He loves those girls so much," I admit as I flip another pancake on the griddle.

"How's it going? Any luck yet?" She scrunches her nose. Reagan knows I've been trying to get pregnant and I've voiced my concerns of it not happening as quickly as I'd hoped. She advised that I speak with a specialist in her office if nothing happens in the next couple of months.

"Nothing yet," I say quietly.

"Don't stress about it," she says with a sympathetic smile. "It'll happen when it's supposed to; it always does."

"I know."

"I know I told you to wait to see the specialist, but why don't you come in tomorrow? We'll just do some basic lab work. Run some blood and urine tests… just to see if there is anything *off*." I immediately feel better and smile at her.

"That sounds like a good idea." Anything to help ease some of my fears will make me feel better.

"Good; come early on your way to work. I'll get you in before we start seeing patients."

"Thanks, Reagan."

Abby runs into the kitchen, hugging Reagan's legs. "Mama. Princess," she says, pointing to the TV again.

"Uncle Matt let you watch princesses, didn't he?" She narrows her eyes at Matt. Reagan likes to limit the amount of TV time with Abby, but Uncle Matt won't hear any of it.

"If she's screwed up as a teenager for watching too much *Sophia the First*, you can blame me," he jokes with her, pulling a t-shirt over his head before picking Abby back up and putting her on his shoulders.

Reagan rolls her eyes and sets the kitchen table. We enjoy a nice breakfast with Landon, Reagan, and the girls before they leave and Matt and I spend the rest of the day in bed, watching movies and "practicing."

Reagan shoves me toward the bathroom with a wipe and a small, plastic cup in my hand. "Wipe first, then capture the sample in the collection cup. We'll do bloods when you're done." The bathroom door shuts behind me and I sigh loudly before doing as she told me. I twist the plastic cover back onto the cup, wash my hands, and meet her outside the bathroom.

"Cup o' pee?" I say in my best Irish accent. She pulls the collection cup from my hands and gives it to one of her medical assistants.

"I swear you and Landon are the same person. You both act like fifteen-year-old boys," she scoffs jokingly. I sit in the chair, resting my left arm on the cushion while the phlebotomist wraps my arm in a giant band and pokes me, filling two vials of blood. One Band-Aid later and a quick hug from Reagan, and I'm out the door, on my way to work.

Getting settled at my desk, I begin my morning routine of

checking voice messages, answering emails, and preparing for our morning production meeting. Elaine has been assigning me a lot of feature stories and I've even gotten some anchor time for the noon newscast. My cell phone rings on the desk next to me and I see Reagan's name flash across the screen. I've got ten minutes until the production meeting, so I hit ignore and finish answering the email I've been working on. My desk phone rings and I notice Reagan's number on the caller ID.

"Lindsay Kennedy," I answer, just in case I'm mistaken and it's not Reagan.

"Tell me you're sitting down."

"Uh, yeah, but I'm..."

"Stay sitting."

"Why do you sound out of breath? What's wrong?"

"Lindsay..."

"Yeah..."

"You're pregnant." And that's where my heart stops beating.

"What?" I barely make out in a whisper

"You heard me. Your urine test was positive. You're pregnant. We're waiting on the blood work to come back tomorrow to confirm, but you're pregnant. When was your last period?"

"I don't know. I mean, they're so off. Some months I have one, some months I don't. I just... I don't know," I mumble into the phone.

"Come back to the office. We'll do an ultrasound."

"Yeah, um... let me go let Elaine know that I have to leave unexpectedly."

"I'll see you in a little bit."

"Reagan? Please don't say anything to anyone. I'm just..."

"I know. Just get back here."

I don't remember driving back to Reagan's office. I don't remember her talking to me. I don't remember changing into the gown and doing a full OB check-up. What I do remember is Reagan handing me a long piece of paper that showed me the ultrasound with two babies and a due date. I notice the due date first, "September twentieth." I look up at Reagan, who's standing next to me. "That's Matt's birthday." She smiles at me. My eyes fill with tears and I lay my head back against the pillow on the table.

"You're almost nine weeks along, Lindsay—with twins."

"Well, that would be why my clothes are getting tight." I laugh.

"I know you're healthy and doing well, but Lindsay, as a doctor, I have to say this. I need you to eat and not worry about your weight." I listen as Reagan quietly addresses my past struggle with anorexia. "You and your babies need to be healthy. I want you to talk to your therapist, or me if you feel like you're struggling with this. You're going to gain weight—and more so than normal. You're growing two babies." I nod my head in acknowledgement and she smiles at me. "Everything looks really, really good." She squeezes my hand while I swat tears away with the other one. "Now, go tell Matt," she says, pulling me up to a sitting position.

I get changed back into my clothes and sit in my car outside Reagan's office for god only knows how long. A million things run through my head and every emotion imaginable courses through me. When I returned to work two years ago, Matt changed his shift and now works the day shift. With only a couple of hours left in his shift, I decide to wait for him at home. Arriving home, I immediately begin prepping dinner and start a load of laundry, anything to keep me busy and my mind preoccupied.

"Linds?" I can hear the confusion in his voice just before I hear the front door shut. He usually gets home before me, so I'm sure my car in the driveway surprised him.

"In the kitchen," I holler.

"What are you doing home?" he asks as he walks into the kitchen.

"We have to talk." My tone is serious and his face contorts and loses color. I grab his hand and pull him into the living room. "Sit down." I gesture to the couch. I untie the apron I'm wearing and set it on the coffee table before sitting down next to him.

"I have something to tell you." My heart races in my chest.

"What's wrong? You're scaring me." He pulls me closer to him, wrapping his arm around me in a protective nature.

"I'm pregnant." Matt stills at those words.

"You're pregnant?" he repeats as a question.

"I'm pregnant," I repeat. "But that's not all."

His eyebrows shoot up.

"What do you mean, 'that's not all'?"

I literally crawl into his lap and sit face to face with him. His arms wrap around my waist, holding me in place.

"Just tell me, Lindsay."

"Do you want a girl or a boy?"

"Honest to god, it doesn't matter. I just want you and our baby healthy."

"Good answer," I say, pressing a quick kiss to his lips. "What if I told you, you could get a boy and a girl, or two boys, or two girls?"

"Shut up!" he says loudly. "Twins?" I nod my head and he jumps up from the couch with me still wrapped around him.

"We're having twins?"

"Yes!"

"Oh my god, we're having twins!" He sets me down and holds my face before leaning in to kiss me. "I love you," he says against my lips. "I've never loved anything as much as I love you."

"That's about to change," I mumble back against his lips.

## Six months later

I wake to a sharp pain in my back and groan as I try to reposition myself for the twelfth time tonight amongst the sea of pillows. Another sharp pain takes my breath away and I gasp loudly. Matt sits straight up out of a dead sleep.

"What's wrong?"

"I don't know," I groan. "Sharp pains in my back."

Matt shifts pillows and moves closer to me. "Let me rub your back." I prop a pillow under my belly and lie on my right side. Matt rubs my lower back, paying special attention to the area that the pain is coming from.

"That feels good," I mumble just before another pain courses through me. "God dammit," I bite out.

"I think you need to call Reagan."

"It's just back pain. It's too early for me to have the babies. I'm only thirty-four weeks."

"Call her," he orders me. I reach for my cell phone, which is sitting on the nightstand, and scroll through the call list, pressing Reagan's number. In three rings, she answers, but I hand the phone to Matt when another wave of back pain hits me.

"She's in a lot of pain," I hear him tell her. I close my eyes and try to take a deep, cleansing breath. I push myself up to a sitting position and do my best to lean forward in hopes of stretching my lower back. Standing up, I begin waddling to the bathroom, when I feel the warmth begin running down my leg.

"Matt," I say, trying to get his attention. He's lost in conversation with Reagan when I finally yell louder. "Matt!" He turns his head quickly just before I hear an "Oh shit."

"Need some help here."

"Reagan, I think her water broke. Oh my god, what do I do?" He's freaking out and, for some reason, this strikes me funny. I begin laughing so hard that I bend over slightly, causing more water to leave me, running down my leg.

"Oh my god, it keeps coming," he's yelling into the phone to Reagan. My always calm, cool, and collected husband is freaking out, and I'm laughing.

"Why are you laughing? What is wrong with you?" he's yelling at me. I don't know if it's exhaustion or the situation, but I can't stop laughing. Matt hands me the phone and runs to the bathroom, pulling towels out from under the vanity. He throws them at my feet and orders me not to move.

"Ready, Mama?" Reagan asks me.

"Ready," I reply, still laughing at Matt.

"Meet you in OB triage in about a half-hour. Tell your husband to calm his ass down." She laughs before hanging up the phone. Matt is pulling clothes out of drawers and stuffing them into an overnight bag.

"We are not ready," he says, shoving more items into the bag. I waddle carefully to the bathroom to clean myself up and change before leaving. Twenty minutes later, we're entering the hospital and being checked in. A few minutes later, I'm in a room, hooked up to every known monitor ever made and an IV bag delivering fluids. The contractions are slow at first, coming every seven to eight minutes, but as the evening progresses, they strengthen and come every two to three minutes.

Matt paces the room and honestly provides comedic relief for me while I labor. "Haven't you delivered babies before on the side of the road?" I ask him in between contractions.

"Totally different," he barks at me. "It wasn't you. I don't like seeing you in pain."

I breathe through another contraction and, before I know it, my room is full of family. Landon and the girls are here and my mom and Louis just arrived. Everyone is quiet and respectful, but Reagan orders them all down the hall to the private waiting suite.

"Let's check you," she says, slipping on a rubber glove. "You're ten centimeters and fully effaced. Let's have some babies," she says. Matt runs both of his hands through his hair and breathes deeply. Reagan calls in some additional nurses and positions the stirrups for my feet so I can begin pushing.

"I'm not going to lie, Lindsay; this is going to hurt like hell. Focus on pushing and seeing your babies, not the pain." I opted to do a drug-free delivery. I know I'm insane, but for me, it was important to steer clear of any narcotics.

Matt leans down and presses a kiss to my forehead and squeezes my hand. "This is it, Linds. It's no longer just you and me." I smile at him and begin pushing. Forty minutes later, we are now a family of four with the addition of Liam and Noah. Matt goes with the nurse and the babies to the NICU while Reagan stays with me.

"Good job, Lindsay. That was tough, but you did it." I nod my head, too tired to reply. The nurse has administered some extra strength ibuprofen through the IV line to help with the pain and I finally begin to relax a little. "They look perfect. The pediatrician will keep them for a few hours and monitor them, but if everything is good, they'll be able to come back to the room for a while. They will want you to try and nurse if you're up for it."

I close my eyes and rest while more nurses come and go, checking my vitals and changing my IV bag. I'm not sure how long I've been asleep when Matt kisses my forehead, waking me up. He's pushed a bassinet into the room where both boys are swaddled and sleeping next to each other.

"They're perfect, Linds. Perfect," he repeats. He picks up the first baby and hands him to me. "Noah. He's got the darker hair." I push the little beanie aside and see just a small tuft of dark hair on top of his head. "And Liam. He has the dimpled chin." I spend the next few minutes inspecting my babies and kissing them. There is nothing sweeter than the smell of a newborn. I nurse and Matt changes the boys' diapers as we settle in to a quiet little routine at the hospital.

When Landon, Reagan, the girls, my mom, and Louis have all come and gone, I realize this is the first time my room has been quiet for the last twenty-four hours. Matt has fallen asleep upright in the chair next to the bed, cradling each swaddled baby boy in the crook of each of his arms. I snap a quick picture with my phone and lower the back of my bed so I can rest for a bit.

My heart is bursting with love for Matt and our new family. Two and half years ago, I never would have imagined that this would be my life—married to the man of my dreams with two baby boys. As I close my eyes, I whisper a prayer of gratitude for all that I have and for all that has led me to where I am today. Learning to process my emotions—drug free—while balancing my career and personal life was the biggest hurdle I had to overcome; however, making amends with those I've hurt was the most painful. While I'm healthy today, my past battle with anorexia will always be in the forefront of who I am. The most important lesson I've learned is that forgiveness is a beautiful gift to give, but an even more beautiful gift to receive.

# AUTHOR'S NOTE

As the "Unbreakable" series comes to an end, I want to thank you for taking this journey with me. What started out as a single book, *Unbreakable*, grew into something so much bigger because of your love for these characters.

At times, I've wanted to quit—I felt I couldn't give these characters the story they deserved, but then I'd get a message from a reader begging me for more. So thank you. Thank you for helping me write Gabe, Jess, Ava, Luke, Lindsay, Landon, Reagan, and Matt. I have loved crawling around in the heads of these characters so much that they almost feel real to me (is that weird?)

I plan to continue writing, but the "Unbreakable" series has reached its end. I know many of you have asked for a story for Ava and Adrian, and Luke and Heather and, at this time—I just don't know if that will happen. "Never say never" is my motto, but for now, I'm on to writing something new.

Thank you all for your support and encouragement and loving this series as much as I have!

Giant hugs to all of you!

~Rebecca

# ACKNOWLEDGEMENTS

Many, many thanks to my family for your never-ending support. You are everything to me.

My betas, Christine, Amy, Katy, and Lauren, and my editors Beth and Beth, you ladies made this a better story—thank you!

Sara Celi and Amanda Clark for helping me with the "TV" parts. You two girls have the coolest jobs ever. Thank you for your help and making this story authentic.

Gretchen, Amy, Hadley, Renee, Emmy, Julie and Toni— because you balance me. Love you all fiercely.

## ALSO BY REBECCA SHEA

**Unbreakable**

**Undone**

# CONNECT WITH REBECCA SHEA

Website: www.rebeccasheaauthor.com

Facebook: https://www.facebook.com/rebeccasheaauthor

Twitter: @beccasheaauthor

Goodreads: www.goodreads.com/goodreadscombeccashea

Email: rebeccasheaauthor@gmail.com

14854328R00184